SUN DRAGON

By

Michael Brookes

DEDICATION

I have a lot of people to thank so here goes! To Dave and Umit – the best friends anyone can have. To my family for their support. – I hope you like my latest book! To Adam and Simon for their valuable test reading.

The biggest thanks of all goes to you and all my other readers - you make the effort worthwhile.

And of course, a shout out for the Ely Writers Group.

© 2014 Michael Brookes - All rights reserved

Cover image provided by Magic Owl Design
http://www.magicowldesign.com/

Editing service provided by Storywork
http://storywork.co.uk/

Chapter 1
Lift Off

7th June 2022, 06:29 local time

With less than a minute until launch, the roar of the engines' ignition shuddered through the vessel. Commander Samantha Collins glanced to her left where Doctor Colette Laurent ran through the final safety checks. Samantha commanded the mission and, even after spending so many years in training together, still admired the older woman's youthful looks.

Samantha frowned at her momentary distraction and returned her attention to her own multifunctional displays. On each screen she checked the key systems for the spacecraft.

Engine controls – green.

Life support – green.

Communications – green.

Flight controls – green.

Mission management – green.

"Mission Control, I'm showing green across the board," she reported.

"Confirmed, Commander. Our board is also in the green. Launch is a go."

The tension in her stomach increased. In part it came from bracing in preparation for the weight about to be piled on her, but for the most part it came from the thrill. She loved lift off, and she experienced a similar, although lesser, thrill even when taking off in an aeroplane. This was her third proper launch. The first had been a decade ago, on the one of the old Russian Soyuz rockets. They'd been dependable launch vehicles which had provided reliable service for decades and had only recently been phased out of service.

That launch had taken her up to the International Space Station for the first time. It had been smaller back then, with a crew of four – herself, two Russians and an Indian astronaut. That had been her first and only orbital mission while an active astronaut with NASA.

She had been grounded after that all-too-short trip, along with most of the other astronauts, thanks to a series of budget cuts during the early years of the 21st century.

That grim reality had all changed three years ago with the news that had stunned the world. Now here she was with a new international crew on the most important launch NASA, or any other space agency, had ever seen.

This launch was on the new Delta V Heavy, now approved for manned missions. The programme had needed to be accelerated as there wasn't enough heavy lift capability available. This was the second time the rocket had launched into orbit – the first had taken the crew on their first visit to the space station.

She glanced again at Colette, who nodded in reply, indicating she confirmed the safety checks.

"Launch is a go."

"Confirmed, Mission Control."

With that instruction, the six crew members settled into their seats. Everyone checked their safety webbing for the last time. They were all committed now.

Samantha kept her face calm, but her excitement still fluttered inside her stomach. More than the thrill of the launch, she had always dreamed of going into space. She had achieved that goal already, and now she was about to start a mission that had been the dream of every astronaut for decades.

A launch into space also represented the ultimate expression of trust. Once the engines ignited and lift off began, there was nothing they could do to affect anything until they entered orbit. In theory, there was the emergency escape capsule. If they or anyone at Mission Control were quick enough, it might catapult them far enough for safety.

In reality, that was unlikely.

Astronauts trained hard. They trained for months, years in the case of the current mission; their training had a single purpose. That purpose was to make sure they could control any situation that developed, but during launch they relinquished that hard-earned control.

And Samantha loved every moment of it.

The vibration intensified, while in her ear she listened to Mission Control count down the final seconds.

And there it was.

The weight piled up upon her, although slowly at first. She heard Colette grunt in a soft voice as she experienced the same. The world resisted their launch with all of its might and pulled her down in her seat. Not even a lover's grip could compare to that feeling.

With a roar that shuddered through her body, she felt the powerful rocket lift from the pad.

The pressure on her body increased as the rocket built up speed, slowly at first, then lurching into the sky. The sinking feeling in her stomach had been crushed from existence by the weight of gravity's resistance to their launch.

Minutes later, a new and sharper vibration shook the speeding craft as the explosive bolts fired and released the first stage. Despite the great power of the rocket's engines, it had to be divided into sections to reach beyond the atmosphere. The second set of rocket engines fired, propelling them faster as the spent stage fell away. With the mass of the ship reduced, this second stage would now push them out of the atmosphere and into space.

It was almost disappointing when the shaking stopped and the crew capsule settled into its arching orbit. The capsule would now coast along its transfer orbit. The mission used the new rapid transfer procedure, so they would have to circle the Earth twice before docking with the ISS. On her last visit, they'd required twelve orbits. Not that she had minded, as the view from orbit was amazing, even through the tiny portals in the crew capsule.

Samantha once again checked the readings on the displays in front of her. That had been another important part of their training. They had developed an odd paradox of trusting their instincts (although instincts tended to be training doing its own thing) and trusting their instruments.

The launch hadn't been perfect, but was well within the required parameters. Next she checked with the rest of her crew.

"Is everyone okay?"

"I'm fine," Colette replied, her accent warm, her voice trembling with excitement. Samantha wasn't alone in enjoying the thrill of a launch. It was no coincidence that they'd both been pilots in their respective air forces.

Ronald Larsson's deep Southern drawl sounded next across the intercom. "I'm A-OK. I don't think I'll ever get used to that."

"Steady there, I think I'm going to be sick." Professor Stephen MacQuire's clipped British accent irritated Samantha. If anyone was going to puke, she would have bet it would have been him. "Just joking." And then he did that nasal laugh of his.

It was going to be a long voyage.

"All good here." Juliet Jakes was the third American in the crew.

"Da. I'm fine," Piotr Vasilevitch confirmed. His accent was thick, but he sounded as calm as he always did. He spoke perfect English, but sometimes he enjoyed letting the accent run free.

"Good to hear. Stay in your seats until we dock with the ISS," Samantha instructed.

Not that there was any space for anyone to move. The original design of the Orion capsule allowed for only four crew members, so with six on board, things were more than a little cramped. Extensive modifications had been needed to facilitate the launch of the entire crew in a single capsule.

Still, they only needed to suffer the cramped conditions for the short ferry to the space station, so it would only be for another hour or so. Then they'd be inside the space station, and that had grown to accommodate the construction crew. With the two extra habitation modules, there would be sufficient space for them all.

On their first pass, they couldn't see the ship clearly. It appeared as a vague cross-shaped silhouette behind the International Space Station. Samantha watched through the small windows, even though she could have got a better view from the camera displays.

On the second pass, the procedure for the docking approach kept her too busy for sightseeing. Juliet and Ronald started describing the scene to the others. Samantha switched them to a private channel so that she could focus on the approach.

"Orion 4. This is ISS, we have you on approach. We're seeing you on a clean vector."

"ISS, this is Orion 4. Confirmed."

The chatter back and forth remained business-like as they performed the delicate ballet of docking the capsule with the station. The station was huge, a large sprawling structure with several cylindrical modules. Each of the modules was larger than the capsule that approached it in a delicate manoeuvre.

Despite its superior size, the station was fragile. A collision would risk the ten astronauts on the station as well as causing damage that could cost millions, if not billions, of dollars to fix.

Minutes of subtle adjustments later, the capsule connected with the station's docking ring, and with several mechanical clunks a seal formed.

Then it became a simple matter of waiting.

It took the two Russian cosmonauts on the station another fifteen minutes to secure the connection and open the capsule.

Samantha looked through the porthole again, but found her view blocked by one of the vast solar panels. A brief hiss of escaping air announced the opening of the airlock. A grinning, bearded face greeted them in Russian. Samantha replied in kind – everyone visiting the ISS had to be fluent in Russian.

The crew took a little while to find their space legs. All of them except Colette, who floated through the airlock with her usual natural grace. They'd all been in orbit before and they'd all trained in the 'Vomit Comet' to prepare them, although weightlessness in the diving plane didn't feel anything like microgravity in orbit.

Samantha followed Colette into the station. After being cramped in the capsule, it appeared spacious and bright. A brief smile crossed her face as she realised that the current crew and construction team, who had been stationed here for the past six months, would surely disagree.

The station looked oddly primitive. Wires and tubing lined the connecting tunnel, which opened into a wider space. There the theme continued. Given all the money required to put and maintain this station in orbit, it was difficult to appreciate why so much had been spent from the décor alone.

The simple truth was that putting anything into space was expensive, and by an order of magnitude more costly if humans had to live there.

The construction crew weren't here to welcome them – they were still busy on the vessel making it ready for the next day's departure. Instead, the normal crew of the station waited for them. The first thing she thought was how young they looked. Samantha was the youngest of the arrived crew and she was at least ten years older than any of the astronauts who welcomed them.

For this mission, going so far into space without the protection of the Earth's magnetic field, they would be exposed to the radiation dangers of the solar wind. For such prolonged exposure, only crew aged between 45 and 55 and with the correct genetic disposition had been considered. That gave them a greater chance of surviving the long journey than a younger crew.

She thanked them for the offered tubes of juice, drinking the cool liquid with some relish. As the remaining four crew members entered the module, it didn't take long for the space to become cramped. The first Russian led them to one of the two new habitation modules. She saw the personal effects of some the construction team attached to the walls.

They'd be there for the rest of the day. The ISS crew were busy setting up their tasks for the coming launch, but would join them for a celebratory meal that evening. The next day, the crew would transfer to their vessel and finalise preparations for their departure.

Chapter 2
Mars Voyager

7th June 2022, 19:15 station time

The International Space Station's crew pulled out all the stops for the Mars mission crew's last meal in Earth orbit. It would be three years before they returned to Earth.

The ten astronauts squashed into the same module that the crew would be bunked in for that night. This was one of the new modules that they'd added to the station to accommodate the construction crew and was a little larger than the station's older modules.

Without realising it, everyone steered the conversation clear of the subject on everyone's minds – the mission to Mars. The reasons for doing so were complex. In part there was more than a little jealousy at the crew heading farther than any astronaut had ever gone before.

There was also an element of superstition. Like actors not mentioning the 'Scottish Play', they kept the talk clear of the impending mission. Instead they told anecdotes from their training, as despite their different nationalities they shared that common bond.

"It was the flight training that worried me the most," Professor MacQuire told the eating crews. The Mars mission was unusual in that every crew member had to be flight qualified. For all space missions, skill redundancy formed standard procedure, but for the crew being so far away from Earth, the mission planners had determined that everyone should be able to fill any other team member's role in case of an emergency.

"It wasn't the flying. I've always loved flying. I wouldn't be here if I didn't. Right?" A few grins of agreement from the others in the module. "No, my real worry was flying the plane. It took me ages to pass my driving test in my younger days. I had a terrible time. I imagined this would be the same. Thanks to Colette here," he smiled at her, "I soon mastered the basics."

Despite their national rivalries, the Englishman and the French woman had formed a quick friendship. They made an odd pair. At first glance he appeared the stereotypical bumbling professor. However, his intelligence matched his quick wit and fit physique. 'Long walks in Welsh hills,' he claimed with his usual self-deprecation.

He was also a prankster and had caught out Samantha, who hated practical jokes, a few times during training. He'd promised there would be none on the voyage, but no-one believed him.

As well as co-pilot, Colette was the crew's medical doctor. She'd started her career as a pilot in the French Air Force. After giving up flying following a year-long deployment in French Guiana, she had trained to become a doctor. Colette had then stayed with the Air Force until joining the European Space Agency six years ago.

"For me it was the neutral buoyancy training." Juliet Jakes entered the conversation. "I'd scuba qualified years ago, too many years ago. I love being in the water. But being in the water wearing that big old suit. Well, that was something different."

The conversation flowed along with the tubes of food. At least on the ship they'd have some gravity, well, spin to be accurate, but it was almost the same thing. They'd at least be able to eat food in a somewhat civilised fashion.

As Ronald started telling an anecdote from his time with the Army Corp of Engineers, Samantha excused herself from the table. She headed to the Tranquillity module, intending to use the latrine. The cupola at the far end caught her eye. The segmented window enabled the ISS crew to observe Earth and provide a view when controlling the station's robotic arm.

More than a few astronauts had made the view famous with their antics over the years. It was a glorious view of the Earth that kept the public and the astronauts entranced. Below her, Africa flowed towards the dawn. It was dark under the night sky except for a few cities which stood out with their glow in the shadow. She twisted her head to see if she could view the Mars Voyager vessel.

Everyone agreed that it was a silly name, but of all the negotiations this had proved to be the stickiest. A delicate multifaceted negotiation that had dragged out between several national space agencies and the three major space corporations involved in the mission.

Many industry commentators considered this mission to be the first step of the commercialisation of space. Samantha smiled at that thought. The commercialisation of space had started decades before, although in recent years private launch vehicles became busier than the national space agencies. That had been a tipping point and it hurt the pride of some of the nationalities in the programme.

Samantha found what she was looking for. A large cross shape, almost obscured by the space station's shadow. This ship would be their home for the next three years. The modules had required nine launches to put them into orbit. They included three European Space Agency Arianne 5s, two Russian Protons and four launches from Chimera Industries' own rockets.

Without the involvement of the fledgling space launch industries, the mission would have taken many more years to put together. Without their assistance, the mission would never have made it off the ground. In more ways than one, this mission was making history.

At the ship's base was the first stage, comprised of three twelve-metre-tall fuel tanks that would power the vessel out of Earth orbit into its transfer trajectory. As well as providing thrust, the bimodal nuclear engines had a low-power mode to generate electricity for the ship and crew throughout the extended journey.

Above the first stage she saw the second stage. Smaller than the first, it would push the ship into the right orbit to rendezvous with Mars in ten months.

The top of the cross was comprised of two more modules. At the very top, with its single engine pointing into the sky, was the hangar module. Inside the hangar were two landers, which would take them to the surface of Mars and back into orbit. Below that was the Mars science observatory. This module would remain in orbit around Mars, acting as a base for the landing mission, but also for any future missions to Mars.

The two arms of the cross came from thin tubes which connected the two modules, one on each end. At a diameter of seventy metres, the arms would be spun at a fraction under four revolutions per minute. The spin would produce an effect almost the same as gravity, although to about a third equivalent of Earth gravity. This approximated the gravity they'd experience once on the surface of Mars.

One of the biggest dangers to human beings when living for extended periods in space was bone and muscle loss. This was especially true in zero gravity. The fake gravity created by the spin along with a specially designed exercise programme would aid in preventing that problem. An experimental drug treatment had also been developed, although everyone hoped that it wouldn't be needed.

On the left arm was the habitation module. All six of the crew would live in that space. It would also act as their return craft, bringing them back home when the mission was completed. The other arm comprised the Mars science laboratory. The long trip provided an opportunity for a lot of experiments, both along the way and while they were in orbit.

A hand upon her shoulder startled Samantha from her thoughts. She glanced over the gnarled hand and saw Piotr's smiling face. He wasn't alone, the whole crew had joined her. They knew what she was looking at. Each of their faces also wore the same excited expressions as she felt in her heart.

The ISS crew floated in the background, they wanted to share the moment but knew that it wasn't theirs and kept out of the way. Everyone who dreamed of going into space dreamed of going to Mars. This was the ultimate journey. And in just over a day's time, they would be heading there.

Chapter 3
Safety Checks

8th June 2022, 06:23 station time

None of the crew slept well on that last night in Earth orbit. Except for Ronald, who maintained that his tours in Iraq and Afghanistan in his younger days had taught him the ability to sleep anywhere. "You never knew when you'd get another chance to sleep," he told them. Besides, he'd told Samantha that a sleeping bag attached to the walls was quite comfortable, although that was true of sleeping in zero gravity anyway.

Samantha agreed they were, however this was another plus for the Mars Voyager's spin-created gravity. It wasn't the comfort or lack of it that had kept her awake. The tension of the next day's events made sleep fitful at best. She usually handled stress well. She wouldn't have been selected for the mission if she didn't, but in this case excitement interfered with her usual calm.

The orbital launch was meticulously planned, but that didn't stop her from reviewing the procedure over and over in her mind. It came as no surprise to her when the others told her they had done the same. Ronald joked that he'd done his in his dreams.

They joined the ISS crew for breakfast and then suited up for the transfer to the Mars Voyager.

When first constructed, the ISS had just a single airlock; with the addition of the new habitation modules for the construction crew, a second airlock had also been added. They needed this to support the increased traffic to and from the station. Connected to the airlock was one of the two tugs used to ferry the construction crew between the station and the Mars Voyager.

The tugs were simple devices. A central harness had enough space for four astronauts to clip onto. Attached to the central strut were three canisters. These would thrust the tug to the ship. Samantha, Colette, Ronald and Juliet would ferry across first and begin the handover procedures.

The Mars Voyager floated several hundred metres away. The tugs weren't built for speed and the journey took twenty minutes. Nothing in space ever moved in a rush. To hurry brought the risk of something going wrong. Despite the excitement of moving towards her new ship, Samantha didn't mind the delay, as the journey to the ship provided her with ample time to appreciate the view.

At the halfway point, they passed four of the construction crew travelling in the opposite direction. The two remaining engineers met Samantha as they entered the ship after cycling the airlock.

"Ms Collins. Welcome to the Mars Voyager. She's in pristine condition and has zero miles on the clock."

"Jake, it's so good to see you."

She meant it as well, they'd first met during one of many planning sessions soon after the mission's initial announcement. Then he had been Chimera Industries's Lead Engineer. He'd designed the Chimera launch vehicle and then transferred from his follow-up project to work with the assembled planning team.

Samantha remembered how chaotic everything had been in those early days and the buzz of everyone's excitement at being involved in the project. The Mars mission wasn't just a dream job for the astronauts, every aeronautical engineer had wanted in on the project as well.

As part of the deal, scientists and engineers from NASA, the ESA and the three commercial partners would be responsible for the design and planning for the mission. In those early days the discussions lacked organisation, if not energy.

Ronald and Jake had stepped in and taken charge. Ronald had also worked for Chimera Industries and knew Jake to be a genius engineer. As well as his technical abilities, he was a skilled leader who knew what would be needed to make the project succeed.

It had been a hell of a risk.

The news of Curiosity's discovery of life on Mars had astounded the world. This wasn't bacteria or traces of life long extinct. The rover had captured a brief glimpse of a worm-like creature burrowing through the ancient clays.

Never had such a brief glimpse of any creature generated so much excitement.

Despite the worldwide euphoria at the announcement of the discovery, the national space agencies had suffered a gradual decline for too many years. The fledgling private launchers lacked the maturity and infrastructure to go it alone.

Neither of them could complete the mission without the other. However the inclusion of private space corporations caused a lot of friction, in particular at NASA. As a long-term NASA astronaut, as well as being the mission pilot, Samantha's role included helping to smooth over some of the organisational difficulties. It had been difficult at first, but as a plan coalesced so too the team came together.

"Here, let me help you with that."

Jake helped Samantha from the bulky suit. It was difficult enough under gravity, in microgravity a helping pair of hands was essential. She noticed the other engineer helping Ronald from his suit.

Once freed, she hugged Jake.

"It's so good to see you again."

They'd last seen each other on her previous trip into orbit. That had been their orientation visit when they'd been getting to know the ship's systems. Off the record, it led to her induction into the 250 Mile High Club. The discovery after the fact that the club wasn't as exclusive as she'd thought had surprised her.

With the private quarters in the habitation module, she'd thought they'd been discreet. But the grins on the rest of the crew's faces at breakfast the next morning had soon dissuaded her of that notion. Much like the mischievous grin Ronald now beamed at her.

She'd hooked up with Jake soon after meeting him. He was smart, charming and funny. He also understood the pressure of her job, as she understood his. She wasn't looking for a relationship, not with a three-year mission in her future, but that didn't stop her enjoying good company.

"Well, we should get started. We have a lot to go through for the hand-off," Jake said as he pulled away from her embrace. Ronald still wore that giant grin. He even winked at her just to make sure that she got the message.

She couldn't help but laugh and then followed Jake into the habitation module, still chuckling. Each module formed a cylinder twelve metres long and eight metres wide. She followed Jake through the central tunnel. After passing through the cone, she used the rungs to move into the first floor.

The ship's rotation wouldn't be started until they had departed from Earth orbit, so for now they had to manoeuvre in zero gravity. They each took a seat at the main command console. He placed his hand on hers, she smiled at him in response.

"It's good to see you."

"You keep saying it so it must be true. Anyway it's always good to see me," he joked in response.

Ronald's voice interrupted them over the radio. "Okay lovebirds, let's get started." He sat at the other command console. Each of the main modules contained multifunction displays that accessed any of the ship's systems. If for any reason any of the modules failed, they could still control the ship from one of the others.

"All right. Colonel."

"Ex-Colonel if you please. I'm a well-paid civilian now."

That had been a long running sore point between the staff of the national space agencies and the private companies. Government jobs didn't pay as well for the same roles and lacked some of the perks from previous decades. Ronald didn't care either way, although like everything he enjoyed making a joke of it.

"We've got a lot to do today, we have to complete this safety pass so I can return to the ISS. Don't worry, I'll be sure to catch you all on your press conference this evening."

Samantha cursed under her breath. She hated cameras. Well, those pointed in her direction at least. She should have become used to all the media attention by now, although it constituted a part of her job that she'd never quite managed to become comfortable with.

"Right, let's start with the power system," Jake told them. "The grid is already online and drawing power from the stage one NTP."

The NTP was a bimodal Nuclear Thermal Propulsion, the first operational one of its type. This drive was an experimental engine that Chimera Industries had been working on for their project to mine near-Earth asteroids. With help from NASA and the ESA as well as their rivals Hermes Enterprises, development of the drive had been accelerated.

The drive was a wonder of technology. It would provide the thrust they needed to get to Mars and supply them with all the power they needed as well. However they did have a flaw: the helium-2 fuel flow had to be exact. Even in low-power mode, a sophisticated computer's sole duty was to monitor the fuel entering the system and make constant adjustments to the flow.

Side by side with Jake, Samantha started working through the hundreds of system checks they needed to complete. Ronald did the same with the communications systems. The vessel had several different communications systems. His test list was almost as long as Samantha's. In the Mars science module, Colette and Juliet followed a similar procedure with the life support system.

Two hours later, Professor MacQuire and Piotr arrived on the tug that had passed them on the trip to the ship. MacQuire began with the landing mission checklist and Piotr the experimentation equipment. Long boring lists for everyone to complete, but without the checks they couldn't leave.

Of the construction crew, Jake was the last on the ship. By the time they stopped for lunch they were less than a third of the way through the checks.

"Looks like I'll have to stay for the night," Jake quipped.

A few mock groans from around the table. The table was useless without any spin to hold anything down. They were supposed to depart that evening, after the live press conference. With the checks not completed, that couldn't happen.

"Linda contacted the ISS. She's postponed the press event until tomorrow. She wasn't happy about it and its caused quite a few political complaints, but David Richards agreed we shouldn't go live until the checks and hand-off is complete."

David Richards was the mission controller back on Earth. He was a calm but purposeful man whose three decades of experience at NASA and the Jet Propulsion Laboratory made him the ideal choice to lead Mission Control. In many ways, his was the hardest job of all. Like the rest of the ground team, he had all the stress of the mission, but none of the glory or the thrill of going into space.

"Shall I make you the guest bed in the lander?" Colette teased.

He laughed before replying "I think we best get back to it. Mission Control are requesting for updates, we're already behind schedule."

She received serious nods from everyone around the table, before they all barked "Yes, Commander Collins!" in mock military fashion.

Despite the levity, they all knew how much they had to do and so they set to it.

* * *

Twelve hours later, the exhausted crew had completed their checks, all fourteen thousand of them. Every system was in the green and ready for launch. Exhausted, everyone gathered for a final meal before retiring to their quarters, or in Jake's case Samantha's quarters.

"We haven't left yet and we've already eaten a day's worth of the emergency rations," Professor MacQuire grumbled. Samantha didn't disagree. The mission relied on them growing almost half of the food they would consume on the mission. To supplement this, they also had four months of emergency supplies.

"Quit complaining," Jake told him. "I'll get the ISS to send some additional supplies in the morning. You'll end up ahead of the game."

"Flavoured toothpaste, delicious!" Juliet retorted.

"You should have tried the MREs back in the Army. They had a sandwich that would never go out of date, so you can give me toothpaste any day." He chuckled, "At least this beef stew tastes of beef."

"What is an 'MRE'?" Juliet asked Ronald.

"Meals Ready to Eat."

"I thought it was Meals Rarely Edible?" Samantha joked.

"You got that right," Ronald laughed. "Well, once we get going we'll be growing and cooking our own. I hope you all like rabbit food."

Ronald wasn't as happy at that prospect as the others already knew all too well. Although they had plenty of dried and condensed meat products to vary their diet, Ronald was correct, the bulk of their food would be vegetarian-friendly.

"Okay everyone, we've had a long day. We should consider getting some sleep."

"Sleep? Is that what you kids are calling it these days?" Ronald said with a lecherous grin.

"Well, sleep might be involved at some stage. Are we all clear on tomorrow's schedule?" Despite the nods around the table she told them anyway. "While Jake returns to the ISS, you'll all have time in the morning for final messages with your families and loved ones."

The ship contained ample communications hardware and bandwidth, so keeping in touch will people back on Earth wouldn't be a problem. However the farther they travelled towards Mars, the longer it would take for messages to reach the ship and Earth. The signal lag would make real time communications problematic and when they had travelled far enough, impossible.

"At midday we have the live press conference. Make sure you've read the briefing packs prepared by Miss Hayworth. The press conference should last no more than an hour. We'll then conduct the final checks and countdown will commence."

Samantha raised her juice.

"Assuming everything goes well, we'll launch at 1800 hours ship time."

They synchronised the ship's clocks with Mission Control, that way the shift pattern for both the Earth-side teams and the ship's crew matched each other.

She smiled and everyone returned the smile and raised their drinks, all non-alcoholic of course.

"To the mission."

She caught Jake's eye and left the dining area.

The personal quarters were all on the second floor of the module, the same floor as the kitchen and living space. The rooms were small, just enough space for their few possessions, a bed and an entertainment system built into the walls. The walls and mountings were constructed from composite plastic, giving the ship's interior an almost sterile look.

Each of the crew had a small case for personal possessions, and it hadn't been easy deciding what mementoes they should bring with them. Samantha imagined the others would be going through the few possessions they'd brought with them. They would be unpacking, making their new quarters home for the next three years.

For tonight she had other plans. It was a tight space for two people, but they'd manage.

Chapter 4
Fond Farewell

9th June 2022, 08:40 ship time

"Hello my darling granddaughter." Piotr greeted the cherubic face of his only grandchild. As he had with his own daughter, he had spent too many years away and missed too many treasured moments. He'd spent many of those years with the Russian Antarctic scientific expedition. There he'd searched for new life in lakes that had remained undisturbed for millions of years.

And now, for this trip to Mars he would be away from them for another three years. He did regret that, but how could he refuse such an opportunity?

"Grandpa! You look funny!"

"You don't like my new blue uniform?"

"It's better than your old green one."

"I liked my old green one."

"It smelled funny."

"No it didn't! Now, are you working hard at school?"

"Of course. My teacher says that I speak the best English in the whole class."

"Your teacher is quite correct, your English sounds perfect. It sounds like you've been practising!"

He always insisted that they spoke in English as he had grand hopes for his granddaughter. Piotr wanted a life for her in Europe, or maybe in the United States, somewhere she could prosper and live without fear. He feared that his country was returning to the old ways and not a place for his family to live.

"Mother bought me a puppy."

"She did, did she? And what have you called this puppy of yours?"

"I wanted to call her Rex, but mummy wouldn't let me."

"Why not?"

"She said that was a boy's name and the puppy is a girl."

"Just like you?"

She giggled. "Not like me. I don't have a tail."

"Are you sure?"

More giggles. "Of course not. When are you visiting me?"

"I told you, princess. I'm going to be away for a long time."

"You'll phone me?"

"Of course. I'll phone you every day. And I have your picture next to my bed. Now is your mother there?"

The goodbyes to his daughter were even harder, but underneath it all, the excitement for the coming journey bubbled. He wanted to get going. He felt a little guilty for that, but the expectation far outweighed that negativity.

When he had finished, he exited the communications booth, constructed to allow privacy for those using it during the trip. Similar facilities were also available in their quarters. Colette took her turn and he heard her greet her mother in French as he propelled away.

* * *

In her quarters, Samantha dressed as she said her goodbyes to Jake. She'd already said her farewells to those back on Earth that she wanted to. She had no family, her friends were all professional rather than personal. Although the time with Jake might change that.

While it was true they hadn't developed more than a 'friends with benefits' relationship, she felt closer to him than any other person she knew.

There wasn't enough space for them both to get dressed so he remained in the sleeping bag and watched as Samantha pulled on her uniform. Once she finished dressing, he slipped free and drifted into her embrace. The stubble on his face scratched her cheek.

"I guess this is goodbye then."

She kissed him in reply.

"So will you look me up when you're next in town?"

"Of course. Now get out here, you have a tug to catch. I'll message you once we get going."

"With some naughty pics?"

She laughed. "The comms booth isn't that private."

"You could take them in here."

"I think not."

Jake kissed her this time and then left her to get dressed. She joined him for coffee a few minutes later. Professor MacQuire was taking his turn in the booth. She guessed that he was talking to his ex-wife. He complained about her all the time, but they still kept in touch.

"Time for me to get suited up. Jones will be on his way."

"He is. The ISS have confirmed his departure. He's bringing the extra supplies with him."

"I should get ready then."

Samantha followed him to the airlock and helped him suit up. They kissed one last time before twisting the helmet into place.

"I'll see you in three years."

"I'll see you before then."

She frowned at him.

"The press conference. Remember?"

And with that he pulled himself into the airlock.

* * *

All six of them crowded into the living area and sat facing the large flat screen. On the screen, a young blonde woman spoke to them. They all knew her well, her name was Linda Hayworth, NASA's principal press officer.

Linda had been and still was an ambitious woman. She saw government service as her route to high politics. Unfortunately for her, NASA started dying a death of a thousand cuts soon after she joined. Continued reductions reduced NASA to a backwater, a problem for someone seeking a political career.

The discovery of life on Mars changed everything. NASA once again became the focus of attention. There were calls for a new mission to Mars, and a manned mission at that. That hope faded when a hostile Congress refused to fund a mission. The President, sensing an opportunity to create a legacy for his presidency, gave his full and public backing.

His position didn't convince Congress to approve the needed funding, although after considerable political manoeuvring they did agree partial funding. The Europeans were eager to join in and committed themselves to the mission. Even after the Russians added their resources, it still wasn't enough.

When the new players of the private space industry became involved, finally the astronomical funding required was raised. As well as their own funding, a huge international groundswell of sponsorship and donations added millions of dollars to the project. In fact it was that early enthusiastic crowd-funded support that paid for the first few months of design and negotiations.

The negotiations had been complex and conducted in secret. An amazing feat that blindsided the President's opposition when he announced the collaboration. That wasn't the end of the resistance, but despite their further efforts, the project went ahead. Their resistance also lost them support in the face of public opinion. The public's imagination had been captivated by the mission despite, or perhaps because of, the worldwide financial difficulties at the time.

Some analysts thought that the huge investment around the world in this most expensive scientific endeavour fuelled the current global economic recovery.

And it also had been Linda's salvation.

The thought of men and women walking on the surface of the red planet fired up the public's imagination. Not just in the United States, but all across the globe. That put Linda on TV screens and websites in front of billions of viewers. She became famous and she made sure it stayed that way.

The budget cuts had reduced the press office to a skeleton team, with her as most senior. At every key moment, she became the face of NASA. She was skilled at her job and the senior officials at NASA appreciated that and saw their own opportunity.

For the past ten years, NASA's operations had been reduced to supporting the International Space Station and few robotic probes. They had become reliant on the Russians, the Europeans and private industry to even maintain a small manned programme.

The voyage to Mars changed all that. They were smart, they understood that there was no way NASA could return to its old glories. The world had changed, but perhaps there would be a new path for NASA to follow. They imagined a role where NASA would become the arbitrator of space as well as a lead partner for human expansion into space.

And so Linda became a household name and as a result she also gained more influence within the programme. She sat on the selection panels for the crew, making sure that those selected were suitable public faces for their roles as well as experts in their respective fields.

For Samantha, these had proved the trickiest part of her selection. She didn't enjoy the public relations part of the job, she never had. Despite her own discomfort, her looks and quick wit made her popular and, Linda knew, a valuable figurehead for the mission's brand.

Linda also arranged the documentaries that featured the crew while they trained for the mission. Never had the public had such access to astronauts preparing for a mission. She wasn't popular with the crew, since she added to their workload and not in a way that they considered critical to the mission. They understood what she needed though and as dreamers themselves, they wanted the dream to continue.

"Thank you all for agreeing to this press conference, I know how busy you all are right now. We're briefing the world's press about the mission as we speak. I appreciate that they should all know the details by now, but we're hosting this as a live event so it's best to make sure everyone is up to speed. When the introduction and overview are finished, we'll move onto the question and answers section with you."

"What happens then?" Samantha asked.

"While you go through your final preparations for the launch, we'll feature your friends and family, as well as various celebrities for their comments and thoughts. Just before we enter the final countdown, we have a live speech from the President and then we have the departure from orbit live."

She cocked her head as she listened to her headset.

"Are you all ready?"

Everyone affirmed that they were.

"Okay then. Let's begin. And don't forget to smile."

Chapter 5
Q&A

9th June 2022, 17:01 ship time

"Welcome back, ladies and gentleman, to this live broadcast for the departure of the most important manned space mission since Apollo 11 in 1969.

"After seeing how the people in Mission Control are preparing to support the Mars Voyager when it leaves orbit, now we'll meet each of the six crew members. Even though they're all real busy with final preparations for the launch, they've agreed to answer a few questions from our guest representatives from the worldwide press."

Linda had vetted all the questions in advance. She didn't want any surprises for what would probably be the most important television broadcast of her career.

"I'm pleased to introduce everyone to Commander Samantha Collins. Like many astronauts, she joined NASA after serving in the US Air Force and has been an astronaut for over ten years. She is the mission's senior pilot and commander of the Mars Voyager."

The negotiations to ensure that NASA held the primary crew slot had been protracted, but their established expertise in long missions and ownership of the ground facilities swayed the final decision.

Samantha appeared on screen, wearing the familiar blue jumpsuit that all of the crew wore. Once the mission departed, the dress code would be more lax, although the uniforms were comfortable and practical to wear.

She might not have liked having the camera pointed at her, but many of the men in the audience appreciated the view nonetheless. She was short, slim and pretty in a classic American way. Linda had capitalised on that as often as she could – she knew her audience. Most of the men wished they were with her and many of the female audience wished they were her.

"Hi everyone. How's everyone doing tonight?"

She knew how to charm an audience as well, her open smile and capacity for light banter made her the perfect representative for the mission. Linda had devoted considerable time into schooling Samantha to create the best impression on screen.

"We're all great down here, Samantha. Thanks for taking the time to be with us, we know how busy y'all are right now."

"No problem at all, Linda, we're touched by the well wishes that everyone has sent our way."

"That's great, Samantha. Our first question is from Dale Carlton from CNN."

"Good evening Ms Collins and to everyone on board. You can't imagine how excited we all are in this final countdown. The question voted by our viewers to ask you is: What will you say when you first step onto Mars?"

"That's a tricky question, Dale, are you sure your viewers don't want to pick another?" The audience laughed dutifully. "As you can imagine, I've given it a lot of thought and Linda's provided some good suggestions, but I haven't decided yet. I think Neil Armstrong already beat me with the best line."

She received a few more polite chuckles from the audience and Linda.

"For Samantha's second question, we turn to Victoria Morgan from Fox News."

The negotiations for the order of the news organisations presenting the questions had also been a tricky process. Linda had dealt with these herself rather than allow any of her assistants to do the work, and as a result extended her contacts considerably. She was a hot ticket and at that moment could have asked for whatever she wanted to join any of the news channels.

Linda, however, maintained a view for the long game. Public relations for her was simply a means to an end. Even with her gruelling schedule, she still found the time to continue her law and political studies. Her network of contacts spanned big business, politics as well the news media and they would all come in useful for her future. But for now her task was to make the Mars mission the most talked-about event in history.

"Hi Samantha. Our viewers would like to know: How do you prepare for such a long voyage?"

"Another good question, Victoria. A big part of our selection has been psychological testing to make sure all of the crew members have a suitable temperament for living as a small group for so long a period.

"We've also trained with each other for almost four years now, so we all know each other pretty well. The Mars Voyager has more space allocated for the crew than any other spacecraft ever constructed. We even have our own private quarters. It's not five-star accommodation, but we all have our own space."

"Thank you Samantha. And now let us welcome Colette Laurent. She joined the European Space Agency after eight years of service with the French Air Force. She is the crew's medical doctor and also the co-pilot for the Mars mission."

If Samantha was popular with the male audience, then Colette stole the show. Her classic looks were almost a stereotype for French beauty which, combined with her soft accent, meant she should have been selling perfume rather than exploring deep space. She complemented Samantha's home-grown presence in a way that helped keep the fickle public interested in the crew. Everyone knew that a pretty face alone wouldn't have passed her through the selection process. She was smart, had earned several degrees and was one of the world's foremost experts on space medicine.

"Thank you Linda. It is a pleasure to be here. I can't tell how excited we all are up here."

"I'm sure. And we're all excited with you. Your first question is from Marcel Phillipe from the FRANCE 24 news channel."

"Bon, oui Mademoiselle Laurent. The whole of France is proud to see one of their own preparing for this historic journey to Mars. As a doctor, what challenges do you face on this journey?"

"Bonjour to all of my countrymen. As a doctor, this mission provides us with a unique opportunity. The years of operations on the International Space Station have provided great advances for medical science in space. But the ISS is within the magnetic belts that protect our planet from the solar winds.

"Radiation from solar flares and these solar winds present a danger for those travelling outside of Earth's protection. We are well protected within the ship, but we are explorers into a new realm. I'm thrilled to be a part of that exploration."

"Thank you Colette. Your second question is from Margaret Leroux from BFM TV."

"Hello Colette. Our viewers have been eagerly following your progress ever since your selection. After running a poll on our website, they would like to ask why you changed career from being a fighter pilot to a doctor?"

Colette appeared surprised by the question. Linda may have vetted the questions, but she hadn't checked with Colette. She'd answered the same question many times during the selection process. Linda had seen no reason not to allow this question.

Colette clearly didn't agree, but she was live on international television. A few torturous seconds passed and Linda glanced at the monitor.

"That's a complicated question." She paused. "As part of the Air Force, we helped many people across the world. I loved flying, but I wanted to take a more personal and immediate involvement with the people I encountered.

"The Air Force was very supportive and helped me as much as they could to achieve what I wanted to do."

In the silence that followed, Linda noticed the follow-up question building on the reporter's face so she intervened.

"Thank you Colette. We'd love to talk with everyone for longer but we're running out of time before the launch, so let's move on to the rest of the crew. Next we meet the mission engineer, Ronald Larsson. He served with the US Army Corp of Engineers before joining the Jet Propulsion Laboratory's propulsion research programme and then helped to form Chimera Industries, which as you know is one of the major partners of the mission."

Ronald took his turn in front of the camera. His face was rugged, handsome in a way that inspired trust. His straight bearing marked him as an ex-military man and the easy smile on his face counterbalanced the stern posture.

"Good evening Linda and hello to all of our viewers, it's swell that you all could join us for the countdown."

He waved at the camera. Somehow his infectious grin looked wider than his face and the crowd responded to his charm with cheers.

"Hi Ronald, thanks for joining us. I understand that you have a message for someone special."

"I sure do, Linda, we're not the only people celebrating today. We might be going to Mars, but my mother and father are celebrating their golden wedding anniversary. Congratulations you guys!"

"That's wonderful news. Everyone here at Mission Control sends their wishes as well. Now Ronald, your first question is from Mark Reynolds from The Washington Post."

"Thank you Linda. It looks like we weren't the only ones to use an online poll to select our question and congratulations to your parents from the staff and readers at The Washington Post. Here's the most voted question for you: How involved were you in the design of the spacecraft?"

"Hi Mark and hello to everyone at The Washington Post and thank you for your well wishes. As for your question, everyone in the crew was deeply involved not only in the mission planning, but in the design as well. We all have particular skills and experience that are vital to the mission.

"My favourite example was Piotr's improvement to the toilets after a nasty experience on the ice in Antarctica."

Linda intercepted any follow-up to that comment.

"Thank you for that image, Ronald. Your second question comes from Leanne Porter from the New York Times."

"Thanks Linda. And thanks Ronald and let me wish the crew good fortune for your trip and of course many best wishes to your mother and father."

"We appreciate that, Leanna. What's your question?"

"As the mission engineer, what do you think will be the greatest challenge for the mission?"

"Well, there are many potential challenges, that's what makes the whole mission so exciting! We've worked hard to anticipate any problems we might encounter. We've identified the landing mission as the most problematic as there are more potential points of failure during that part of the operation, but also the most rewarding.

"It's also the most vital part of the mission. After all, we're going there to find out more about the life form we know inhabits that region of Mars."

"Thank you, Ronald, for answering those questions. Up next is Professor Stephen MacQuire. He has been a theoretical physicist at Cambridge University in England for many years. He has more recently been working in partnership with the Asteroid Mining Corporation, another of the mission's major private business partners."

Even in the NASA blue jumpsuit, MacQuire looked every bit the professor. His hair stood out at angles around his lined face and his glasses gave him an academic look. Linda was convinced he deliberately made himself look like a stereotypical English professor. His accent also had a tendency to become more pronounced whenever he was in front of a camera.

"Good evening everyone, and thank you Linda for the introduction."

"It's great to have you, Stephen. For your questions we start with your fellow countryman, Bob Knowles from the BBC."

"Thank you Linda. Stephen, can you tell us why a physicist is going to Mars?"

"That's a great question, Bob. We'll actually be spending more time travelling to and from Mars than we will at Mars. This is a unique opportunity not only to discover how deep space affects us as humans, as Colette has already mentioned, it's also a splendid chance for us to learn more about what space is like beyond the Earth."

During the selection process, Linda had almost vetoed MacQuire's selection to the mission. However, she wasn't one to make decisions on instinct and had been surprised when focus groups responded positively to his odd mix of schoolboy charm and lecturing officiousness.

"Let me explain what I mean by that. While there have been many robot probes over the past decades, there hasn't been a manned presence beyond the Moon. But as a physicist, going there and being able to decide what we're looking for while we are actually there is very exciting.

"I can't wait to get started!"

"Thanks Stephen, we're almost as excited as you are! Your next question is from Blair Hodges from Sky News."

"Hi Linda. Hello Stephen. First let me wish the whole crew our best from all of the viewers of Sky TV. They want to know, is this a moment you have always dreamed of?"

The huge grin on Stephen's face answered the question better than his words would.

"Of course, Blair. I never thought I would ever go into space, even when I started working with the AMC. For me to experience and live the science that has fulfilled me throughout my life in such an extraordinary way is incredible."

He might sound strange, Linda thought, but his enthusiasm was felt by the crowd.

"And the Mars Voyager will be departing in just a few short hours. We will be showing the launch live on this channel, but before then let's meet the last two members of the crew.

"Here's Juliet Jakes. After spending twenty years working with oil and mineral companies around the world, she joined Hermes Enterprises as their lead geologist."

Juliet adjusted herself in the camera, beaming a bright smile at the audience. Besides Samantha, she was the only other member of the crew under 50 years old. Her accent still contained traces of New York where she grew up. She lacked the obvious beauty of both Collette and Samantha, but even so she was very photogenic, although some of her mannerisms did lead people to underestimate her intelligence.

"Hello everyone. It's good to see so many people interested in our little trip."

"The pleasure is all ours, Juliet. Your first question is from anchorwoman Kirsty Morgan from ABC News."

"That's great Linda, and thanks for joining us, Juliet. Can you tell us why a mining geologist is going to Mars?"

Linda hid a frown, that wasn't the tone of the question that they'd agreed beforehand.

"Well, Kirsty. I worked in the oil and mining industry for a long time, but I've also been studying and publishing papers on planetary evolution for most of those years.

"When I left the industry, I looked for a new challenge and considered teaching and received some generous offers. However, Hermes Enterprises contacted me and told me about their dream for mining asteroids in space. I thought that this was my opportunity to have a real impact on the future of the human race."

Linda cut in. "For those watching who want to learn more about how asteroid mining can provide benefits for us all, check our website. The address is shown at the bottom of the screen. You can also check the live feeds from the International Space Station and from inside the Mars Voyager."

With the length of the voyage ahead of them, the crew were happy that the cameras wouldn't be switched on all the time...

"For your second question, we are joined by Caroline Davis from MSNBC."

"Thanks Linda and hi Juliet. Thanks for taking the time to speak with us. What will you miss most on your journey?"

"Okay, I wasn't expecting that question! I'll be missing my sister and her family a whole bunch. It's going to be hard being away for so long from them. We have the best communications equipment so we'll be able to keep in touch.

"Other than that it would have to be ice cream. I love ice cream."

"I think I would too," Linda joked. "And now let's meet Piotr Vasilevitch. He represents the Russian Federal Space Agency's partnership in the Mars Voyager mission. He is the world's leading microbiologist and has spent much of his life hunting unusual life in extreme conditions, such as in the buried lakes in Antarctica.

"I think it would be fair to say that you are the happiest biologist on the planet right now, Piotr?"

Piotr's grinning face filled the camera. His peppered hair afforded him a distinguished appearance, although the crinkles around his mouth and eyes showed his obvious happiness.

"That's not true, Linda. After all, I am no longer on the planet."

"Very true, Piotr. For your first question, let me welcome your countryman Mikhail Gorsky from the ITAR-TASS news agency."

"Thank you Linda, and thank you Piotr Vasilevitch. Our question is an obvious one, but what does the discovery of life on Mars mean to you?"

"You're correct Mikhail, it is an obvious question, but also one that is very close to my heart. My entire career has been hunting life in places where no life was thought to exist. We've found life in the deepest holes ever dug into the Earth's crust and in lakes that haven't seen the Sun in over a million years.

"Every time we discovered a new organism, it gave more weight to the argument that life will find a way to exist, no matter what the conditions. Despite that we'd never discovered life, or even signs of it, beyond the confines of our planet.

"When I first heard of the discovery of life on Mars, it was a moment of splendour. It was not just traces of ancient life, but an actual living organism. The odds were good that simple microbial life existed somewhere in the Solar System and here we have a complex organism."

Indeed, such a simple creature had never inspired such excitement across the globe.

"This is the greatest news anyone could have ever told me... apart from the birth of my beautiful daughter, of course!"

Linda responded with her own warm smile. "It was a monumental moment for everyone." The viewing figures confirmed that. The voice in her earpiece confirmed that the current viewing figures were over 1.7 billion viewers. And they were all looking and listening to her.

And the crew of course, but she was the one running the show.

"Our final question for the crew comes from Iba Samara from Al Jazeera."

"Thank you Linda, and welcome to you Piotr and all of your crew. Our viewers wish you every success with your journey."

"Thank you and what is your question?"

"Now that we know there is life on Mars, is there any danger that we could harm that life by landing on the planet?"

"The sad fact is that earlier probes may have already created that threat. With that in mind, for this mission we have taken the possibility very seriously. We have taken the most extreme precautions we can with the landing equipment to make sure we don't add any contamination to the surface.

"The very same is true of the probes that we'll send down before the manned landing. One of the major tasks for the probes is to assess the situation on the surface to make sure that we do not pose a danger to the indigenous life."

The camera cut back to Linda.

"Thank you all aboard the Mars Voyager. We'll let you continue with your safety checks and prepare for the final countdown. While we do that, let's meet some friends from around the world..."

Chapter 6
My Fellow Americans

9th June 2022, 18:03 ship time

The crew all had the live broadcast visible in windows on their secondary screens. The checklists were now all complete. Mission Control had paused the countdown at T minus ten minutes. After the President's address, the countdown would resume and with it they would be ready to leave Earth orbit.

The President's distinguished face filled the screens and the crew sat strapped in their seats in rapt attention. He looked proud and that was understandable. He had, after all, invested a lot of capital, political and otherwise, into the Mars mission. His advisors had considered it unwise when he had publically backed the project while still battling for election to his second term.

This moment was a personal triumph as well as a historic one.

"My fellow Americans. Over fifty years ago, the proud American Neil Armstrong was the first human being to step upon an alien world.

"That first footstep was in his words 'a great leap for all mankind', but more than that, it was a pinnacle of American ingenuity and achievement. A victory over our enemies of that time. We had won the Space Race.

"Once again we stand before the world on the brink of history. The world has changed in many ways since that monumental moment. This journey is no longer a race between two contesting super-powers. No, it is now a race of co-operation.

"Without the involvement of countries around the globe, including former opponents, we would not be here, heralding this greatest journey ever undertaken by mankind.

"So my address is not just for my fellow Americans, although we should be proud as a nation of our participation in this mission. Let me start again, but rather than my fellow Americans, let me instead say, my fellow citizens of the world."

The President had left out the three other major players in space, as well as China and India. The early negotiations had included representatives from these nations, and the goal had been for an inclusive international effort. However, competing goals had stalled these negotiations and so to maintain any progress, these nations had been sidelined and ultimately shut out.

While they weren't taking part in the mission itself, both India and China had agreed to provide full access to the data from their orbiters already in Mars orbit. China's space programme had become a powerhouse with the recent Moon landing and launch of their own space station in low Earth orbit.

China already planned to send their own manned Mars mission within the next five years. That had provided some additional impetus to the urgency of the international mission. Simply put, they wanted to get there first.

"And this moment sees not only the restoration of great agencies like NASA to their purpose, but also the rise of private industry on this last great frontier.

"I think even my colleagues in the Republican Party would be pleased at the economic and technological boom this mission heralds. Although I'm sure they wouldn't care to say so in public."

He flashed a wry smile for the camera.

"We're all gathered here, whether in person or watching the countdown on our televisions, computer monitors, mobile phones and tablets. The sharp end of the mission is the six astronauts, who are at the moment waiting for me to finish this speech so that they can resume the countdown and depart Earth orbit.

"I know how hard they have worked to arrive at this moment, but they are the lucky ones. They are the ones who will see Mars up close. Four of them will be even more fortunate, they will actually walk on the surface of another planet, something humanity has dreamed of for thousands of years.

"Yet at this moment, let us not forget everyone's hard work and dedication which made this moment happen. The engineers and technicians, the computer programmers and the secretaries. The factory workers and the caterers. And yes, even the accountants and the lawyers."

Another broad smile for the camera.

"Without the thousands of people working together, this tremendous undertaking couldn't have been completed. So I would like to thank all of you who have toiled and supported the project.

"That all said, let me wish the brave crew of the Mars Voyager Godspeed, and like all of you listening, I will be awaiting their mission updates."

Chapter 7
Departure

9th June 2022, 18:15 ship time

The launch countdown resumed moments after the President completed his address. Now they heard the final countdown in stereo, first on the command channel and then in an echo seconds later on the live broadcast. It soon became distracting, so they muted the broadcast so they could focus on the channel from Mission Control.

Like a mirror, the broadcast displayed the views of the three command panels. Each of the crew sat at their designated positions. Any of the consoles could take charge of the ship should any of them fail.

At the main control panel in the habitation module sat Samantha and Piotr. In the Mars observatory module waited Colette and Stephen. Even though Samantha had primary control, they were ready to cover if needed. Juliet and Ronald occupied the remaining console in the Mars science module and also stood ready as a third level of redundancy.

At T minus ten minutes, they scanned through the readouts of the core systems. Each checklist item was highlighted in green by the computer. At the secondary and tertiary consoles, Colette and Ronald confirmed the same readings.

Their proximity to the ISS meant they couldn't fire the main engines. Even when they did, it would be much less dramatic than the rocket launch from Cape Canaveral two days ago. Chemical rockets mixed liquid hydrogen and oxygen in a raging firestorm that provided immense thrust, but they lacked endurance and required a lot of heavy fuel to do so. This made them impractical for the long haul to Mars.

The nuclear engines used by the Mars Voyager would be far less visible, to the naked eye at any rate, although it possessed several advantages over the older and more ostentatious rockets. Rather than its might being spent in mere minutes, the nuclear engines would run for weeks. And in low-power mode, they could generate all the electrical power the vessel needed for months. As far away from the Sun as they were heading, solar panels wouldn't provide anywhere near enough power.

The bimodal nuclear engines provided the main thrust for the vessel. For manoeuvring they used hydrazine thrusters, the same technology as used in most satellites and probes. They were a safe and well-established technology, unlike the main engines. This would be the first long-range mission using the revolutionary new drives. The technology had been used before on small probes, but never for a ship of this size.

The retro thrusters fired, slowing the vessel's orbital speed.

In a few minutes, the Mars Voyager fell behind the ISS and out of its shadow. The ship soon slowed enough for its orbit to decay. If it continued, it would eventually decay enough for the ship to catch on the Earth's upper atmosphere and burn up on entry. Except for the lander and habitation module, none of the other parts of the ship could survive the intense heat and forces of re-entry.

At T minus eight minutes, the retro thrusters stopped firing.

Samantha cycled the main engines' coolant flow, preparing for ignition. These engines were experimental. Ronald had been part of their development with his friend Jake. They'd tested the engines successfully and had even passed the stringent stress testing, but this would be their first real use.

At T minus seven minutes, Colette initiated the communications check for the ship's three main communications systems. The main system connected to the three-metre high-gain antenna placed on the habitation module. It would provide a data channel capable of five megabits per second, slower than most people's home broadband connection.

The second system was a high-bandwidth laser communications system provided by the European Space Agency. It was an experimental system that had been tested in Earth orbit, but it supported a thousand times the bandwidth of the standard high-gain antenna.

When designing the mission, the engineers and planners tried to utilise as much established technology and systems as they could. However, a mission of this duration was unprecedented so they had to include more experimental systems than they would have liked. Everything had been rigorously tested, but even so, operating them as a combined package was new to the crew and the team back at Mission Control.

The final system was a series of high-bandwidth secure wireless transmitters. They had a short range, about a thousand kilometres, but they provided high-speed links to the ISS and ground control while in Earth orbit. While in Mars orbit, they would link with the deployed orbital satellites and rovers on the surface.

"All communications are in the green," Colette reported.

At T minus six minutes, the crew locked down their seat restraints. The thrust would be much lower than the rocket launch, but it was best to lock everything down.

Ronald activated the life support system's auto switch mode. If any part failed, it would automatically switch to the back-up systems.

T minus five minutes passed and Samantha activated the stage one engines. For the next five minutes, the engines would idle, their output kept at zero thrust. The ISS had now moved far enough away to be out of danger from the engines at T minus four minutes.

At T minus three minutes, Colette re-checked and confirmed the telemetry connections with Mission Control. The team back on Earth would now receive a constant stream of data from the Mars Voyager. The main stream provided the basic navigation and command data, while further secondary channels compressed and transmitted data from all of the ship's sensors both internal and external.

Tension stretched those last few minutes. On the consoles' secondary screens, the images shifted between faces of their excited family and loved ones. It felt strange for the crew to be focused on the impending launch and to have everyone watching every moment.

At T minus one minute, the countdown changed to seconds. The crew had nothing left to do except hope the systems performed as designed. They glanced at their loved ones on their screens and waved goodbye to the cameras.

The countdown ended and Samantha triggered the stage one's thrust. She increased the power in increments, they didn't want to stress the system too quickly. For the first three minutes the crew felt nothing, then they experienced weight. Nothing compared to the immense pressure of the launch from Earth, but still an odd sensation after their time weightless.

Samantha took a moment to look at the Earth on one of her monitors. It wasn't as good as seeing it with her own eyes even if the image was clearer. On the high-definition screen, the Earth looked so blue it might not have been real. The Pacific Ocean almost glowed, and in the halo of black around the planet no stars could be seen, the reflection of the Sun's light was so bright.

In that short moment, she wondered how the rest of her crew were feeling. For herself, she felt a pang of homesickness. That struck her as odd, since the only person of importance was on the International Space Station, no doubt watching the Mars Voyager depart.

The moment passed and the thrill of the mission filled her once again, as she focused once more on the control screens in front of her.

Everyone remained restrained in the seats as they departed Earth orbit. After checking that the crew remained secure in their seats, Samantha initiated the spin. Hydrazine thrusters jetted and over several minutes, Samantha increased the rotation speed until it reached the required 3.8 revolutions per minute.

With the spin established, they felt their weight pushed towards the outer circle of the rotations. Samantha selected the cruise mode for the main drive controller. The thrust would be kept at a minimum level to keep accelerating the craft along its course. With beaming smiles all round, the crew released themselves from their seats.

They were on their way to Mars.

Chapter 8
Early Days

1st July 2022, 06:35 ship time

Samantha recalled the first week, only Ronald managed anything resembling decent sleep. For Samantha it was primarily the excitement of being on their way that kept sleep at bay. After so many years of training and hard work, it felt amazing. For the others it varied, although excitement played a big part for them too.

This wasn't unexpected, as the mission psychologist had warned them early in their training that this would be a likely situation. Routine would adjust them to their new situation, although it would take time. So for that first week, Mission Control pushed them hard to establish a routine and to tire them into natural sleep.

Experience from the ISS and simulated long-term missions highlighted the likelihood and dangers of sleep deprivation, so it was something the crew and Mission Control took seriously.

They operated on ship time, their clocks synchronised with the same time zone as back in Houston. That way they were in tandem with Mission Control. They had been operating on the same time frame before the launch, which helped reinforce the pattern.

During the early planning discussions, the idea of shift teams had been mooted. Naval vessels operated on a similar principle, but they had larger crews to work with. The crew had discussed it at length and decided that it would be better to operate as a single team, rather than create a division between the six of them.

Natural partnerships would evolve over time anyway, so the ground team encouraged anything that helped mould them as a single unit.

So they followed the same timetable. Like good housemates, they divided up their duties between them. Unlike many housemates, they actually kept to them! They even divided the mission-specific duties between the crew to continue building their familiarity with each other's roles. Key tasks would still be performed by the relevant mission specialist.

Ship's lighting was keyed to their day-night cycle to help reinforce the routine. The ship's interior was never completely blacked out, since the risk of accidents was greater than the concern for some loss of sleep. However, the general lighting was dimmed during sleep periods and their private quarters could be blacked out for comfort.

Whoever was on breakfast duty also got to use the shower first. The shower had been designed to work in microgravity by attaching an enclosing sheet and a pump. However, while the ship was rotating the fake gravity allowed them to shower normally, a luxury never available on a spacecraft before.

In emergencies, they could fall back on the wet towels as used on the International Space Station. For such a long journey, the advantage of a real shower improved morale as well as personal hygiene.

They had all the heat and electricity from the drives that they would need and an efficient water recycling system, but even so, the showers had a two-minute timer. Plenty of time for everyone to get clean, apart from Colette it seemed. Almost every morning she could be heard cursing in French as her two minutes ran out.

That morning, Samantha took her turn as the chef of the day. And already the joke was wearing thin. Breakfast that morning consisted of ham and mushrooms, diced and mixed with scrambled eggs. They weren't real eggs of course, but dried and condensed. For preparation, all they needed was some water and heating.

They prepared most of the food in the same way. Their stocks contained as wide a variety as possible, and included many of the crew's favourites. They would also grow some of their own food to add fresh vegetables and fruit to their diet.

Stephen had suggested that they bring a few hens along, so they could eat fresh eggs every morning. He'd said it in jest because he kept a few hens at home, but the planning team had looked into the possibility anyway. They hadn't taken his suggestion for bringing a pig along for fresh bacon as seriously.

"So what's for lunch then?" Stephen asked as he chewed his eggs. They might have been reconstituted but they didn't taste bad, although nowhere near as good as the ones his hens laid.

"I haven't decided yet," Samantha replied as she looked around the table. "And what is on today's to-do list?"

This had become part of their new routine, whoever cooked asking what the day's plan would be.

"I will be checking the equipment in the medical bay," Colette responded. "For the fifth time in three days." She tempered the complaint with a smile. "Then it's my turn in the gym."

Everyone had to exercise at least two hours per day. They didn't have to do it all at once, in fact they were encouraged to spread it out throughout the day. As part of their exercise, they were tested for muscle and bone loss. If the tests were abnormal then Colette prescribed additional supplements and exercise. They also maintained accurate records of their exercises for the medical team on Earth to monitor.

On the second floor of the habitation module, a small gym had been constructed for that purpose. There was space and equipment for two to exercise, but their new routine had them exercising in private.

Stephen swallowed another mouthful. "I'll be first in the gym, but then I'll be in the science module preparing for the first batch of experiments."

"I'll be helping Samantha with clearing this place up." Piotr nodded at the breakfast remnants on the table. "I'll then join Stephen in the lab and help set up the experiments. Solar wind physics isn't my usual field, but I'm sure it will be fun."

"Of course it will be fun!"

Juliet drained her juice. "I'll be running through flight safety checks and then running stock checks on the supplies."

"Well, I thought I'd take the morning off. You know, laze around and see what's on TV."

Samantha raised an eyebrow at Ronald, and he chuckled in reply.

"Okay, I'll be checking our packages we're delivering on the way."

Part of the deal with the three private corporations was deploying three prospecting satellites that would be used to investigate some of the near-Earth asteroids for mining suitability.

The three companies had encouraged the assumption that they still competed against each other. In truth, none of them were big enough to pioneer the space mining industry on their own. It wasn't public knowledge yet, but the businesses had agreed the division of labour and the resultant spoils between them.

Chimera Industries had the most launch vehicle expertise and so would provide the engines and transportation. The AMC designed the mining drones and processing plants that would take the raw ores and refine the pure resources to return to Earth orbit. Hermes was developing the drop pods that would be used to transport the refined metals and minerals to the surface.

They were also investigating the technologies and infrastructure to begin manufacturing in space. The ability to deliver raw materials to Earth was just the start of the process.

To expand into space, they needed to have a manufacturing base in orbit so that fewer expensive launches would be needed to maintain a presence in space.

Each aspect of the plan presented severe challenges. Alone, the cost would be insurmountable to solve everything. Together they separated the problem into smaller parts, in the same way as they had for the Mars mission.

"I, of course, will be cleaning your mess up and preparing your lunch. I think salad will be the order of the day."

Stephen and Ronald, as the crew's resident carnivores, groaned. Samantha smiled sweetly at them.

The living space was small so clearing up the remains of breakfast and cleaning the space didn't take long. Samantha took a leisurely time preparing lunch for everyone. She prepared a salad from their limited supply of fresh leaves, but to keep the boys happy she also cooked burgers, or rather reheated them.

Over lunch they chatted, not about work, but about their latest messages from home. Samantha had received a video message from Jake. It turned out to be a flirtatious message that caused her to blush when she watched it. She blushed again when Ronald teased her when she declined to talk about it.

Piotr showed the collection of bold coloured drawings from his granddaughter. He handed his tablet around so that everyone could marvel and compliment his granddaughter's artistic talents.

Stephen and Colette shared the emails from children in their respective countries. Messages from a dozen children asking them about life in space. A seven year old boy's query about how could they poo in space made them all laugh.

After lunch they resumed their duties. For Samantha that meant clearing the table and then taking her turn in the gym.

Chapter 9
Tending the Garden

18th July 2022, 06:00 ship time

For the first time since leaving Earth, Samantha woke feeling almost normal. Her body had finally acclimatised to being on the ship. She'd slept for seven straight hours and felt refreshed. She enjoyed the novelty of being awoken by her tablet's insistent tones.

Jake's face grinned at her from the screen. Samantha smiled as she stretched and remembered the video call from the previous evening. After nearly six weeks of travel, the communications lag now made live chat difficult. She reflected that all too soon it would be impossible, and it surprised her how disappointed that made her feel.

A rap at her door snatched her attention from her thoughts.

"Shower's free."

Samantha acknowledged Colette's prompt and climbed out of bed, another luxury possible thanks to the ship's continual spin. She'd grown accustomed to the lower gravity and moved with a lazy grace. As she showered, she remembered that Stephen was on cooking duty today. That meant breakfast would be bacon rolls again. She should be thankful that at least they wouldn't be greasy.

Her guess proved correct, it wasn't true bacon of course, but it smelled and tasted pretty close. She chewed the hot roll with gusto. Colette's expression as she pulled faces while eating the salty meat amused her.

Tomorrow would be Sunday and that meant a day of rest. Now that everyone had adjusted to life aboard ship, Mission Control had directed that they reduce their timetables to normal levels. That meant Sundays would be rest days for everyone. Piotr and Juliet would receive a recorded service transmitted from Earth, as they were the only believers on the trip.

As they ate, they followed their tradition of outlining the day's activities. Today Samantha had gardening duties, her least favourite job, but essential to the mission.

With her breakfast eaten, she exited the habitation module and made her way along the connecting tunnel. The tunnel had been constructed from inflatable walls, the outer layers comprised of multi-weave micro-fibres far tougher than Kevlar. A core lining of liquid metal as used in the US Army's latest body armour provided a self-sealing layer in case of punctures from meteorites.

A line of rungs helped Samantha pull herself along the tunnel. The gravitational effect from the spin lessened the farther towards the central junction she travelled.

Samantha had to take care as she manoeuvred herself through the central spindle. The arms with the attached habitation and Mars science modules spun, but the central spindle didn't. The Mars observatory and the landing module were attached to the top end of the central spur so they couldn't spin. At the speed the spurs rotated, it would have caused motion sickness for the crew when they were in those modules.

She pushed into the central spur. She then pulled herself up towards the observatory module. The feeling of weightlessness again helped make the task easier.

They required sixty square metres of growing space for their crops. Most of the equipment in the observatory module wouldn't be needed until they reached Mars orbit, so this made it the most convenient space for cultivation. Moulded covers placed around the module provided trays for the plants to be grown in.

Experiments on the ISS had helped determine the best plants to grow and they had brought a good variety with them. Each tray contained a different plant and they planted a batch in stages so that they'd have a continuous supply of fresh fruit and vegetables.

The trays were already half full with the current crop and she checked each of them in turn. First up were the salad leaves, lettuces and spinach. They bedded the plants in an engineered mesh that held the growing compound together. Water from the recycling system kept the plants hydrated, while a computer-controlled system injected nutrients into the water. UV growing lamps provided the necessary light and heat to accelerate the plants growth.

The plants had been genetically modified to ensure quick growth as well as resilience to various diseases. Disease was one the biggest threats. In the enclosed conditions and with the circulated environment, any disease would devastate their crop.

Part of the gardening duties involved a visual inspection of the crop as well as random sample testing. Some of the plants also required structural support in the low gravity, so the tall plants like tomatoes were held up with plastic rods.

Samantha checked the rest of the crop, which consisted of beef peppers, carrots, green onions and cabbages. There was also a small herb garden for flavouring their meals and Samantha's favourite treat – strawberries. The first batch would ripen in a few more weeks and she couldn't wait to taste them.

The current crop all looked fine so she turned her attention to the empty trays. This was her first planting. The task was easy enough, but Stephen obviously felt otherwise. He popped his head through the hatch from the central spur.

"Do you need a hand?"

He'd been paying her a lot of attention in the last few weeks. While that wasn't unexpected it wasn't welcome, not for Samantha, or at least not yet.

One of the reasons for the mixed crew was to allow for personal relationships, romantic or otherwise. Psychological experiments and studies into single-sex crews for long missions had shown that problems occurred with unreleased sexual, romantic or even just intimate relationships.

She'd already noticed that Juliet and Ronald were spending more time alone, syncing their off-hours. Samantha didn't think they'd joined the Million Mile High Club yet, but she was willing to bet it would only be a matter of time.

Stephen was a handsome man, but Jake was still too fresh in her mind to consider partnering up with anyone yet. Maybe farther into the voyage she'd change her mind, but for now she was content with the video messages for company. That was odd for her, sleeping with someone had never been that big a deal.

"I'm good, thanks."

"Are you sure? I've got the time."

"No I'm all right – thanks. It's not rocket science after all."

The joke fell a little flat.

"Uh. Okay. I'll catch you later."

Samantha returned to the task at hand. She planted more strawberries. She'd need to plant the other crops as well, but strawberries was what she wanted. It was a shame none were ripe enough to indulge in just yet.

Chapter 10
Public Relations

20th August 2022, 13:01 ship time

Almost three months into the journey, Samantha had her wish granted. The rest of the crew were well aware of her desire so didn't use the strawberries and waited for her to use the small harvest when it was her turn as cook. Tempted as she was to eat them for breakfast, Samantha maintained her willpower and saved them for lunch.

For the first time, they prepared lunch using only the food they'd grown themselves. A picnic atmosphere graced the meal despite the close white walls of the module. They were the farthest away from Earth any human being had ever been.

Their initial excitement from starting the mission had faded under the grind of the routine that made the experience seem normal. That simple meal rekindled their excitement.

During lunch discussion turned to the main reason they were all here – the discovery of life on Mars.

"Why now, Piotr?" Colette asked.

"What do you mean?"

"Why have we discovered these worms now?"

"We don't know that they are worms, Colette."

"Whatever they are, why did we find them now? We've had probes and rovers in that region for years."

"Well, the Curiosity Rover did dig into the soil and these creatures, whatever they are, aren't common. Even since the first find and we know what we are looking for, we have only found trails, and not many of those."

"So what do you think they are?"

"Worms is a good guess, but apart from that first image, we don't know for sure. The trails in the clay are reminiscent of worms' trails here on Earth. Whatever they are, there aren't many of them. They appear to be solitary creatures."

"What are they feeding on?"

"That we don't know either, but we have some good guesses. I would have assumed they're feeding on bacteria or some other microscopic creatures. If that's true, we haven't seen any sign of them and that was the type of life the rovers we have sent have been searching for. It's also possible that the worms are extracting minerals from the clay. It might be rich enough."

"Okay everyone, speaking of food, it's time for dessert."

Everyone turned to face Samantha as she brought the small bowls to the table. She'd used condensed milk as cream, but nobody minded. They all waited for her to eat the first one.

She grinned as she chewed. Sweet juice burst with flavour inside her mouth, a little taste of heaven up here amongst the stars.

"That is divine."

Everyone ate theirs with equal enjoyment. They had enough for a few each, so they finished them all too quickly. Instead of leaving the table and continuing the day's tasks, they sat content for a few minutes in companionable silence.

Samantha broke the tranquil moment. She didn't want to, but her afternoon task was the daily chat with the mission's public relations feed. These daily conversations and presentations were part of the continued drive to keep the mission's profile high with the public back on Earth.

It wasn't the crew's favourite part of their job, but despite her dislike of the camera, Samantha didn't mind it too much. Sometimes it was even fun. She hoped that today's call would be one of those times.

The time delay now meant that over a minute passed between questions and answers. This would be the last live video chat until the return journey.

"Hi Linda," Samantha greeted her as Linda's face filled the screen.

...

"Hi Samantha."

Linda's voice always sounded like it had a bounce to it, even while they weren't being broadcast.

"It's all good up here. We had our first strawberry crop. I've emailed you some photos. I'll make sure to pin them to our board later," said Samantha.

...

"That sounds great. Make sure that you tweet and post them as well."

"Sure. I'm using the app you provided so they all get done together."

...

"Excellent. Your last post was the most popular one yet."

So guys like watching women work out in the gym, who would have thought it?

"Typical, the blurry video where I'm at my sweatiest."

...

"Everyone just wants to know what life in space is like."

"It's a lot like home, but everything is lighter, the apartment is smaller and there are more cameras."

Samantha's smile took some of the sting out of the comment, but Linda frowned at the comment anyway.

"If you're not feeling up to this then I'm sure one of the others can host the chat."

"No, I'm fine. Honest."

...

"Okay. Today we have a short Q and A with an elementary school up in Maine. Are you sure you're okay?"

"Yes, of course. It was just a bad joke."

…

"All right then, let's get started."

The view on the screen changed to show a classroom with a dozen children, their faces bright with excitement. Behind them, their teacher looked a little nervous. Proud, but also visibly concerned about being live with her children in front of the world.

Linda appeared in a smaller window, inset into the feed from the school. She introduced the kids and then handed over to Samantha.

"Hi kids, thanks for joining us. So who has a question for me?"

…

A dozen hands shot into the air and a dozen voices clamoured for attention.

"Okay, you, the blonde girl at the front. What's your name?"

…

"Sally, miss."

"All right Sally. What's your question?"

…

"Thank you miss. Can you see Earth from your spaceship?"

"We can, we have a few portholes in the modules and we can just about see the Earth as a blue dot. We do have excellent telescopes on the ship that provide a clearer view. Here, let me show you."

She tapped a few commands on the tablet to access the small telescope that they used to align the laser communications system. She then showed the screen to the camera.

"I'm Eric, miss'"

Linda must have prompted the teacher to pick the next child to ask a question; that made sense, the delay was making the conversation next to impossible.

"How fast is your spaceship moving?"

Again Samantha tapped on the tablet, this time to access the navigation controls when the ship's current speed and velocity appeared on screen, she held it to the camera.

"As you can see, we're travelling very quickly. We're moving at more than twenty miles every second. That's the fastest that any human being has ever travelled."

For the next half hour, Samantha continued to respond to the children's questions. A slow and cumbersome process thanks to the signal delay which was growing longer with each question and answer. They were about the usual things, questions that Samantha had answered many times before. The penultimate question came from a quiet little boy near the back of the class.

"Does it get lonely up in space?"

Yes.

Yesterday had been the first day she hadn't received a message from Jake. Was he bored of the wait already?

"No. We're all good friends here on the Mars Voyager. We have a good communications setup so we can talk with our friends and family."

The last question came from the teacher.

"What do you eat up in the space ship?"

It seemed an apt question from the rotund woman, but it helped strengthen Samantha's camera smile.

"We ate strawberries. Today we ate strawberries."

Chapter 11
Prospecting

11th September 2022, 08:46 ship time

Despite their newfound co-operation, the corporations built each probe with different design philosophies. Each reflected the institutional expertise of the different companies.

The Asteroid Mining Company built theirs as a cloud of mini-sats. These were a new form of robot probe that utilised swarm dynamics to gather information. The method meant that a larger volume of space could be more easily covered and provided a level of redundancy impossible in more traditional probes.

These were still quite experimental and had been inspired by the cube-sats developed in the previous decade for enabling cheap (relatively speaking) orbital experiments that could be launched as part of larger mission packages.

The AMC had projected the orbit so that their probe passed close by a few known loose clusters of near-Earth asteroids. NASA and other agencies around the world monitored these groups in case any headed towards Earth.

As they approached one of the target asteroids, it would release a few of the mini-sats from the dense cloud. In turn each mini-sat would split into two. The first part would fire a tiny rocket motor to propel itself into the surface of the asteroid. When it impacted it would scatter dust and other particles into space. The partner mini-sat would then capture the impact and return images and spectrographic data back to Mission Control on Earth. This data would then be used to determine the suitability of the target asteroid for future mining.

The orbiter part would continue to follow its target, mapping it and providing more data for several weeks until its batteries ran dry.

Meanwhile, the cloud would continue its orbit around the Sun, seeking more targets and depleting its stockpile as it went. With all the accumulated data, they could then select the most suitable target. They would also have gathered a considerable amount of data useful for asteroid trackers and researchers on Earth.

Chimera Industries, on the other hand, took a more traditional approach. They placed all of their eggs in a single basket as they intended to land on their selected asteroid and conduct test drills on various spots on the asteroid's surface. Their mission was to test their experimental drilling systems.

The company picked their target asteroid after reviewing data from an ESA probe's flyby two years ago. The data indicated the asteroid had a high metallic content and was therefore suitable for the drilling test.

The lander was equipped with two different drilling systems. One of the key issues facing the mineral exploitation of space was getting the equipment needed to the mining sites. By necessity, equipment for mining was bulky and heavy, two attributes which added to the expense of any venture in space.

To make the project's finances viable, they needed to address these issues and part of that included making the system automated. Human beings required life support and that represented the greatest expense of any space venture.

Both of the experimental systems were designed to be lightweight and automated. The first system resembled the traditional methods for drilling and extracting ore, however the materials used for the drills used the latest technology to manage cooling and keep the system light. Tests on Earth had been promising, but everyone was well aware that operations in space were a different matter.

The other system was more revolutionary as it used lasers to dig into the surface. While tests had been less successful on Earth, the company considered this an alternate plan if the more traditional method failed. At the very least it would produce more useful data for the analysis team.

Hermes Enterprises' probe comprised of three separate systems. Each would follow different orbits and then encounter several asteroids along their journey. Each probe would then fire a laser to create a debris cloud. Sensors would then analyse that cloud to determine the composition of the asteroid and thus its usefulness as a mining operation.

They had now reached the point in their flight path to release those probes on to their own missions.

"Mission Control to MV-1. Hi Samantha."

The signal from Earth now took almost nine minutes to reach the ship. They were farther away from Earth than the Earth was from the Sun. It made live conversations like this tedious affairs.

"Mission Control, this is Mars Voyager. Hi David."

Over the months, the conversations between the ship and Mission Control had grown more casual, still business-like, but much less formal than during the launch phases.

"We're seeing a launch window variance of minus two per cent, are you reading the same Samantha?"

The probe launch parameters included a generous launch parameter variance, more so than would be usual for a probe launch. They couldn't afford to change the Mars Voyager's course even by the smallest margin, so the first stages of all of the probes allowed for extra course corrections if needed.

"We're seeing the same, David. We've already programmed the corrections into the launch program."

...

"Confirmed. We're seeing the update here."

"We've already run full diagnostics on all three units. All systems and sub-systems reported green. We've sent a data burst with the full report."

While waiting for the response, she spoke with Colette as they began their manual checks on the primary systems.

"Data burst received and opened. We're scanning the results, but go ahead and start the manual checks."

"Already started. Colette is here to confirm the readings."

"Propulsion, in the green."

"Propulsion in the green confirmed."

"Navigation, in the green."

"Navigation in the green confirmed."

"Communications, in the green."

"Communications in the green confirmed."

They continued until they completed and confirmed all of the checks on the Chimera Industries probe. They then had to wait for Mission Control's confirmation.

Over four hours later, the checks for the three probes were complete.

"Samantha, you are go for launch. Keep the telemetry feeds open, but you are now the launch control for the probe launches."

"Thanks David."

Samantha looked through the readouts on the displays in front of her one last time. She then turned to Colette.

"Let's get started."

Colette nodded and checked the same readouts on her own screens.

"Launching probe one."

An electromagnetic pulse pushed the smooth cylinder containing the probe away from the vessel. The Mars Voyager was no longer accelerating so it took only a few minutes for the container to drift clear of the ship.

"Probe is clear," Colette reported.

"Opening pod."

Tiny explosive charges along the seams of the pod curled the container into petals, revealing the lumpy sphere of the probe, with the rocket stage beneath.

"I'm starting drive ignition countdown."

It was a short countdown, and ten seconds later the flare of the single rocket motor bloomed on the screens for the cameras recording and monitoring the launch.

"Ignition confirmed."

"Monitoring trajectory," Colette responded. "First vector monitoring is well within the green."

Every minute, Colette checked the probe's trajectory and confirmed it was within the expected parameters. After ten minutes, the engine died and the rocket stage separated from the probe.

The telemetry data from the probe fed into Mars Voyager's computers and ten minutes later back to Earth. Both Mission Control and the ship's computers would continue to monitor the feed.

An hour later, they'd completed the same process with the Chimera Industries probe and the second telemetry feed connected with the ship and Mission Control. With two of three missions launched and just the one left, they relaxed a little.

In that moment, everything went wrong.

On the third launch for the Hermes Enterprises probe, the rocket stage failed to fire.

"Mission Control, this is MV-1. We have a problem with the third probe launch. We're running diagnostics, but we'll lose the high-bandwidth connection soon."

Samantha and Colette were both exhausted. They'd already spent seven hours at the controls. The last thing they needed was a problem here at the end. Samantha checked the flight controls and the system responded to her command codes as expected, but the engine still didn't fire.

Ronald brought them coffee and sandwiches. They ignored the sandwiches and drank the coffee.

"Juliet's gonna be pissed at you," he joked.

"You're not helping," Colette replied.

They heard him laughing as he retreated.

"Hey! Where are you going?" Samantha shouted.

"What?"

"Get your ass back in here!"

Ronald returned to the command area. "So you need a man's help then?"

"No, we need an engineer. Stage one isn't firing."

"I know, I've been monitoring back in the science lab. Have you checked the command code interface?"

"Of course. It seems okay."

"What about the communications interface?"

"That looks clear too," Colette replied.

"Have you tried the other channels?"

"It shouldn't make a difference, but I'm about to try that?"

"Okay and use the low-bandwidth command set."

"What? Why?"

"I suspect that you're experiencing some network collision."

"From what?"

"The other probes."

"But they're on different frequencies."

"They are, but coming from the same comms system. It should be cycling the frequencies, but what if the software isn't synced with the frequency change?"

"Surely we'd see a similar problem on the telemetry feeds?"

"They're on different channels, telemetry and commands run on different systems. And don't call me Shirley."

Even Samantha smiled at the old joke.

"I'm getting a response," Colette said. "Here we go, the engine's firing. Stage one ignition confirmed. Initial trajectory is good."

"Thank God for that," Samantha replied. "I'll let Mission Control know."

"I told you ladies that all you needed was a man's help."

They heard him laughing as he returned to the living room.

Chapter 12
Feel the Burn

16th September 2022, 10:20 ship time

Samantha pedalled hard on the cycle exercise machine. The equipment monitored her effort. It would complain if she didn't push herself hard enough. Two hours of sustained exercise had to be completed by each of them every day.

They were now three months away from Earth. While that was far from the longest time astronauts had spent in space, no astronaut had been out of the protection of Earth's magnetic fields for such a length of time.

Outside of the magnetic fields the solar wind raged, invisible to the naked eye. The wind was full of charged particles that posed a health risk to the astronauts. The Mars Voyager's function was to protect the crew from its fury. The skin of the ship contained a dense layer of hydrogen-rich polyethylene.

Throughout the ship, radiation detectors monitored the radiation levels at all times, but so far they'd detected no major radiation events. The Sun was a turbulent beast and at any moment could throw a fit and cast a storm of energised particles out into space.

Samantha pushed herself harder. The mask on her face measured her breathing and the composition of her exhaled breath. The crew had to test themselves by various means as a part of their exercise and health regime.

Their blood, their urine and even the air they breathed was tested and data compiled for the doctors to analyse back on Earth. Colette was also conducting her own research with the crew as willing volunteers.

Twenty minutes into her routine, Samantha stopped pedalling and breathed in deep for a minute. With some relief, she removed the mask. The mask made the exercise more difficult, it also made her face sweat.

She crossed the small space and sat in the weight resistance machine. Samantha set her weight level and started pumping her arms. She pushed with even, straight movements and timed her breathing to match the motion. She preferred the weight machine to the bike, as cycling felt too passive. With the weights it felt more like she was fighting against something.

As she completed each exercise set, she made sure to record it on her tablet. The medical team back in Mission Control counted their calorie intake and calories burned in detail.

Jake had got in touch, a casual video message. The tone of the message sounded distant compared to the videos he'd sent in the early weeks of the mission. It still sounded friendly, but lacking the intimacy of previous communications. It might be true that she hadn't wanted anything serious, but she still felt slighted.

Those feelings complicated her thoughts, and she knew that if she tried to bury them then they would compromise her ability to command. The sensible choice would be to talk with one of the other crew members. They were all friends and she trusted them with her life. Even so, she couldn't open up to them.

Instead she imagined her anger pushing the sweat from her skin, not the exertion with the machine. Her arms burned so she shifted to her legs. They'd lost a little tone since leaving Earth, but they still looked good.

The thought surprised her, she wasn't as a rule given to reflecting on her body shape. Not that she'd ever had to worry about it. Her years in the Air Force and then with NASA had forced her to keep in shape.

Samantha checked her watch. Another twenty minutes done, almost time to start winding down. She then started the stretching routine. Right on time, Colette entered the small gym.

"How's it going?" the French woman asked.
"Almost done."
"Good, it's time for your daily prod and poke."
"Wonderful."
"I'll meet you in the medical bay."

A few minutes later Samantha entered the medical bay, a quick enough journey as it was opposite the gym and next to the command area. She waved at one of the cameras as she passed.

There were cameras all over the ship, and the feeds remained popular viewing back on Earth. The bathroom, private quarters and medical bay were safe zones, places where they couldn't be observed by the watching public.

They still received daily data packages containing emails and messages from their fans all over the world. They all devoted a part of their day to responding to the ones that Linda had flagged as important. With the lack of loved ones back on Earth, she spent additional time to respond to some of the ones not flagged by Linda.

"Let's get this done."
"Of course Samantha, take a seat."
"And what poking and prodding will there be today?"
"The usual, we'll start with downloading your bio-monitor data. Hold your arm out, we might as well check your blood pressure while the tablet syncs."

The crew all wore a device that looked like a wristwatch. It contained a number of sensors that monitored the vital signs in real time. As part of the daily examination, they downloaded the data into the ship's computer where Colette and the medical team at Mission Control reviewed it.

Colette checked Samantha's downloaded data. Like the rest of the crew, she was keeping in good shape. She also took a blood sample from Samantha's arm. The medical bay had a number of advanced systems that tested samples, all the more data to add to the collection.

As well as monitoring the health of the crew, Colette also researched some of the feared effects of travelling through interplanetary space. Her current focus was effects on the immune system.

So far, only a small decrease had been detected. The exercise routines were also helping prevent muscle and bone mass loss. The artificial gravity provided an additional reduction in the problems experienced by astronauts compared to those in the ISS when living for extended periods in microgravity.

"There you go. All done!"

"Thanks."

"How are you feeling, Samantha?"

"Okay."

"You seem a little distracted."

"No, I'm fine."

"All right. If there is anything then let me know."

"Of course."

For a brief moment, Samantha resented the inquiry from Colette. She realised that Colette was simply doing her job but Samantha felt fine. True, she wasn't feeling as sociable as perhaps she should be, but that was just tiredness and she was sure that it would pass.

Samantha headed down to the lower floor. The rest of the crew were watching a film, laughing at the comedic action on the screen. She recognised it as an old classic from the Nineties and considered joining them, but she decided to shower and return to her quarters instead.

Chapter 13
Disaster

5th October 2022, 09:31 ship time

Familiarity didn't make gardening duty any more pleasant for Samantha. Easier, yes, but that didn't make it any more fun. Back on Earth, she owned an apartment and was happy that meant she didn't have a garden to worry about. It always seemed like a lot of effort for limited reward.

Of course there was a very real and essential purpose to the horticulture they practised on the Mars Voyager. Despite its critical nature, it remained her least favourite chore. It did, however, provide one positive aspect and that was the time alone and away from the rest of the crew.

It wasn't a constant need and she still spent much of her time, whether working or otherwise, with the crew. But she did find that she needed more time alone and she still couldn't make herself talk to someone about it.

On an intellectual level, she understood that this posed a real threat to the cohesion of the crew and from that it created unnecessary risk to the mission. Her pride in her abilities suppressed that worry so that it didn't affect her waking thoughts, but it did disturb her sleep. Sometimes she woke and saw dark shadows under her eyes. Military service and the intense training at NASA had ensured her ability to function for extended periods so none of the other crew had noticed her deterioration.

They had been warned of the dangers of sleep deprivation and several studies had concluded that such issues would be common in astronauts on extended missions. During mission planning, it had been decided that sleep monitors wouldn't be fitted to the crew as standard. Although Colette did have some in storage if she felt that one of the crew needed monitoring.

Another reason for her to interact with the doctor as little as possible. She didn't want the fact that she wasn't operating at her best shared with anyone else.

Repeated trips to the module had allowed her to perfect her movements along the connecting tunnels. She moved through the changing effect of the rotation in a balletic move, her body now well used to its changes. With a single smooth motion, she entered the central spur and looked up towards the observatory module.

She now even enjoyed the disconcerting feeling as the ship's spin tugged her in one direction and then, after flipping through the junction, it pulled from the other direction.

She noticed that the hatch was closed.

It shouldn't be closed.

She activated her comms mic. "Who closed the observatory hatch?"

Samantha heard Juliet's voice, she was currently on command deck duty. "No-one as far as I know."

"Well, I'm looking at a closed hatch now."

"Hold on, let me check."

Samantha continued climbing up the spur while waiting for further information. As she neared the closed door, she discovered that the red safety seals were visible. They should only be visible if the door had been sealed by the automatic system and that could mean only one thing.

A sinking feel hollowed her stomach. Her training kept her voice calm.

"Hey Juliet."

"Go ahead Samantha."

"The hatch is showing the emergency seals."

"What?"

"I can see the emergency seals of the door."

"That can't happen. It should have triggered the alarm."

In the case of life support failure, especially an atmosphere leak, the hatch would seal itself. When that happened the system should have sounded an alarm and transmitted the problem to everyone's tablets.

"I know. What are the sensors reading in the module?"

"Atmosphere looks fine. Wait a minute. That doesn't make sense."

"What's going on?"

"Hold on, I need to grab Ronald."

"Ronald? Why? What's going on?"

A frustrating minute passed before Ronald's voice came on the line.

"Samantha, don't open the hatch."

"What the hell is going on? Juliet said the atmosphere was okay."

"It is, but it's freezing in there. I'm reading minus thirty degrees centigrade."

"That's impossible."

"Well we either have a faulty sensor suite, or some sort of life support failure. Either way, we need to be careful. I'll meet you at the junction."

"Okay, heading back now."

Twenty minutes later, they finished installing a temporary airlock just above the junction with the connecting arms. Samantha and Ronald had also suited up in the internal emergency suits. They couldn't be used outside the ship, but would protect them from temperature extremes and the cold vacuum for a short time.

These suits were far less bulky than the external suits and used a recent development in materials technology. Spacesuits were made from dozens of thin layers that provided the required protection, and these new materials made the layers thinner and more flexible.

At the command deck, Juliet and Stephen worked on the computer to try and establish what had happened. So far the diagnostics revealed that there had been a sudden temperature drop a few minutes before midnight ship's time.

"I don't understand why the hatch was sealed, but the alarm wasn't also triggered?" Samantha asked.

"We're still working on it," Stephen answered, "it looks like the alarm isn't activated by sealing the hatch. It goes through its own assessment heuristics."

"How the hell did that get through testing?"

"I can't tell. We'll keep looking."

"All right. We're suited up and ready to enter."

They used Ronald's tablet to check the sensor readings in the module. The temperature still read minus thirty degrees centigrade. The atmosphere pressure looked normal and they saw no elevated radiation readings.

"We're going in now."

Samantha led the way. It was a tight squeeze in the temporary airlock, but it didn't take long to seal the entrance and then open the hatch.

She stepped inside the module, followed by Ronald who had attached a portable sensor unit to his tablet. He frowned at the readings.

"This doesn't look right."

"You're right about that."

"What?"

"Look."

Ronald glanced up from his screen and saw what Samantha had seen the moment she entered the module.

Their crops were dead.

All of them.

"Oh shit."

All of the growing trays contained dead plants, their leaves curled and turning brown.

Samantha nodded her agreement, before asking, "What the hell killed them?"

"Thirty seconds ago I would have said flash freezing, but look at this." He showed Samantha his tablet. The tablets linked to the ship's network and they also had their own basic sensor suite.

"The air temperature is normal. Broken sensor?"

"It must be, I'll take a look. We should keep the suits on until we figure this out."

While Ronald checked the sensors, Samantha examined the crop remains. There were no signs of frost or obvious cause for their demise. She looked around, the trays were all fixed to the surfaces of the module. A few of the trays were askew, as if they'd been knocked by something.

"Take a look at this," she said.

"What?"

"These trays have been moved."

"So?"

"They are fixed in position, they can't move, something must have moved them."

"I can't see how."

Samantha moved further into the module. It was faint but she noticed a mark along one of the walls trailing towards the central ladder. After following the mark she found another mark in parallel to the other, but along the floor.

She couldn't imagine what could have caused the marks.

"Ronald, this is weird, what might have made these?"

Ronald joined her at the wall.

"You're right, that is strange."

"Well, what is it?"

"I've no idea, we'll need to take a sample and analyse it. We're going to conduct a full investigation anyway. I'll check the sensors. You take a look on the other levels, and let's hope that the damage is restricted to this level."

Each of the modules was divided into levels. The rotation that provided their fake gravity pushed everything outwards, so climbing up the central ladder was actually climbing down. It had taken everyone a while to get used to that and they climbed up backwards to avoid the weird sensation.

This time she climbed forward as she wanted to see the state of their plants as soon as possible. Climbing towards the floor was still disorientating. After she climbed onto the second level, it took only a quick glance to confirm that the crops on this level had been destroyed as well.

Samantha reported the news to Ronald, who cursed in response.

She continued the climb to the top floor, where the ceiling arched towards the nose cone. The plants were all destroyed here as well. She observed that the marks she had found on the bottom floor were visible here too and were much more pronounced.

"Everything is fucked up here as well." Only then did she realised how stressed she felt. She closed her eyes and breathed deeply, willing the anxiety away. "Those weird marks are up here."

"There's something very strange with this sensor cluster," Ronald responded.

"Does it explain what's happened here?"

"Not that I can see, I'll have to replace it and take a closer look. We'll have to check everything in this module."

Samantha keyed her mic. "Stephen."

"Yes Samantha."

"The crops are all dead."

"Bloody hell. How?"

"I'm not sure. Ronald's found a problem with the sensors as well. The readings you told us were wrong."

"So what do we do?"

"We follow procedure."

And there was a procedure for just this occurrence. The plants and their growth medium would have to be destroyed and sealed in case of contamination. New growth trays would have to be set up and new crops planted.

"Can you send Colette down and we'll get started. You and Juliet continue searching the code; we need to know why the alarm didn't trigger. You'd better send Piotr to help Ronald."

Chapter 14
Loner

16th October 2022, 12:46 ship time

Samantha sat on her bed in the cramped quarters. She hated typing on the tablet's touch screen, but she didn't want to leave her solitude and use the command desk terminals. She could have dictated the report, but the sound of her own voice echoing back at her seemed too weird.

She was typing the final incident report, not that they had found any satisfactory answers. They'd provided regular updates to Mission Control since the incident. They were as concerned as the crew, although they hadn't been able to provide any clear explanation either.

At least they experienced some good news. They'd completed the replanting and the new crop had now sprouted. They'd set up the growing trays into the Mars science module and more in the habitation module. Until they'd cleared the observatory, they didn't want to risk the new plants in the same environment.

It made working and living difficult, especially in the already cramped habitation module. But even though they had sufficient emergency food supplies, they needed to get the fresh food available as soon as they could. To stay in Mars orbit for the planned nine months, they needed the additional food supplies. In addition to the better nutrition from fresh food, the crew's morale also benefited. On top of that the life support, in particular oxygen generation and waste recycling, relied on having the crops in progress.

The next part of the report contained less favourable news. Ronald had replaced the damaged sensors and ensured that they now operated as expected. After running checks on all the other systems in the module he found some other damaged units, all sensitive electrical systems.

Once he had tested and declared all the systems operational, he investigated the damaged components. That's when the difficulties that were hard to explain in the report emerged. He called in Stephen for his help. Ronald had seen something similar to the damage he'd found before, but it seemed too crazy. He wanted to be sure of his conclusion before sharing it.

That annoyed Samantha, although in fairness almost everything seemed to annoy her these days. It wasn't the disaster with the crop; this stretched feeling had started before then. She could blame Jake, wanted to blame him in fact. He'd resumed their text and video messaging and they confirmed that they were back in the 'friends zone'.

She realised that blaming Jake wouldn't be fair on him. It wasn't true either. She found the company of her crew mates tiring. The sensible thing to do would be to speak to Colette, and a small part of her mind kept screaming at her to do exactly that.

That small voice seemed like too much effort to listen to and besides, she had too much work to do. To keep up appearances and make sure that the mission remained on track required all of her energy and focus.

She thought that some music would help calm her thoughts, so she activated the screen built into the wall of her quarters. Like the tablet, it was touch controlled and she selected one of her playlists, then returned her attention to the report.

The damaged circuitry looked like it had been fused by an electromagnetic pulse. That couldn't be the case, since an EMP couldn't occur by accident. The causes she knew about were nuclear detonations and specialised military devices. Ronald had some familiarity with both and he knew that neither would have produced the damage he'd seen on such a small scale.

Besides, something like that would have registered in the other modules' sensors.

Ronald was also certain that there were traces of plasma burns as well. He found them on the damaged circuits, but also on the marks that Samantha had seen on the module walls. Stephen confirmed Ronald's findings, although neither of them could explain how this occurred.

They inspected the wiring between the damaged components and found no damage. For seven separate components to be fried without showing any connecting damage didn't make any sense – they should have discovered something.

The experts at Mission Control were equally mystified. They had conducted experiments trying to replicate the problem, so far without success. The current theory was that somehow a series of capacitors had malfunctioned at the same time and had created a power surge that had caused the damage.

That theory didn't explain all the facts, but the crew and Mission Control rolled with it anyway.

In better news, Juliet had conducted the investigation into why the alarm hadn't triggered and discovered that the fault was a simple problem. The computer code that monitored the environment was a different routine to the code that sealed the hatch. The alarms only cared about decompression, not that the door had been sealed. The programmers had assumed that both would occur so the system required separate criteria. A quick software patch, verified by Mission Control, fixed the problem.

The investigation into why the plants died added to the mystery. Piotr confirmed that flash freezing had killed the plants, the problem was that he and Ronald couldn't explain why the freezing had occurred. They theorised that was why the sensors registered such a low temperature, the error had occurred in the same instant or immediately after the flash freeze.

As to why the flash freeze happened at all, that was more problematic to explain.

They speculated that somehow a plasma flow could have caused a localised temperature inversion. That didn't explain how the plasma flow occurred at all. A powerful magnetic field might have created a plasma flow if it had enough energy to change the air. If that had been the case, then it should have done more than blow a few sensors.

The problem gnawed at everyone in the crew. They were all concerned and they knew it. Samantha handled it by retreating, spending less time socialising with the rest of the crew. She realised this was the wrong thing to do as the commander, but did it anyway.

Colette and Juliet started arguing about every little thing. To be in their presence for any length of time became a trial. Ronald and Piotr focused on the problem, trying to find an explanation. It might be a fluke accident, but if it wasn't, what would happen if the same fault struck the habitation module?

If they suffered another complete crop loss, they would be in real trouble. They would have to abandon the mission and return to Earth. They wouldn't have enough food to stay in Mars orbit.

An even worse thought surfaced: what would happen if the problem occurred during the landing?

Samantha sighed and completed the report. She signed and encrypted it ready for the next data burst. For a while she lost herself in the music that filled her quarters. The moment didn't last long before the spell faded and she checked her emails for new messages. A new video file from Jake waited at the top of the list. She ignored it and started replying to the public relations requests from Linda Hayworth instead.

Chapter 15
Changing Orbit

30th October 2022, 15:56 ship time

Two weeks passed and the depressive cloud over the crew dispersed. They hadn't solved the problem, but every test had pushed the likelihood of reoccurrence further away. The crew spent more time together and even resumed the breakfast ritual of reciting their plans for the day.

Samantha knew from the private communications from Mission Control that the team on Earth had become worried about the crew's state of mind. The problem for them was that her mind was the bleakest of them all. She functioned enough to respond to the messages, assuring them all was well even though it wasn't.

The guilt from her deception added to her burden although things had improved somewhat since then. The crew returned gradually to their previous enthusiasm. For the most part this was due to the approaching orbit transfer. With another stage of the journey almost complete, the end goal of reaching Mars coming closer had restored their spirit and focus.

At this point they were heading past the point they would intercept Mars. In fact they were already beyond Mars. The second stage would now be used to correct that course and swing the ship into the path of the oncoming planet.

In just under three months they would arrive in Mars orbit. The view from the observatory module showed the red planet far clearer than any view from Earth could have been. That simple sight also reinvigorated everyone's enthusiasm for the mission.

All six of them crowded onto the command deck, with Samantha and Colette at the two control consoles. They all sensed the buzz in the air and it felt good to be working as a team again. The displays repeated on the wall screens and tablets so everyone could watch every detail as it happened.

They weren't the only ones watching, although the viewers back on Earth experienced a thirty minute delay on the signal. To Linda Hayworth's annoyance, the viewing figures had declined from the dizzying heights of the mission's launch. Now only hundreds of millions watched the event, but it still featured on many major news channels and websites across the world.

For the benefit of the viewing public, the crew kept some of their chatter on the internal comms. The severe signal lag meant that Mission Control would have no input on the manoeuvre.

Samantha took the lead. "We're all set here. Checking approach vector. I'm seeing all in the green."

"Confirm all in the green," Colette replied. "All safety pre-checks for stage two burn completed and in the green."

"I confirm pre-checks in the green."

The second stage burn was the same drive as the first stage that had launched them out of Earth orbit. Two of the fuel tanks were now empty and would be ejected from the ship's structure. Once ejected, the lower mass would mean that the single drive unit would be sufficient to change the orbit for the Mars approach and provide the braking manoeuvre once they reached Mars.

"Initiating drive sections one and three release."

"Confirmed."

Small explosive charges shattered the mounting bolts holding the two drive sections to the ship. They all felt the vibration as they separated. Small gas canisters activated on the drive sections and pushed the drives and attached fuel tanks clear.

"Auto sequence for firing initialised. Dial in the adjustment vector."

"Auto sequence showing as active. Adjustment vector entered. Computer showing variance and it's well within the green."

"Confirmed."

"You girls sure say 'confirmed' a lot," Ronald joked, although he had the sense to keep it to the private channel.

Samantha didn't bother to conceal her grin. "Countdown initiated. Burn ignition in six zero seconds."

"Confirmed." Colette just about managed to prevent the giggle.

Nobody said anything through the countdown; on the various displays, they watched the remaining seconds tick away.

"Wait, I'm showing an error with the coolant flow." Colette's voice increased in pitch.

Samantha scanned the engine control board, where the error in the flow control flashed red. She cursed under her breath.

"I'm pausing the countdown. Mission Control, we are holding the countdown at zero minus ten seconds. The computer has identified a possible problem with the second stage drive unit. We're looking into it and will report when we have more information."

There was no point waiting for a reply, it would take at least an hour and they all knew what they had to do. Colette relinquished her seat at the console to Ronald who started the diagnostics routine for the second stage.

At that stage, they all hoped that the fault was a misreporting sensor or maybe a software glitch. Ronald's diagnostics would determine whether it was the first case and Samantha handed her console over to Stephen so he could test for the second possibility.

Colette and Piotr moved to the observatory module and set up on the secondary command console. The first thing they established was how long they had to initiate the burn for successful completion of the transfer.

Samantha waited impatiently for a few minutes until Colette reported in.

"We have a window of just under six hours to complete the manoeuvre."

That was a bit of good news, at least they had a decent amount of time to work with. Whether that time would be adequate depended on what Ronald and Stephen found.

"Thanks Colette, can you maintain comms with Mission Control? Keep them up to date."

"Of course."

"Thanks."

Samantha then hovered for several more minutes, the urge to pester the two men took a lot of restraint to ignore. She knew that they would inform of her of any findings and that her asking them beforehand wouldn't make the answer come any quicker.

"Sam! You'd better take a look at this," Piotr said over the private comms channel.

Ronald and Stephen were both still busy at the primary console so she unclipped her tablet from her leg.

"Send it to my screen, Piotr."

"Done."

She looked at the screen. It appeared to be one of the external cameras positioned all over the ship. They were placed there to enable them to check the ship's exterior without having to leave.

The camera view on her screen showed the lower part of the engine mounting, a cover pitted with micro-meteorite impacts. She recalled the engineering plans, and knew she'd locate the coolant flow control under that cover.

She didn't see the problem Piotr had intimated at first so asked, "What am I looking for?"

"Look at the base of the cover, the bottom cover near the engine exhaust."

"Still can't see it, damn it. I'll try one of the bigger screens, pipe it onto the TV."

"Okay."

The same image was displayed on the large screen used for movies and group chat in the living room. It was the latest in high-definition and showed the camera image of the coolant housing in perfect clarity.

"I see it."

And she did, she saw a mark, darker than the surrounding shadow. A blemish that reminded her of the marks she'd found after discovering the destroyed crops.

"Shit."

"Da," Piotr replied. "I don't think this is a software glitch, it looks like there's been some physical damage."

"What could have caused it?"

"I'm not sure, my first thought was a misplaced explosive charge on the mounting bolt, but that should have caused the damage higher up the cover, even if that were possible."

"Sam," Ronald shouted out.

"Got to go, Piotr."

"Okay."

"Yes Ronald, what have you found?"

"Sensor diagnostics are coming back clean. I've started a deeper scan on that and connected systems, it'll take a while to run, but I don't think it will show anything."

"How long will it take?"

"About an hour."

"Any way to speed that up?"

"I've already set the priority to maximum, there's a lot of sub-systems for it to chew through."

They had limited time, so waiting for an hour for a possible dead end didn't seem like a good bet to Samantha.

"How about you Stephen?" she asked. "Anything with the software?"

"Nothing obvious so far, but this will take some time, there's a lot of code here. I've messaged Mission Control, although I imagine they're already doing the same. The lag will mean no back and forth, so we should assume we're on our own."

"Agreed, keep at it and get Juliet to help you."

"Will do."

"Ronald, how certain are we that the problem is that specific coolant control?"

"The computer seems to think so. Without seeing the component it's difficult to be certain, but you know what they keep telling us."

"Trust your instruments."

He nodded, the smile looked forced though. "Trust your instruments."

"Take a look at what Piotr found, could that have damaged the control?"

Ronald summoned the image on to his screen.

"It's in the right place, although I can't think what could have caused it. I'd have to look under the cover to be certain."

"We have less than six hours, we could lose an hour checking through the diagnostics. To review the software will eat all the time we have unless we get lucky, assuming the computer is correct and we could replace the faulty part."

"Yes we could, we have two spares for the coolant control, it's a modular design so replacing it is do-able and within the time we have."

"How long would it take to swap out the part?"

"It's a simple job, it shouldn't take more than an hour. I see where you're going with this and I agree that it's probably our best plan. We should continue the other investigations, but we can EVA and swap out the broken section."

"I agree."

"All right then, I'll get suited up."

"Sorry Ronald, not you."

She sympathised with the look of disappointment that crossed his face. She'd taken part in an Extra Vehicular Activity on her first visit to the International Space Station. That had been a repair job as well. She'd had to repair a faulty communications module damaged after a fragment from a weather satellite had collided with the station.

Like the space station, the Mars Voyager had been constructed in as modular a fashion as possible, to facilitate easier repair. This was most important for any repairs that had to be undertaken outside of the ship. Spacesuit technology continued to improve but with the life support requirements as well as radiation and micro-meteorite protection, they were still quite bulky.

"I'm the mission engineer and best qualified to complete the repair."

"I know you want to go out there, but anyone can swap out the module. It's a simple job, but a spacewalk this far from Earth has never been attempted, we don't know how dangerous it can be."

"You're right, so who's going out?"

"I am."

"Uh-huh, as the mission commander aren't you just as critical?"

"No, my primary specialty is as pilot and you're all flight qualified and Colette is an experienced pilot. The rest of you are all specialists essential for the mission, out of all of you I'm the most expendable if anything does go wrong. Besides, I am the most experienced."

"If you say so, I'm not going to argue with you, Commander," he smiled.

Samantha nodded with a smile in reply.

"Can you set up the repair package?"

"Sure, I'm on it."

"Juliet."

"Yes Sam."

"I need to suit up, can you come and help?"

"Of course, I'll meet you in the observatory module."

Only the habitation and Mars science modules rotated, the ship's centreline didn't spin as they were too narrow and the spin would cause sickness for the astronauts. The ship had an airlock hatch in each module, but while the modules were in rotation the observatory or lander modules were the safest exit and the observatory was nearest.

"Samantha," Stephen said over the comms channel.

"Yes." She was already climbing down the ladder towards the central spur.

"Message from Mission Control, they're analysing the situation, but have suggested that we swap the controller out."

She chuckled, "You can tell them I'm on my way."

Chapter 16
Walking in the Sky

30th October 2022, 17:05 ship time

While Juliet helped Samantha suit up, Ronald prepared the repair kit. He placed the replacement component and a standard toolset into a case with oversized clasp. The standard toolset was centred around a power tool with multiple attachments, the most useful of which was the bolt remover needed to remove the cover so Samantha would be able to access the damaged component.

The process for suiting up took fifteen minutes, even with Juliet's help, but they were being extra-cautious. Juliet did most of the work, since the suits were not designed to be put on by a person on their own.

As she stood and waited for Juliet to finish the suiting process, Samantha prepared for the excursion outside the ship. The repair should be a simple one, Ronald had already talked her through the procedure. Now she waited and tried to suppress the excitement that bubbled inside her.

The EVA outside the ISS had been spectacular, the globe of the world gleamed a rich blue beneath her. There was nothing between her and the Earth except some expensive fabric and composite plastics.

It had been the greatest feeling in the world.

She checked in with Stephen again once Juliet had finished checking the suit's seals. He had nothing new to report from his investigation into the software, and neither did Mission Control. Piotr had joined Stephen in searching through the flow control software looking for problems. No issues arose from the deep diagnostics either.

"All right, your suit is ready," Juliet told her.

"Okay, pressurising."

"Everything looks good."

"Confirmed, my readouts show that the suit is maintaining pressure."

"Good, let's get you to the airlock."

Juliet guided Samantha towards the airlock. Unlike the full and more conventional airlocks in the nose cones of the modules, the doors in the side wall were a more unusual design. Full airlocks occupied a lot of space, but the side panels weren't expected to be used very often so a collapsible airlock was designed.

Samantha stood by the outer door, her back facing the wall. Juliet secured her to two handholds on either side of the door. Unlike the regular airlocks, this temporary design couldn't depressurise completely. Although only a trace amount of the ship's atmosphere would remain, there was a slight risk that it would be enough to push Samantha outside the ship uncontrolled when the outer door opened.

Ronald placed the repair kit beside Samantha and attached it to the wall beside the door and below the handrail. He then helped Juliet unfold the inner seal from its mounting above the outer door, until it covered Samantha like an oversized blanket. They sealed the bottom into the rubberised seating in the floor.

Compressed air filled hollow ribs inside the layered sheet, giving it a skeleton with enough rigidity to begin extracting the air from the bubble. They could see Samantha as a vague shape behind the translucent sheeting.

They had to extract the air at a slow pace, as the skeleton created from the air-filled tubes could only withstand a limited rate of pressure change. Ten minutes later, the pressure inside the temporary airlock was as low as they could reduce it.

"Samantha, we're ready to open the outer door," Juliet said.

"Yes Juliet, I'm secure and ready to go."

"Stand by, we're opening the door."

Ronald unlocked the release arm and opened the outer door. The little air that remained escaped in a rush into space, the wisps visible due to the sudden temperature change. Samantha felt the tug of the air as it brushed over her suit.

"Is everything okay, Samantha?"

"Yes, I'm preparing to exit now, unclipping the restraints."

"Okay, I'm handing you over to Ronald. Good luck."

"Thanks."

Ronald had moved over and now sat at the command console, a duplicate of the primary console situated in the habitation module. The act of leaving the protection of the ship was never undertaken lightly and part of the established process was that just one person would speak to the astronaut outside.

A single voice reduced the potential for confusion. As the excursion was a repair task, and that put Ronald as the point specialist and he would talk Samantha through the job.

"Samantha, this is Ronald. I see you on the camera. You're just outside the door."

"Confirmed, Ronald."

"I see you waving, now attach your tether to the central guide rail."

"Done."

"I see it. Do you have the repair kit?"

"It's secured to my waist."

"That's good. Now make your way down the ship. Follow the guide rail until you reach the rotation collar. Let me know when you get there."

Samantha edged her way along the central structure, regularly-spaced hand grips helping her progress. She moved with care, every motion methodical.

Halfway along the module, she stopped. Up until then her focus had been on the small patch of spacecraft in front of her and the deliberate movements to move down the ship. She looked beyond the Mars Voyager and its once-pristine white skin now marked with micro-meteorite impacts.

The feeling of awe at the universe around her stopped her movement. She'd seen the glory of the star-studded sky before, she'd been in awe of its majesty while in Earth orbit. Throughout their journey so far, she had spent time gazing at the view through the ship's high detail cameras and even through the higher resolution telescope.

None of it compared to this singular moment.

In orbit, the reflected light of the Sun from Earth's atmosphere subdued the heavens with its own glory. The layers of cloud above the crinkled continents and the perfect oceans. Here, nothing intruded upon the view at all, it was just her and the galaxy. A glorious abundance of stars filled her vision and it amazed her.

Ronald then spoiled the moment for her.

"Why have you stopped, Samantha?"

"I'm just enjoying the view and what a view."

"That's it, rub our faces in it."

"All right, stop bitching, I'm on my way."

"Copy that."

She edged her way further down the ship.

"Samantha."

"Yes Ronald."

"We're slowing the rotation, but you'll still need to cross through untethered. We can stop the rotation if you'd like?"

Standard procedure required the rotation to be slowed. During training they had practised at full speed, but that was to build confidence. Here, millions of miles from home, any risk had to be minimised. However, stopping the arms would lose the fake gravity created by the centripetal force, and without everything in the ship secured, it would cause chaos.

"No, slow it to half rotation as per the standard procedure."

"Confirmed, you're almost there."

Even at the reduced speed, traversing the rotating arms proved scarier than she'd anticipated. Up until that point her movements were regular, but slow. In truth the move between the arms required no extra speed, but not being secured to the guide rail was, in part, a leap of faith.

Her training kicked in and she passed through, hopping between the rotation as one of the spurs swept by. The move seemed to hang for ever although in reality it passed in a smooth motion. She grabbed the next rail and snapped the tether into place.

Fifteen more minutes and she arrived at the base of the main drive module. She located the damaged cover with ease and reported in.

"I'm here, Ronald."

"That's great, I see you on the camera. Attach the repair kit to the guard rail and take out the power tool."

She kept her movement deliberate and extracted the tool from the case.

"That's good, make sure to tether the tool before you use it and then use that tool to remove the cover."

Whenever using objects in space, they always had to take care that everything was kept secure, since it was easy to lose tools if they drifted too far.

Six bolts attached the cover to the engine mounting framework. Five of the bolts came out with ease, but she ran into trouble with the last, located near the scorch mark. The motor in the tool whirred, but the tool head shuddered but didn't move the bolt head.

"The last bolt won't turn."

"That's okay, can you determine why? Does it feel jammed? Or is the cover twisted against it?"

"There's a scorch mark on the cover, it's near the bolt that won't move."

"Can you give me a close-up of the damage?"

"Okay."

Samantha moved so that the camera in her suit helmet captured a close-up of the damaged cover.

"The scorching doesn't look too serious. Is the cover bent or warped in any way?"

"Not that I can see."

"Can you twist the cover clear?"

"Will that prevent me from putting the cover back in its place?"

"It won't fit as tight as before, but that shouldn't be a problem. The cover is there to protect the mechanism from meteorite impacts, a bit of movement won't interfere with that."

"All right, I'm trying now."

She braced herself and gripped the edges of the cover then twisted, and her footing slipped. She adjusted her posture to compensate and tried again. This time it moved, although not by much. She reported that over the radio to Ronald.

"It sounds like the bolt may have fused with the cover."

"What could have caused that?"

"I don't know, the mark on the cover does look like heat damage, however to fuse the cover to the bolt would take extreme heat and that should be more visible. It doesn't make sense."

"Well that's a puzzle for later, what do we do now? I have to remove the cover to replace the component."

"Understood. Our options are cutting it free, or bending the cover to provide you with access."

"Can we drill the bolt out?"

"We could, but I'd prefer to leave that as a last resort, re-securing the cover afterwards would be trickier, although we could use some quick-setting filler putty."

"All right, what should I try first?"

"We should try bending it clear, I'd rather not cut it free as we'd lose the mounting for the corner. While we don't have any turbulence up here, I'd still prefer to have it connected on all points if we can."

"Okay then, I'll give it a try."

Like all good toolkits, the case contained a short pry bar. She braced herself and levered the cover up. It refused to move at first, so she tried again. This time she didn't brace herself and slipped forward when she pulled. She caught herself in time and berated herself for the lapse

She tried again, but with more care this time.

"Ronald, the cover is up. I can see the control module and there's visible scorch damage inside."

"That's good Samantha, at least we can be more certain that this is the cause."

"Has Stephen not found anything with the software?"

"Nothing, he's still searching. I'd rather it was a damaged component than a software fault anyway, much easier to fix."

"Well, I guess that's true."

"Let's get this done then. Before you can swap the control unit you need to isolate it. First shutdown the coolant flow. You should see isolation valves above and below the unit."

"I see them."

They were two red valves with oversized turn switches. Every control was built larger so that the astronauts could operate them when suited up. She turned both switches, making sure that both clicked into the closed position.

"Coolant valves are closed."

"Confirmed, next you need to isolate the power so you can replace the control unit. It's the blue turn switch to the right of the unit."

"Done."

"Confirmed. The control unit is secured by six bolts, remove those."

Six whirrs of the power tool's motor, then she gathered the bolts into a loose pocket on her suit's legs.

"Done."

"Good, you'll need a wrench to uncouple the control unit from the flow pipe."

"On it."

This task proved trickier than removing the bolts. Even though extra space had been provided into the mounting, it was still tight enough to make turning the wrench difficult. The tether line attached to the bottom of the tool didn't help.

"I'm done, the unit is removed."

"Bring the broken unit back with you, I want to take a closer look at the damage and see if I can figure out what caused it. I'll talk you through the replacement."

Thirty minutes later as Samantha returned to the airlock, she took a glance at the sky around her. She followed the angle of the high-gain antenna array, their link with home, the blue dot in the distance.

Chapter 17
Apparition

30th October 2022, 18:45 ship time

After Juliet helped her from her suit, Samantha returned to her seat at the primary command console in the habitation module. On the way there she saw that the slowing of the spin had created some mess, but Piotr had secured most of the items so it could have been worse. She guessed that their personal quarters would have been less fortunate.

Luckily their personal possessions were few and the lack of space in their quarters would limit any clean-up they'd have to do later. After walking in space to repair the engines for a final orbit transfer to Mars, worrying about domestic chores seemed a little strange.

Ronald joined her at the console and they waited for the rest of the crew to secure themselves in their seats at the other consoles.

When they'd all reported that they were in position, Ronald ran through the diagnostics for the coolants and other critical engine systems again. He'd already run through them while Samantha had made her way back into the Mars Voyager, they wanted to be certain before they resumed the countdown.

"I've re-calculated our launch profile," Colette informed her over the comms channel.

"Are we still within the transfer window?" Samantha asked.

"We have just under two hours, if we don't make it by then we'll have to abort and return to Earth."

"We'll make it, we just have the final checks to complete and we should be good to go."

The others checked each of the other core systems. Again they had to be certain everything was still in the green. Thirty minutes later with the checks completed, Samantha opened a channel.

"Colette, inform Mission Control that we are resuming the countdown."

"Done."

"I'm resuming the countdown at T minus ten minutes."

"Okay."

They all watched the minutes count down until they phased into seconds.

"I'm preparing ignition sequence," Samantha reported.

"It all looks fine here," Ronald replied, "Launch is a go."

"Ignition initiated."

"Confirmed."

"I'm reading all systems in the green."

"Confirmed."

For a minute they watched the display as it updated their trajectory. This would be a short burn, less than an hour in duration. They would have enough fuel remaining to push the entire ship out of Mars orbit if they needed to adjust their orbit after arrival. The habitation module also contained enough fuel for the module to return to Earth on its own.

"What the hell is that?"

They all heard Stephen's surprised voice over the comms.

"What's the problem?" Samantha replied.

"We must have some sort of leak."

"Where?"

"Check the rear view."

Samantha called up the rear external camera. On the screen she saw a pink ribbon, running across the width of the screen.

"That can't be a leak, its perpendicular to the motion of the ship."

"Of course, you're right."

"Access the observatory sensors, see if we can identify what it is."

Samantha zoomed the camera view at the strange sight while Colette took control of the sensor clusters on the observatory module. With nothing else in view, Samantha couldn't gauge the size of the ribbon. It appeared to twist inside itself as if made from more dimensions than the universe possessed. The ribbon was shaded with pink and purple, and some of the edges flashed green. Already it was appearing to fade as the ship moved away from it.

"It looks like a jet," Piotr said.

"Yeah, but from what?" Samantha asked.

"Whatever it is, I don't think it's from the ship, but I do think the ship's engines are illuminating it. How are the observatory sensors looking?"

"I can't get a clear view," Colette replied.

"Keep trying."

"What do you think I'm doing?" she snapped.

"Once it's out of the engine's wash we'll lose it."

"I know, I'm on it."

"We need a spectrographic reading."

"I don't know what you're getting excited about; it's no doubt just some weird interaction between the engine exhaust and the solar wind," Juliet interjected.

"Not a chance," Stephen responded. "Look at the direction the ribbon is twisting; it's the wrong direction. And we have never seen anything like this before."

"Okay, I've got it."

"Pipe the feed onto the wall display," Samantha instructed.

"Running the spectrograph now."

The results took a minute to compile before they displayed on the screen.

"Hydrogen and helium. I can't see anything unusual."

On the screen, the ribbon shimmered and then faded from sight.

Chapter 18
Love is in the Air

5th November 2022, 07:02 ship time

"So it's finally official then?" Samantha asked with a broad grin as Juliet and Ronald entered the living space. Like most of the ship, it was an open-plan design with the kitchen to one side, a table and chairs and then a seated area below a large screen display.

Everyone else laughed as well. Juliet and Ronald's developing relationship had hardly been a secret. In such confined living arrangements, nothing could remain hidden for long.

"Okay, get your jokes in now," Juliet challenged, her face defiant, but with her smile wide. She knew that they were all happy for them both and they'd anticipated this sort of relationship in the mission planning. The reason for a mixed crew was to allow relationships to form.

"What's for breakfast?" Ronald asked. He preferred telling jokes to being on the receiving end, although he didn't bother to hide his own happy grin.

Piotr glanced up from his preparations in the small kitchen. "Today we have traditional Russian breakfast, black bread and sausage."

"Sounds great."

They'd eaten the same many times before and they all appreciated the care that Piotr put into his cooking duties.

"And black tea."

"Sorry buddy, I'll stick with coffee."

"Heathen. Tea is the proper drink for breakfast."

Ronald sat at the table. "Yeah. Yeah. So what's the plan for everyone this morning?"

The question stirred Samantha from her reverie. Despite the jovial camaraderie around the table, she felt apart from the rest of the crew. The darkness that had plagued her during the early weeks of the mission had abated, but it still lurked in the depths of her psyche.

Jake sent her daily video messages that provided her a lifeline to a world beyond the mission. He told her of the latest happenings on Earth, although they kept up to date with current affairs through the daily data burst that contained updates from the crew's favourite TV and web channels.

She still valued his messages, although the lack of intimacy in his voice hurt. She missed his flirtation, but more than that she missed the promise of something beyond the mission. That feeling confused her, she'd not experienced it before and worried about what that meant.

Instead she focused on what she knew and that was the mission.

"Gym first and then medical exam for me. After my date with Colette, I'll be in my office going through paperwork."

As the mission commander, most of the required reports had to be compiled by her. The automated ship's system helped reduce her workload, but even so, there was a lot of data to be collated and filtered back to Earth.

Stephen took his turn. "I'll be continuing my research into the phenomena we discovered last week."

He'd been working on this side project as often as he could for the past week. It didn't interfere with his other duties, although Colette had to complain a little to ensure that it didn't encroach on their shared time. In fairness, she didn't have to complain too loudly. His analysis of the ship's sensor data had revealed a few new tantalising hints.

The first came from the solar wind detectors positioned all over the surface of the ship. They formed a key component of the ongoing experiment to learn more about the solar wind. For the duration of their journey, the detectors measured fluctuations in the energised particles ejected by the immense turbulence of the Sun's surface.

Data from the surface sensors had kept Stephen and teams of researchers back on Earth busy for months. Now he had discovered something new.

The detectors made their measurements several times a second. The amount of data this produced was too much to stream back to Earth, so aggregated data as well as periodic slices were sent back instead. However, the local buffer stored the full data for several days.

Within that buffered data, Stephen found what he thought was the anomaly they had seen. Even better, it seemed that they had passed through the anomaly. The data showed distinct differences between whatever it was and the background solar wind readings.

His analysis revealed a structure within the ribbon; it looked like chains that twisted in and out of each other. He cursed that the resolution of the data wasn't sufficient to reveal more than that.

The other revelation came from another suite of sensors, these traced magnetic fields. This far away from the protection of Earth's magnetic fields, they had little work to do. However, as the ship passed through the anomaly, they had registered a sharp increase. The low sample rate of the data couldn't reveal anything further about its structure.

Even more puzzling for the physicist was that magnetic fields didn't exist in the middle of deep space, they had to be connected to something. Besides the Mars Voyager, there were no objects capable of emitting a magnetic field for millions of miles in any direction.

"Have you got anything new to follow?" Samantha asked.

He frowned. "Only what I told you last night. Although I did some research on the net and I may have something."

"What did you find?"

"It's not much, but I found a paper on plasma flows and how they can form complex chains like helices."

"I've read that," said Piotr. "It was presented at an extremophile conference I spoke at. It postulated the possibility of rudimentary life forming from dust grains in the plasma flow, but it requires an immense electromagnetic field, doesn't it?"

"Yes it does," Stephen replied. "Although it looks like we have that out here."

"Yes, but if I remember, it mentioned the magnetic field of Jupiter. You've found a field and yes it's not something ever discovered before, but it doesn't even come close."

"I know. I have no explanation for what it could be."

"Okay, so Stevie's going to continue his pet project," Ronald brought the conversation back on track.

"Please don't call me that."

"Sorry Stephen." He didn't look sorry. "I'll be on maintenance duties, checking the environmental controls and the lander module. What's on everyone else's schedule?"

Ronald responded next. "I'm on gardening duty."

The new batch of crops was almost ready for harvest; they'd be able to include fresh ingredients in their meals soon.

"I'll be performing some observations of Mars, calibrating the sensors in the observatory module," Juliet told them.

"And I'll be cleaning up after you all," Piotr said as he placed their breakfast on the table.

Chapter 19
Party Time

3rd December 2022, 19:33 ship time

"SURPRISE!"

And it really was. How the crew managed to keep the secret from her, Samantha didn't know. They'd wished her a happy birthday at breakfast and even gave her token gifts. Even though she'd brought her own stash of gifts for the others, she'd still been surprised by the gestures and appreciated them.

Ronald had demonstrated an unknown artistic talent when he gave her a hand-carved figurine. She recognised herself in the statue.

From Colette, she received a small box of what looked like expensive chocolates. Samantha planned to share them with the rest of the crew after the evening meal.

Stephen had given her a tiny book. She had to squint to read the title and had laughed out loud when she discovered that it was 'An Idiot's Guide to Astrophysics'.

Piotr had winked at her when he gave her a tiny wrapped bottle of vodka. There was enough for a single drink, so there was no danger of her getting drunk. It had been months since leaving Earth and her last drink. Alcohol hadn't been banned from the mission, in fact they had a small supply of wine and even a bottle of champagne that they planned to open once they had landed on Mars.

Juliet revealed herself as the second artist in the crew, she had drawn a pencil sketch of Samantha. She looked at the drawing of herself and discovered that she appeared sad and withdrawn. Samantha thought she'd hidden that from her crew mates and realised that they had known all along.

She didn't know whether she should feel grateful or embarrassed. Either way it inspired her to try and remedy her mental woes.

She'd thanked them all with obvious gratitude and they'd followed the day's routine as they had every day.

As they enjoyed a quiet lunch, she read her email and one from Linda revealed that she had received over a quarter of a million messages and e-cards from fans all over the world. Some of them were less than tasteful and some of them were hilarious. Linda assured her that she wouldn't have to deal with them; the public relations office already had it in hand.

Samantha highlighted a few and informed Linda that she'd respond to them herself.

There'd been a few personal messages in her inbox, including one from Jake. Their relationship had evened out over the past few weeks. With Mars approaching, her thoughts reached an equilibrium. She realised that she'd been irrational and unfair to him. Jake had been a good friend and even so far from Earth – especially so far from Earth – she needed some personal connection.

They might not have the intimacy she desired, but they did provide a high point for her day. Something to look forward to at the end of the day's tasks.

After lunch, she replied to him and to the other personal messages. She then helped Stephen with his afternoon's duties. Or rather she ran the tests on the lander controls that he should have been doing while he carried on investigating the anomaly.

He hadn't made any real progress except to sell Piotr on his theory. Piotr had also become quite excited at the potential of the discovery. They'd stopped sharing their thoughts with Mission Control, arguing that they wanted to solidify their conclusions before discussing them further.

Samantha didn't mind, as long as they returned their focus to the mission when the time came. Which would be soon.

Christmas was just a few weeks away and they'd arrive at Mars shortly after then.

In the afternoon, she recorded a video for the dedicated web channel. The time delay had stabilised at twenty-three minutes, still far too long to allow any form of interview or conversation. Instead Linda had emailed her the script along with a video of everyone from Mission Control singing 'Happy Birthday' to her.

She watched the video twice, the first time with a smile on her face and the second still smiling, but with tears in her eyes. Samantha didn't know where the emotion poured from and for a few minutes she couldn't stop crying. To her surprise she didn't feel sad, or angry, or upset in any way, but that didn't stop the tears from flowing.

The moment passed and she washed her face to make herself presentable for the camera. Piotr performed the role of cameraman. He waited for her to pull herself together, and when she did she flashed her best smile at Piotr and the camera.

"Hi everyone back on Earth, and thank you all so much for the warm wishes and messages. There's so many I won't be able to read them all, but it means a lot to me that so many people care.

"And a special thank you to the guys and gals at Mission Control, I loved the video!

"As well as it being my birthday, today is a very special day, we are now sixty days away from arriving at Mars. We're already getting some great shots from our observatory. Here's an image showing one of our possible landing sites."

After answering the questions Linda had sent through and sending the video, she hit the gym. A quick shower later she dressed and walked into the living area.

"SURPRISE!"

She didn't shout out in reaction, she stood there unable to move instead. At the table Stephen and Colette sat together, so close they were almost touching. Piotr and Juliet held a cake with a single candle burning in a sphere in the still air. Candles don't burn as you'd expect without real gravity and the flame wasn't fooled by the fake gravity created by the spin.

Samantha just stood there.

She felt in awe, a wonderful feeling of belonging. The feeling washed over her and cleared away the remnants of the depression that had haunted her throughout the journey. A rogue thought waved a flag and warned that it might come back. She didn't heed the warning, it didn't matter, in that moment of shock nothing mattered, she felt complete.

She realised that she was crying again. Not sobbing, just silent tears that streaked down her cheeks. This was all the family she needed.

"Hey honey." Colette stepped to her and gave her a hug.

"I'm all right. Thanks for this."

The tears wouldn't stop, they pooled in the smile of her lips.

"Of course. We are always here."

"And we have cake," Piotr boomed. His English was perfect, but sometimes he let the accent ring through. Samantha suspected that he did this on purpose.

"How did you bake a cake?"

"Wonderful American invention, microwave cake mix."

"Sounds delicious."

"Not as good as my mother's, that is for sure."

"I didn't realise we had any in stock."

"We didn't, I stashed a few in the science locker," Stephen grinned.

Ronald selected one of her favourite playlists and music filled the module.

"Who wants a low-G dance with me?" he joked.

"I think we can spare one of these," Stephen revealed a bottle of wine from under the table.

"Guys we shouldn't, they're for big celebrations."

"Seems like a celebration to me."

She laughed and he nodded and pulled the cork from the bottle with a smooth flourish.

"Colette assures me that that this was a very good year."

"Isn't that a Chilean Red?"

"So, she's French, she knows her wine."

Colette elbowed him in the ribs.

"Let's eat some cake," Piotr prompted.

Everyone gathered around the table.

"Make a wish then blow out your candle," Juliet told her.

Samantha blew out the candle, but didn't make a wish. She didn't need to, it had already come true.

Chapter 20
Christmas Greetings

24th December 2022, 20:12 ship time

The weeks leading up to Christmas passed all too quickly for the crew. As Samantha had hoped, both Stephen and Piotr put their side project on hold as the red planet increased in size on the view screens. A significant part of their daily routine now included landing drills to prepare for the highlight of their mission.

The Mars Voyager carried two landers in the foremost section of the ship. In the same module were the orbiters and rovers with which they would survey the landing sites. The landing units were stored in pods within the module, the orbiters and rovers in blisters on the outer skin of the craft. The module also contained a simulator for the crew to practise the operation.

Although Samantha and Colette would be the pilots for both landings, all of the crew had to spend at least an hour a day in the simulator so that any one of them would be prepared if needed.

The pilots controlled the landers using multifunction panels in the same way as the Mars Voyager. They were much simpler than the Russian Soyuz capsules they'd had to become familiar with before their first visit to the International Space Station. In theory the controls followed the same basic pattern as the Mars Voyager, but to properly prepare them the simulator had the same capsule layout.

All of the core controls also had physical back-up variants if the main control consoles stopped functioning for any reason. Samantha had been looking forward to this part of the mission the most, since she would pilot the first capsule for the historic first landing.

As an astronaut and a pilot, this was the ultimate dream, to land on an alien world. Like any good pilot, her skill was a blend of natural instinct, talent and repeated hours of dedicated training.

Her improved emotional state had continued with the approach and even though she devoted as much time as she could in the simulator, she also made sure to spend time socialising with the rest of the crew. They still had their regular duties to perform so it was a busy time for everyone on the approach to Mars.

On Christmas Eve they paused their preparations. Mission Control had insisted that they take a break for the three days of Christmas. It turned out that they all had the same secret plan and laughed when they tried and failed to surprise each other. No-one had discussed it beforehand, but everyone had put aside a small part of their personal baggage allowance to bring some Christmas decorations with them.

The serendipitous moment occurred as they all tried to sneak into the living space to put up their decorations. Between them they had sufficient decorations to make the living room look festive, rather than the token gesture they had expected individually.

This festive cheer carried them through the day. In the afternoon, they recorded joint messages amongst the cheap tinsel decorations for Mission Control and the support teams at their respective organisations.

They also recorded a public message for the holiday season, making sure that they included the talking points that Linda had emailed them. The crew had been pleased to hear that the popularity of the mission had remained high and had increased as the public thought about the six astronauts so far away from home.

They weren't as happy as Linda with that news, of course.

Linda also warned them that public interest would rocket (they felt sure the pun had been intended) as they approached and entered Mars orbit.

For their evening meal, they gathered again. The mood became more subdued as everyone thought about what they would say to their families and loved ones. Once their meal finished, they cleared up the mess and then retreated to their quarters. For the first time in weeks even Ronald and Juliet went to their own rooms.

* * *

Samantha sat and stared at her tablet. She'd already sent festive messages to a few friends and people she'd worked with at NASA and served with in the Air Force. She also made sure to send a message to the crew of the International Space Station. The Mars Voyager crew wouldn't be the only people spending Christmas in space and away from their families.

That left Jake.

She didn't know what to say. She wanted to somehow share the feeling the crew had enjoyed with her closest friend. Samantha experienced a eureka moment, it was as simple as that.

"Merry Christmas, Jake. I really wish you could be here with me. I know, I hope, you feel the same."

She paused as another flash of understanding struck her. He would have wanted to be on this trip. Perhaps that desire explained his strange behaviour soon after they departed?

"I know you want to be here, with me on this journey. When I look back on the months we've been in space I can't believe that we, no I, didn't experience the joy that we should have done.

"In fact Jake, there's so much I should have shared with you along the way. It's only now that I realise this and want to share those memories with you."

Samantha continued to talk until the tablet beeped and informed her that the hour slot for the recording was up.

* * *

Piotr sat on his bed. The private quarters were small, although they were comfortable. He recorded his first message for his daughter and darling granddaughter. They were the brightness and joy in his life.

The thought of how excited the young girl would be filled him with joy. There was a little sadness at not being with his girls for Christmas, but they knew how much the mission meant to him. They had become used to him being away for extended periods, but nothing as long as the trip to Mars. It saddened him to miss out on so much of Mishka's growing up.

With that thought he placed the Santa hat that he'd brought with him. The crew had laughed as he wore it throughout the day. With his beard turning to white with age, they joked that he even looked like Santa Claus.

"Merry Christmas, my little angel. Were you a good girl and has Santa brought you many presents?"

Piotr left bundles of gifts for the two Christmas celebrations and three birthdays that would pass while he was away.

"I'm sure that you have been, I know that you do as your mother tells you. Well, most of the time at least!

"Thank you for the paintings, my favourite is the one with the bear. Although your mother tells me that it is me. Do I really look like a bear?" He chuckled. "I have that picture as my wallpaper on my tablet, have a look."

He held his screen to the camera.

"I'll miss not being with you this Christmas and I'll miss your mother's cooking. We'll be having Christmas dinner, but it won't be what I'm used to. She is a wonderful cook, a talent she gets from her mother."

He paused for a moment, reliving the memory of his last Christmas with his wife. Ill as she was by then, she still spent hours cooking a feast for all of the family.

With a deep breath, he pulled himself together and continued talking to his granddaughter.

* * *

"Hi Laura. It seems I can't escape bloody Christmas even up here!"

Both Stephen and Laura, his twin sister, hated Christmas. It wasn't just the falsity of it, but also the crass commercialisation that filled the streets and the airwaves. Even worse for them was how they were forced to participate in the celebrations. As part of the crew, Stephen made an effort not to put a dampener on the mood, especially now that everyone seemed to have pulled free of the funk they'd slipped into.

Still, at least when talking to his sister he could be more honest about his feelings. Not too open of course, that wasn't him.

"I'm sure you are following our fine tradition of hiding from the world on this day. Anyway, enough of Christmas nonsense, you will not believe what I've been working on.

"I didn't want to say anything to you until I was more certain, but I've had to put it to one side as we get nearer to Mars. I don't have the proper time to apply to the problem and I know it is something you'd be interested in."

Laura was a notable physicist in her own right, not as gifted as Stephen (at least in his opinion), but he considered her capable enough to continue his work. Assist in the work would be a better description. He had a high opinion of his intellectual capabilities, that opinion wasn't unwarranted though.

"I've sent you two papers that gave me the idea and I believe they are the key to solving the problem. It's an amazing find. I think we've encountered something never seen before. It's so beyond what I expected to find out here that I hesitate to say it, even to you, but Piotr Vasilevitch agrees with my conclusion that this is a self-sustaining entity.

"I know it sounds incredible and I've not shared my thoughts with anyone but the crew. Not yet, I want to be absolutely certain before going public, it's too big. I've sent the data we have collected back to Mission Control. They took some convincing, but they've agreed to allow you access to the data.

"You should have received my email by now with some of my lines of enquiry and a few thoughts. I'd rather you kept this quiet for now, until we can prove what the phenomenon is."

Even though he'd explained his research so far in great detail in the email he'd already sent, Stephen talked about his thoughts. It was much more fun than thinking about Christmas.

* * *

Colette recorded a message for her mother. The latest email from the care home wasn't encouraging. Her mother's periods of lucidity were drifting further apart.

Her mother suffered from dementia. She'd turned 80 a few weeks before the mission had launched. Without Colette's constant visits, her condition had deteriorated.

She tried not to think about it. On an intellectual level she knew it wasn't her fault, but sometimes a traitorous thought indicating otherwise would emerge.

This might be the last Christmas her mother might be able to understand, or even recognise her daughter. Colette wanted to make the most of this opportunity, but she couldn't think of what to say. She sat on the fold-out seat and stared at the camera.

* * *

"Best Christmas ever. I don't know how else to describe it," Ronald enthused in his message to his brother. He'd already recorded his well wishes to his son and ex-wife. In all his years of sending messages from far off places, he still couldn't quite get used to talking to a camera.

"We can see Mars bright in the sky now. It's more prominent in the sky than Earth, which looks no more than any other star in the sky. Actually that's not quite true, you can see that it's blue even this far out, and when I'm looking at it I think of home. Don't worry, I'm not going soft, but this is the longest deployment I've ever been on."

He paused for a short while, his thoughts drifting. Ronald wasn't usually one for melancholy introspection. Sometimes, though, the enormity of what they were doing gave him pause. He rode with the moment, allowing it the respect it deserved and then he smiled at the camera.

"Do you remember how we used to play at being astronauts? We'd walk in the sand pit pretending to explore the surface of alien planets.

"It's hard to believe that in a few weeks that I will be in orbit around an alien planet.

"We've had some freaky shit along the way though. I still haven't figured out what caused the failure in the observation module. Stephen and the Russian think it's an alien. Can you believe that?"

Ronald didn't. That being said, he couldn't explain how an immense magnetic field and a plasma flow could appear in deep space. Perhaps it was something to do with the engines interacting with the solar wind after all?

"Sure is crazy."

* * *

"Hi Emily, Julia here. Merry Christmas, honey. And what are you doing for Christmas? Are you visiting Aunt Judy? Make sure to give her my love. I know she doesn't like email.

"I've sent you some more pictures for your blog. You'll like these. I got one of each of the crew as well as the views of Mars and Earth that you asked for. It was Ronald that took those.

"There's a great one of Piotr gardening in a Santa hat that I think your followers will love. He does look a bit like Santa, doesn't he?"

"We'll be recording our Christmas meal for the news feeds. I think that's what Linda wanted for Christmas! I'll take some more photos, don't post them until Linda's done her thing though. She moaned at me when you posted those pictures of the stories before they'd been featured in her release cycle.

"Anyway, that's enough work stuff. I still find it hard to believe that we're on our way to Mars. I know, it sounds stupid after all the training and the time we've been in space. So much for no more work stuff, not that it feels like work.

"I'm signing off now. I'll record another message tomorrow and yes, before you ask, I will send season's wishes to all the girls at the club. I bet they're not doing so well without me on the team. Which reminds me, I'll start another game, I've been practising my moves. Piotr is a mean chess player and it turns out that he's good at checkers as well so you're going down this time.

"Merry Christmas Emily, take care and I'll chat to you soon."

Chapter 21
Mystery

11th January 2023, 11:31 ship time

"This doesn't make any sense," Stephen muttered.

"What?" Samantha asked.

They were now less than a week from arriving in Mars orbit and an atmosphere of excitement filled the ship. For the bulk of their time, they focused on preparing for their arrival. Samantha and Ronald were busy checking the landing modules. This was the fourth time they'd run through the detailed checklists that preceded each landing mission.

In the neighbouring observatory module, Stephen calibrated the sensors, checking their settings. While checking the radio receivers, he discovered a new anomaly.

"These radio readings are wrong. Not just wrong, they're impossible."

Samantha moved down to his position. Here on the centreline of the ship, they received no artificial gravity from the ship's spin, so she could glide with a few well-placed pushes and pulls on strategically-placed grab rails.

"All right Stephen, tell me what you're seeing."

"We're receiving radio waves from Mars."

"A transmission? It's probably from one of the orbiters."

"No, this isn't a coherent transmission, it's more like the background noise from Jupiter or Earth."

"That's impossible. They're generated by energetic magnetic fields, aren't they?"

"Yes and Mars doesn't have one. Well, not one worth talking about and that's what puzzles me."

"So, impossible?"

"Yet there it is."

"Could it be an equipment malfunction?"

"That's what I thought at first, but every part of the system checks out. I've run full diagnostics on each component and everything is in the green."

"Have you tried samples from Earth or Jupiter?"

"Yes and the system is reporting the readings that I would expect from both those sources. I did the same for the Sun as well."

"So we're back to the impossible again. What do you think it could be?"

"I don't know. I'm mapping the frequencies and field strengths to create a 3D picture. It'll take me a little while to finish, but even with the first pass results it's clear that it's no ordinary magnetic field."

"How so?"

Stephen indicated one of the screens. "Here's the Earth's magnetic field. You know how it's formed?"

"Of course." Samantha had become used to Stephen always assuming that everyone else knew less than he did, however on this occasion it did annoy her, since this was basic physics. "The Earth's core rotates and because it's molten iron it produces a strong magnetic field."

"Indeed and without it, life wouldn't have evolved on Earth as it has, maybe not at all."

"It protects us from the ravages of the solar wind."

"Exactly, although it has a distinctive pattern, in effect it forms a shield around the Earth."

"And this field around Mars is different?"

"It looks that way. For starters it's more evenly distributed and it seems to have a relatively consistent field strength which is also impossible. I'll have to complete several passes to build a decent image. While we wait, take a look at this."

Again the screen changed. It displayed a close-up of Mars. Its thin atmosphere provided a clear view of the red desert that formed its surface. She could make out the blurred form of a dust storm below the equator, raging south.

But there was something odd.

Something so strange she didn't register it at first.

"Oh my God! Is that what I think it is?"

"I think so, but I can't see how."

On the screen they watched ribbons of green and purple shimmer across the northern pole of the red planet. They were pale, more ethereal than the auroras on Earth, but still distinctive. Especially to those who had seen them from orbit as she had on her first trip to the ISS.

That had been one of the highlights for the rotation. Every astronaut was awestruck by the vision of the world beneath them. During the day, the splendour of nature dominated the view. At night the power of mankind rose into ascendance as the lights of the cities pushed against the night.

One night she witnessed the aurora towards the north pole. The lights of the cities studded the night, but that technological prowess was shadowed by the sight of magical fire that filled the sky.

To see the sight on Mars shouldn't have been possible.

"Are we feeding this to Mission Control?"

"Of course. I'm expecting a response in the next forty minutes."

"It'll be interesting to see what they think of it." She glanced at Stephen. "But of course you already have a theory, don't you?"

He nodded. "Look at this." The screen switched to a thermal view. For the most part it showed a confused mess of blues and greens. This far from the Sun, very little heat was absorbed or reflected.

"What am I looking for?"

"Where the aurora is, there are hotspots. It's difficult to detect them, I didn't at first. We're still too far away for a decent resolution, so I can't be certain. Yet. My theory is that the hotspots are causing the aurora and I think they are the plasma flows."

His smile appeared almost as bright as the aurora.

Samantha shook her head. "I agree this is something strange. Something none of the previous probes have observed, but let's not jump to conclusions."

"Okay, so what is causing this?"

"I don't know and that's what worries me."

He pursed his lips, but didn't respond.

"Keep investigating this new situation on Mars, we'll need to do another safety review to account for the changed parameters. Give me a shout when you have something new. I'll carry on helping Ronald with the lander checks."

For the next hour, she continued the pre-checks with Ronald. They checked each system and sub-system, as they had several times before. Sometimes it felt like a lot more, the checklists were so long. They joked about how Ronald had found aliens again. No doubt Piotr would already have heard the news and be on his way to see what Ronald had learned.

Samantha pondered the theory that the two scientists had formulated. She thought that they were jumping the gun on the idea of it being an alien. While she agreed that there was something strange going on, her main worry was whether it would affect their mission profile.

As expected, they heard Piotr join Ronald in the observatory. After being shown the new readings, he sounded very excited and the two scientists got down to work.

Chapter 22
Love is All Around

17th January 2023, 06:35 ship time

To everyone's surprise, Colette and Stephen arrived together for breakfast the day before they were due to arrive at Mars. Samantha had expected something to happen, the signs had been there for a few weeks now. She hadn't been sure whether they'd actually get together. Their attraction was plain for all to see, but they both seemed too reserved to commit.

"I see you're celebrating early," Ronald said with a not so subtle wink.

They both looked a little embarrassed, as if unsure what they had done was okay.

"Lay off them," Samantha instructed in her best commander's voice. "We didn't give you and Juliet a hard time."

"Yes you did," Ronald replied.

"Okay. Maybe we did a little."

"Isn't there a law against English people and French people sleeping together?" Piotr grinned.

"That goes for you as well, Piotr!"

Piotr held his hands up in mock surrender. Juliet stepped between them, serving pancakes for their breakfast. She made them with powdered milk and dried eggs, but they still tasted pretty good.

"So we have a day off," Samantha told the crew as they ate their breakfast. The established routine was that they got Sundays off from the work schedule, although the domestic chores still needed to be done. When they arrived at Mars, that schedule would be thrown out as they'd have so much work to do to get ready.

They'd completed all the necessary pre-checks for their arrival, so in agreement with Mission Control, today would be a rest day. Everyone assumed it would be their last for some time. The team back on Earth were still analysing the data for the electromagnetic anomaly at Mars. The field strength registered much lower than the field around Earth so they didn't expect any change to the mission profile.

Stephen said "Well after eating these delicious pancakes, I'm going in the observatory for a while. I want to see if I can get any more data on whatever is going on around Mars. I also want to start some preliminary modelling of the readings. I know Mission Control will be doing the same, but I want to play with some thoughts I've had, thanks to a beautiful muse."

Colette smiled and said, "I'll be joining Stephen, help him out with his tests."

"This is supposed to be a day off, you know," Samantha told them.

"I know, but with the mission preparations keeping us so busy I haven't had chance to go through any of the recent data. Besides," and Stephen smiled at Colette, "I'll be in good company."

Piotr looked as if he was about to declare his intentions in joining the research, then sat back and remained silent at Stephen's last comment. He could review the data on his tablet or one of the other consoles easily enough and keep out of their way. Young love was a wonderful thing, he thought with a smile.

"Well we're having a lazy day watching movies and munching popcorn," Juliet told them. "And Ronald will be helping me with kitchen duty as well."

"I don't remember agreeing to that!"

"Where would you like to sleep tonight?"

"Kitchen duty it is."

Samantha watched the interchange with a smile on her face. She also experienced a guilty feeling of envy on the inside. It had been several months since she had last slept with Jake. It would be nice to share a bed with someone again. It didn't have to mean anything on an emotional level.

She glanced at Piotr.

"And you Samantha?" Ronald asked. "How will you spend your day of rest?"

"Me? I'll be catching up on email. I might even listen to some music."

"You party animal, you."

* * *

Over dinner, Stephen told them of his findings.

"I'm getting some decent readings now we're closer, in fact I'm now getting enough resolution to determine its structure. There's a complicated structure to the field, a coherence that I can't explain unless it is self-organising in some way."

Piotr joined in. "We can't be sure until we arrive in orbit, but the pattern looks very similar to the double helix."

"You're kidding?" Samantha said.

"No. I'm certain we are on the verge of something monumental."

"Until we map it in better detail, we can't be certain." Stephen tempered Piotr's enthusiasm, although everyone around the table realised he hardly kept his own in check.

"Is it a danger to our arrival?" Another question from Samantha.

"I don't see how," Stephen replied.

"Are you forgetting the short-out in the observatory module?" Ronald entered the discussion.

"The entity sitting around Mars doesn't pose a threat to us."

"I'm not convinced there is an entity, but there is a strange magnetic field around Mars where there shouldn't be one. A magnetic field that no-one has encountered before in all the years we have been observing the planet. We've had two encounters on the journey here and one of those occasions caused us severe damage."

"The damage wasn't severe, it was just a few blown fuses."

"It was severe enough to destroy our crop and we still don't know how it managed to get inside the ship."

"We don't know that the cause of the malfunctions is linked to the anomaly."

"You're suggesting that we have encountered two different phenomena with the same general effect?"

"The data suggests exactly that. Look at these field lines. You know as well as I do that we can determine the strength of the magnetic field from the radio emissions."

Ronald took the tablet and examined the data as Stephen continued.

"As you can see, the field strength is much lower than the belts around Earth. The same belts we flew through without incident."

Ronald handed the tablet back.

"Okay, but we're not just talking magnetic oddities. The damage in the module looks like plasma burns."

"First, we haven't been able to prove that and second, Earth also has a plasma bubble that we travelled through when leaving orbit. And it's much more energetic than the few flashes we're seeing here."

The argument continued in circles, but in the end everyone except Ronald agreed that there wasn't enough evidence to abort the approach.

Deciding to play it safe and also to assuage Ronald's concerns, Samantha sent a message to Mission Control. She also included all of the assembled data and Stephen's latest conclusions. Another argument then ensued over what film to watch while they waited for the reply.

Some perverse whim caused them to settle on watching Apollo 13.

Samantha wondered if they should take it as an omen when the go-ahead arrived from Mission Control as things went pear-shaped on screen. She kept that thought to herself.

With the decision made and the film finished, the two couples made their excuses and retired to their quarters. That left Samantha and Piotr alone in the living room.

They shared a glance and an uncomfortable moment. It occurred to them both that spending the night together might be a pleasant as well as a comforting diversion. Although the reality was that they both felt a little left out.

The moment passed and they both said their goodnights and went their separate ways. It would be a big day come the morning.

Chapter 23
Arrival

18th January 2023, 06:40 ship time

Breakfast on arrival day was a subdued affair. Like their first night of the mission after launching from Earth, sleep was fitful at best. Samantha had lain awake for two hours. She didn't want to disturb the others even though she suspected that they were having the same trouble.

As sleep eluded her anyway, she decided to use the time for good purpose and set about completing the various routine communications that had to be sent on a daily basis. She found herself distracted by the image of Mars on one of her secondary screens mounted on the wall in her quarters.

The image came from one of the high-definition cameras mounted on the Mars Voyager's hull. As well as providing a constant stream of data for the planetary scientists back on Earth, it gave Linda some incredible footage for the news and web channels.

Public interest in the mission now exceeded that of the launch with almost two billion people watching the news channel or logging into the website. Linda had arranged for commentary to be provided by experts on Earth, so keeping the crew free to focus on their main task. Once they settled in orbit around Mars, they would resume their media duties.

The sight of Mars growing larger on her screen had captivated Samantha the closer they travelled. Now that they were only a few hours from entering orbit, the image of Mars appeared so clear that she could almost reach out and touch it.

In the end she gave up and in doing so managed to claim the shower first. After dressing, she brewed coffee and waited for the rest of the crew to join her.

The few attempts at conversation while they ate faltered. Everyone felt too keyed up to even complete the morning ritual, their thoughts already focused on their respective tasks for the day ahead. This was the culmination of their long voyage and later this day would be the moment they all dreamed of.

After breakfast was eaten and cleaned away, they conducted the final checks for the approach. They then moved through each of the modules ensuring that everything was properly secured. They would need to stop the spin while they performed the orbital insertion manoeuvre.

At 11:00 they all sat in their respective seats at the command terminals around the ship. Samantha and Piotr were at the main console in the habitation module. Stephen and Colette sat at the desk in the observatory module. In the Mars science module, Ronald and Juliet sat strapped in.

Once everything and everyone was secure, Samantha initiated the reversal manoeuvre. They approached Mars too fast to enter orbit, and at their current velocity they would swing by Mars and off into the far reaches of the Solar System. Their speed was too great for the thrusters to halt, instead they had to turn the ship so that the main engines could be used.

First she had to stop the spin providing artificial gravity to the habitation and Mars science modules. The strain of the manoeuvre would be too much for the connecting arms if they were still rotating. Once the arms locked into position, she fired the thrusters. With delicate control, she flipped the ship so that it travelled backwards.

"We're entering the magnetic fields," Ronald called over the comms.

"How's it looking?" Samantha replied.

"There was a sudden spike in the field."

"To be expected."

"Of course. We're well within safety limits."

"Understood, I'll be initiating the retro burn in ten minutes."

"Roger. I'll keep monitoring the sensors."

"Will you look at that!" Juliet's voice, filled with wonder filled the comms channel.

Samantha checked the external camera views and it was indeed a sight of wonder.

A large portion of the red planet filled the screen. They had arrived. They all saw the green fire as it danced across the upper reaches of the thin atmosphere.

"That's one hell of a fireworks show," she replied.

They watched the sight as the countdown continued.

The counter reached zero.

"Initiating retro burn."

The exhaust from the main drives was invisible to the naked eye, but on the screen a ribbon of energy shimmered into life. She recognised it as the same phenomenon they'd witnessed earlier in the voyage.

That's when all hell broke loose.

Chapter 24
Attack

18th January 2023, 11:11 ship time

The shimmering ribbon flared and convulsed throughout the forward visible arc. It writhed like a tentacle, retreating at first and then lashing against the ship. Alarms sounded on all of the control panels.

"I'm reading power surges across the board." Samantha barely heard Ronald's voice over the static that now polluted the comms channel.

"What the hell is going on with the comms?" she demanded.

"We're experiencing massive electromagnetic interference on all channels and radio frequencies. It's as if we're under attack from an EMP."

"Can we stop it?"

"No, we're right in the middle of it. I told you we shouldn't have..."

Samantha cut him off. "You can save the 'I told you so' until later. What are we dealing with?"

"The same as what we saw from afar, a complex magnetic field with energised plasma. Now we're close enough I can see the structure is more complicated than Stephen thought."

"Can you pipe the data through to me?" Stephen's voice was hard to hear through the crackle.

"Sure."

A sudden creak rang through the ship.

"What the hell was that?" Samantha asked.

"The support struts in the arms are registering tension."

"From what?"

"I don't know, but the EM readings are now off the scale. Hold on, I'm also receiving elevated thermal readings."

"I'm aborting the approach. I'll increase engine thrust, so we'll overshoot and then slow into a higher orbit as we go by."

Their targeted orbit was 350 miles above Mars; if this worked, they'd be ten times higher than that.

Stephen transferred the data onto his tablet. He instructed it to render a 3D map of the field. With a few simple commands, the data displayed in real time. The field wasn't uniform, but instead made up of tendrils.

And the tendrils were moving.

Those near the engine moved away from the exhaust, but the others moved towards the ship.

Everyone heard another wrenching scream.

"The forces on the connecting arms are rising, they're twisting the connections," Piotr said.

"How is that possible?" Samantha replied.

"I don't know, but we have a problem."

"I'm aware of that."

"No, we have a new problem, the connecting tunnels aren't designed to withstand this kind of torsion. The bracing struts are twisting, look at the camera feed."

"How is that possible?"

"I don't know, but I do know that if this continues it's going to rip the ship apart."

"Shit. How can we stop it?"

"We need to get out of this field."

"We're facing the wrong way and we're already travelling as fast as we can."

"I realise that."

"We could flip the ship again."

"That would be too risky; it would also increase the stress on the central hub."

"What choice do we have? I'm open to suggestions, people."

No response from the rest of the crew.

"All right, I'm doing this."

Samantha dialled down the engine, reducing the thrust to zero.

On his tablet, Stephen watched a nest of tendrils surge forward, like tentacles from some deep sea monster. He remembered an old etching from school, 'The Kraken Rises'. As he was about to call out a warning, another screech echoed from the central spur.

Fresh alarms rang out loud throughout the ship.

"We've got a hull breach. We're venting atmosphere from the central spur."

The ship's automated systems detected the air leak and sealed the modules. The crew were now divided and cut off from each other.

Another scream from the ship's arms and Samantha felt the ship shift around her.

"Oh Christ. The ship is coming apart."

The forces acting upon the central spur twisted and ruptured the connections, and tore the ship into four separate pieces.

Chapter 25
Separation

18th January 2023, 11:21 ship time

The closing hatch shut out the squeal of tortured metal and hiss of escaping air. Colette checked the life support system readouts.

"We're okay, the hatch closed the seal in time. We're not venting any atmosphere anymore."

"I don't think we are okay, the thing has torn the ship apart."

Colette hadn't agreed with Stephen's theory that the anomaly was a life form, but her opinion changed with what now seemed like a directed assault on the ship.

It didn't matter anyway. Like the rest of the crew, her training kicked in. The first priority was to establish the situation so that they could formulate a plan of action. She started this process by bringing up the navigation controls and comparing what she saw with the sensor readings.

What she saw didn't provide any good news.

"We're drifting away from the rest of the ship."

"That's not good."

"Normally I like your British way of understating a situation, but it's not going to help us. We are fucked."

Stephen shrugged and continued analysing the data.

"Stop looking at the light show outside, we have a real problem here."

"I know, we're drifting."

"It's much more than that, look at this."

Stephen looked at the indicated screen, showing their projected course. They would swing by the planet. The really bad news was that they were travelling too fast so they wouldn't enter orbit and would continue out into deep space.

"We need to slow down. If we can at least get into orbit then we have a chance."

"A chance for what?"

"To link up with the rest of the crew."

"And how are they going to manage that? They're just as screwed as we are."

"They're smart and have had the same training that we've had. The hatches sealed so they must have atmosphere like us. Each of the modules has enough supplies for an extended period and they all have manoeuvring thrusters."

"That's not going to be enough. "

"I think I preferred your understatement. Now sort yourself out, I can't do this alone. I'll see what we can do about slowing down and reaching orbit, you see if you can contact the rest of the crew."

"All right, I'm on it."

Stephen switched his tablet to connect with the communications system. The local network connecting the ship's systems registered as active, but showed severe signal degradation. He couldn't maintain a consistent connection, so he tried voice comms instead.

"This is Stephen in the Mars observatory module. Is anyone receiving me?"

He heard nothing but static on the radio.

"Can anyone hear me? This is Stephen in the observatory module. I'm with Colette. Can anyone hear me?"

Still he heard only static.

As he was about to try again he heard a voice in the crackle of static.

"Hello, can anyone hear me?"

"Yes this is Stephen. Who is this?"

"Ronald... science module... decaying orbit..."

The voice disappeared into the static.

Stephen turned to Colette. "That was Ronald, he said something about a decaying orbit."

Colette looked on her screen for the science module's position.

"I can see them. Merde! They're in a spin and approaching the planet too quickly. They're not going to overshoot. They're going to clip the atmosphere and get dragged down."

"We have to help them."

"A moment ago we couldn't help ourselves and now we have to help them?"

"We can't leave them."

"We're not, but unless we can slow down we won't be able to help anyone. Although we would be the first human beings to reach Jupiter, not that we'd live that long."

"That's the spirit, now what's the plan?"

"The thrusters won't do it, they don't have enough thrust. Hold on, we have two lander modules! If we can fire the engines on those it might be enough to slow us down."

"We can't do that."

"Why not?"

"It was firing the engines that caused the alien to attack in the first place."

"You can't know that."

"Take a look for yourself."

He showed her his tablet with the animation of the tendrils and their reaction to the ship's engines.

"The tendrils recoil while the engine is firing. Now look, the moment it stops they swarm in."

"Why?"

"I have no idea. My best guess is that some of the exotic particles in the exhaust harm it in some way."

"Well that's all right then."

"What do you mean?"

"The main drive is a nuclear thermal engine, the landers use old-fashioned chemical rockets. They need more immediate thrust to lift off the planet."

"Of course. I'm so stupid."

She smiled. "Only sometimes."

"Okay. How do we fire the engine?"

"I'll have to do it from within the lander. It'll take a while to rewire the controls, but I should be able to do it."

"What can I do?"

"Keep trying to contact the others."

Stephen did as she instructed while Colette entered one of the landers. For several minutes he kept trying the radio without any discernible response in the static. He also tried sending text messages across the data network. He doubted they'd get through the chaos, but it was worth a try.

"I'm done."

"Okay, shall I come through?"

"No, I'll come through once I've completed the burn."

"What shall I do?"

"See the course correction I've programmed into the navigation system?"

"Yes."

"Initiate the program and tell me when to fire."

"Countdown has started. Five, four, three, two, one, fire."

The engine roared its defiance of Mars's gravity. Its power shook the module and pushed him against his seat. Stephen watched the new countdown. The engine had to fire for precisely ninety-four seconds. As the seconds passed, the shaking grew ever more violent.

"Ten seconds to go," he warned Colette.

"Ready and I'm shutting the engine down now."

The shaking continued.

"Shut the engine down, Colette."

"I'm trying."

"What's happened?"

"I don't know!"

The trembling stopped for a split-second and in the same moment the engine's roar intensified.

"No!"

Stephen couldn't hear her voice.

He didn't hear her scream as the rear portion of the ship peeled away and the landing module tore itself from its mounting.

He did hear the alarms as the hole sucked all of the air from the module. The straps of his chair held him safe against its savage grip so he wasn't sucked into space. The sudden cold numbed him. He reached for his safety mask, but it was too far away. His vision dimmed and the last thing he saw was the landing module falling towards Mars.

Chapter 26
Red Sky at Night

18th January 2023, 11:23 ship time

"We're spinning out of control."

The scene inside the Mars science module was one of complete chaos. The hatch to the module closed a fraction too slowly, its primary systems fried by the electromagnetic storm from the tendrils that gripped the module.

Ronald fought with the system, as every critical system shut down. He managed to restore life support and then checked on Juliet. The violent spinning of the module made movement difficult.

Juliet's chair had torn loose from its mounting. She lay unconscious, still strapped in and bleeding from a severe head wound. He dressed the deep gash as best he could and then strapped her seat down to prevent it floating free again.

He returned to the command desk and ran through the primary systems. Communications were down, life support operational, the thrusters were also offline but looked like they might just need rebooting.

While the thruster controls restarted, he focused on the communication system. As far as he could tell, it was just the main transfer bus that had failed. He unstrapped again and pushed himself across the module. Ronald opened the access panel and saw that all the circuits within looked fried.

Ronald cursed under his breath, but remained calm.

A storage locker beside the panel contained replacement boards so it didn't take long for him to replace the damaged ones. He found that repairing the damaged connections wasn't quite so easy, as the module's movement made intricate work difficult. But he worked through them one by one, forcing himself to remain calm and focus on the task at hand.

Ronald returned to the command desk and was relieved to see that the communications system now displayed as online. He scanned the wireless frequencies, at first only hearing static. He kept scanning and brought up the navigation system.

"Shit."

The navigation system reported that the module's path headed straight towards the planet. The single good news on the screen was the fact that the approach angle didn't appear too steep. A small push from the thrusters would be enough to put them into a stable orbit.

The computer calculated the required burn vector, and following its countdown Ronald initiated the thrusters. A sudden bang shuddered through the module as the control circuits blew. The thrusters misfired in sympathy and pushed the module into a steeper approach angle.

"Oh shit."

Juliet groaned as she regained consciousness. Ronald pushed his way over to her.

"My head."

"It's okay, don't try to move."

"What happened? Ah, my head."

"There's been an accident."

"What?"

"It's okay," he lied.

Ronald checked her dressing, and as soon as he finished she released her seat straps. He tried to stop her, but she pushed him away.

"All right, what's going on?"

"Shit is going on."

She took a look at the screen. "I should have stayed unconscious."

He snorted. "Our first problem is our current orbit approach."

"Tell me."
"We're heading straight in."
"Thrusters?"
"The controls are dead."
"Shit."
"My thoughts exactly."
"Have you tried the radio?"
"Yes. I can't get a signal, and the data network is down too."
"Keep trying, I'll take a look at the manoeuvring controls."
"Are you okay?"
"I've been better."

She moved over to another access panel and opened it. A cloud of smoke escaped, polluting the air.

"Christ. This panel is totally blown."
"There should be replacement boards..."
"No, the whole panel fried, including the mounting board. The whole panel needs replacing."
"Shit. We don't have any panels in this module."
"Have you had any luck with the radio?"
"None. Hold on. I'm getting something."
"Who is it?"
"I'm not sure. I think its Stephen. Stephen? It's Ronald. Can you hear me? This static is terrible, I can't hear anything."
"Try again."
"I am. Can anyone hear me? This is Ronald in the Mars science module. We are in a decaying orbit. Scratch that, we're heading straight towards the planet."

Juliet closed the access panel, she then returned to the command console.

"How long?"
"How long until what?"
"Don't be obtuse! How long until we hit the atmosphere?"
"Less than an hour."
"What can we do?"

"Nothing. There's nothing we can do. The thrusters were our only hope."

"There must be something we can do?"

He shook his head. "The thrusters are the only way to slow our approach."

"What about venting the atmosphere?"

"What?"

"Vent the atmosphere. We can use it as thrust."

"There's not enough pressure in the module to push us fast enough."

"Then we have to fix the thruster controls. There must be something we can do. I'm not just sitting here waiting to burn up. Now help me."

Ronald followed Juliet to the damaged panel. She opened it again and began pulling out the damaged boards.

"I'll swap the boards. You're the engineer, fix the mounting panel."

"How?"

"I don't care, think of something!"

"All right. I can try to bypass the more damaged parts."

"Are the panels a common component?"

"Yes."

"Why don't we use the other panel?"

"We'd lose communications and life support."

"Communications isn't doing us any good. And how long will life support work without the control panel?"

"A few hours."

"All right then, go grab it."

It took ten minutes for Ronald to remove the other panel and clear the installed boards. A new alarm rang as the life support primary system shut down. A new red countdown appeared on the control console.

Meanwhile, Juliet took out the fried boards and then lined up the replacements.

After three more minutes, she'd removed the fried mounting panel. It then took Ronald another five minutes to put the replacement in. Aware they were running out of time, they both added the installed boards.

They grinned at each other.

They would make it!

Mars's atmosphere was much thinner than Earth's, but it still reached high above the planet's surface. As Juliet placed the last replacement board into its slot, the uppermost molecules of Mars's atmosphere touched the module.

They both rushed to the control panel. The screens were now a mess of alarms and warnings. Ronald activated the thrusters. Sensors along the skin of the module registered sudden heat as friction from the air scorched the module's outer skin.

The thrusters on the underbelly caught in the grip of the red planet's atmosphere, tearing them from their mountings. Fragments of the outer skin disintegrated under the heat and panels tore away in the howling wind. The module burned up seconds after hitting the atmosphere. Ronald and Juliet's final screams were lost in the storm of burning air.

Chapter 27
Escape

18th January 2023, 11:24 ship time

The screens on both of Samantha's and Piotr's consoles flashed white and fell dark. They were blind except for controls patched to their tablets.

"What's going on?" Piotr asked.

"I'm not sure. We need to restore access."

"The circuit breaker for the displays must have tripped. It must have been a power surge from the entity."

"You check it out, I'll see what other options we have."

The tablet's screen had seemed adequate up until that moment, now she wished it was larger. She couldn't fit all the screens she wanted to see on it. The action of flicking between them took too long, it slowed her down.

"Ah, here it is."

The screens snapped back into life.

"Nice work, Piotr. Now let's see what we have."

Samantha read through the displayed readings.

"We're off course. Comms are up, but all I'm receiving is a wall of static."

"Life support is good," Piotr added.

"I'm checking damage control. Holy shit, it looks like the ship has broken apart. I'm trying to find the other sections."

"Internal sensors are reporting a small leak somewhere near the main hatch. I'll check it out."

He unstrapped himself from the seat and, in the zero gravity, pushed himself towards the nose where the habitation module once connected to the central arms.

"Radar is useless with all this interference. Hull sensors are fried, and we lost most of the observation packets with the observatory module. We're getting a few readings though, it looks like we're still meshed in the field."

"You still don't believe it is a living entity?"

"Does it really matter?"

"It should. We need to think about how it will react."

"Well right now we need to determine how we're going to survive."

"That is true. Can you see any sign of the others?"

"I can't tell. I've initialised an automated handshake trying to established contact with the other parts of the ship. How's that leak?"

"It's only a micro-fracture by the looks of it. I've applied a seal. Sensors indicate pressure is stabilising."

"We need to get out of the field's influence, it's interfering with our systems. If we can get free then we can search and help the others."

"How can we get free?"

"This module is also the return module, it's equipped to get us home. I can fire its engine to get us clear."

"No, we can't do that, that's what caused it to attack us in the first place!"

"Piotr, we have no choice. We cannot stay here."

She'd said moments ago that they should break free and try to help the others. The reality was that they had to get clear, sweep around Mars and head back to Earth. There was no way they would survive another encounter with whatever now owned Mars.

How could she tell Piotr this harsh truth?

She reviewed the readings on the navigation screen. The computer was experiencing difficulty matching their exact position, but it was clear where they were heading. The retro burn had done its job and they were now heading into low orbit.

With the back of the ship pointing forward, they couldn't change course.

"We need to flip the ship and thrust into higher orbit."

"What about the entity?"

"Piotr, this isn't an alien, we're caught in some strange electromagnetic effect."

"You saw how it reacted. We're facing an organism, an alien being. We've already seen how it reacted to the exhaust from the engines."

"We have no choice, we have to risk it."

Piotr didn't look happy at that decision, but he nodded and strapped himself in.

"Programming burst sequence."

They felt the module rotate, but whatever was around them didn't react to the hydrazine thrusters and few minutes later the Mars Voyager faced forward.

"Ready and initiating burn."

The module rumbled as the main engine fired up. The entity reacted against the nuclear exhaust as it had before. It lashed with tendrils of magnetic force at the small module.

Everything went dark.

Emergency lights pushed back the gloom.

"It's shorted the main power distribution."

"I will take a look."

Piotr released himself from his chair again and glided to the main junction box. His motion was made more difficult by the engine's thrust that pushed him in the direction of its vector. Its control circuits were isolated from the main distribution, as was the life support system.

"I'm reading power surges all over the hull."

"How long until we're free of the creature?" he asked.

"I can't tell without the screens, but I'd guess several minutes at least."

151

"I'm working on it. It looks like it's just the main fuse that's blown."

"Okay, but be careful."

"No problem, I just have to replace the fuse."

Simple enough, except...

"Wait!"

Too late.

A blue flash illuminated the module. The smell of ozone accompanied it with a loud bang. Piotr issued a strange keening noise. With a trembling arm, he pushed the cartridge into place and the lights came on before passing out.

"Oh shit. Piotr, I'm coming."

Samantha read the screens as she unbuckled from her seat. Their new course would take them past Mars. The engine's burn would need to continue for another fifteen minutes.

That provided her with enough time so she rushed over to Piotr. By then his body had drifted against the far wall. Before touching him, she checked that he wasn't in contact with any power source. Once certain that he was clear, she felt for his pulse.

She found none.

She checked his breathing and that had stopped too.

Samantha began CPR, first chest compression and then breathing into Piotr's mouth. She followed the rhythm she'd learned in training and she kept at it.

As she did so, the countdown in her head continued. She had to stop the engines at the right time. Too early and they'd be trapped inside the field. She still couldn't (didn't want to?) consider the effect as a living being. Too long and they would sweep past Mars and onwards, out towards the asteroid belt and then on to the outer regions of the Solar System, far beyond any possible rescue.

On the sixth attempt, Piotr spluttered as his heart kicked in and he breathed again. Samantha cried out with relief. Without realising, she had been praying to a God she didn't believe in.

Relief flowed through her. She allowed the moment and then she focused on his other wounds. One side of his face had been disfigured by a horrific burn that had melted one eye and his cheek. The burn continued down his side. It didn't look as bad as his face, but still looked serious.

The mental timer seized her attention.

With a single push, she returned to the controls and turned off the engine. She checked the limited readings on the display; they looked to be reaching the edge of the entity's reach.

The ship shook as a tendril of energy lashed out against the fleeing habitation module. She heard the tortured metal along the upper surface of the module and then, with one last shudder, they were free of the creature's grip.

Chapter 28
Rough Landing

18th January 2023, 23:57 ship time

The lander spun along its lateral axis as it tore itself from the mounting. The acceleration from its single rocket motor twisted its trajectory and increased the erratic spin. Through the tiny porthole, Colette watched the observatory module shrink with each rotation.

At first she screamed Stephen's name, not wanting what she had witnessed to be true. Hoping that in some way that he could save her.

The horror of those initial seconds were too much for her to accept. The disorientation from the spin dragged her back to the reality of her own predicament. Her training took over, here was a problem to be solved.

A 'solution opportunity' as one of her lecturers had once joked.

The first problem she needed to address was the spin. The engines' continued burn exacerbated the problem, so she needed to act fast. She had already tried disconnecting the override she had constructed without any success.

Another option sprang to mind – the engine needed fuel. She typed on the control console, seeking the correct code routine. The lander's main computer controlled the fuel flow, but if she could access it directly then she might be able to stop the flow.

By now the rapid spin of the ship made her nauseous, even with all of her extensive high-G training. She struggled against the nausea as she scrolled through the subroutines, typing in terse commands to narrow the search.

There.

She found it.

She entered the necessary commands and a few tense seconds later, the engine stalled. It didn't stop the spin, but it at least reduced the increase of its oscillations. Within another minute, the lander's automatic systems corrected the spin using the gas thrusters.

Her nausea subsided as the craft stabilised. Colette then tried the communications system. It was dead, without even the hiss of static on the voice channels. She tried the data channels with the same result.

Next she checked life support, which appeared functional, or at least it reported no errors. That provided some relief, but the lander had only eight days' worth of air. Not good, but the situation could be worse. If she could land then the others might be able to save her. Failing that, she could return to orbit using the lander's return capsule. Although it wouldn't be sensible to return to orbit until she'd made contact with the Mars Voyager.

Colette next reviewed the navigation system, which was a simpler system than that on the Mars Voyager. Its purpose was landing the craft, not long-range navigation.

Still it showed her that she was approaching the planet too fast and at too shallow an angle. In less than three hours, the craft would skip across Mars's upper atmosphere. The module would survive hitting the atmosphere, but would be cast into high orbit afterward.

The craft tilted again and the rocket burned for a few seconds.

That shouldn't be happening.

Colette recognised the manoeuvre from the countless hours of simulator training. The lander had engaged the landing sequence. She cursed in French – the sequence shouldn't have started so high above the planet's atmosphere. There were safety checks in place, it shouldn't have been possible.

She checked the computer again. It confirmed that the landing sequence had initiated. Then the screen died and again she cursed, her words loud in the confined space. The well-rehearsed repair protocol directed her next actions. The console's power supply looked fine.

A quick search around the console revealed a spare tablet. With a few swift commands it interfaced with the main console and displayed the lander's approach. The engine fired again.

She tried various instructions to stop the sequence, but none of her commands registered. She then tried shutting off the fuel, which worked, but too late. She was now committed to a landing.

This was the worst possible scenario for her. Unless... and with that thought, sudden hope blossomed within her. Unless the second lander could somehow be used to rescue her. True, it was a slim hope, but better a small hope than none at all.

All the others had to do was rescue the observatory module and use the other landing pod.

Colette knew full well that would never happen.

She also knew she couldn't give up. Again she cursed as she remembered the return capsule. If she landed without damage then she could fly back into orbit.

Besides, they'd travelled all this way to walk on the desert surface of Mars. Her decision made, she activated the fuel pumps. The rocket roared again, adjusting the approach vector.

As the ship completed its adjustments, Colette climbed into one of the space suits from the storage locker. They were much less bulky than the ones used by the Apollo astronauts sixty years ago, but they were still difficult to put on unaided.

Now enclosed in the bulky suit, she strapped back into the seat. She called up the progress of the landing on the tablet. The module would hit the atmosphere in a few minutes. The engine stopped and the inflatable heat shield deployed with six sharp cracks that reverberated through the craft.

An angry roar consumed the capsule as it struck the thin upper atmosphere. The lander's skin protected her from the raging inferno, but not from the noise and buffeting. She held on to her seat, as the nausea from before returned with a vengeance. She swallowed the acidic bile. The last thing she needed was vomit in her helmet.

After a long minute, the shaking calmed to a mere tremble. She heard more cracks which resounded from the bottom of the craft as the shield was cast away, its protection no longer needed. The firestorm's roar also dimmed to a bearable level, leaving just the wind howling around the plummeting capsule.

The engine fired again, providing the final retro boost for the landing. An alarm shrieked – on the display, Colette saw the fuel gauge reading empty. There wasn't enough fuel to slow the lander for a safe landing.

The dreadful fall slowed with a lurch as the parachutes deployed. Colette cried out at the unexpected jolt, and once again only just managed to stop the rising bile. Three giant parachutes slowed the capsule, but not enough to stop it smashing into the red soil.

Chapter 29
Stock Take

19th January 2023, 00:03 ship time

The habitation module completed its half-orbit around Mars and then swept round to begin its long journey home. Samantha treated Piotr's wounds as best she could. When she had removed the old man's shirt, she discovered that his burns were much more extensive than she'd first thought.

She applied a coolant gel to his burns and injected him with antibiotics to help prevent infection. She had decided against giving him any painkillers as well as he hadn't regained consciousness yet. He often groaned in pain, but it wouldn't be safe to administer anything until she was more certain of his physical condition.

She hated leaving him in pain, but it was the correct decision.

As they completed their orbit, Samantha focused her attention on the surrounding space, looking for any sign of the other sections of the Mars Voyager. The field's presence made scanning the area difficult. The sea of electromagnetic fields confused the few remaining sensors.

While she examined the chaotic readings, she thought about the attack upon her ship. Her body had burned through so much adrenaline that the time seemed so much longer than the few hours it had taken. She had disregarded Stephen and Piotr's theory that the anomaly had been an alien as wishful thinking, even from two so obviously intelligent scientists.

Now she wasn't so sure.

Alongside the screens with the patchy sensor data, she reviewed the information recorded during the attack. The thing had reacted to the engines and that might have been a physical reaction. Although if that had been the case, why hadn't it attacked the engines?

No, it had attacked the whole ship, not just the part that harmed it. That showed some form of decision-making process. Or at the very least some understanding of what was around it.

She should at least be thankful that it had not followed them as they left its presence and she hoped that would remain the case. She didn't know what that meant, but for that moment it didn't matter, she had more immediate concerns.

Her three most pressing issues were life support, flight control and the unconscious Russian. In her mind she tried to label Piotr in that abstract fashion, to diminish the emotional impact of his injuries. In truth, she liked the old man. He had always been good company and she respected his abilities.

The life support system had sustained some damage from the alien's attack. She was pleased to discover that the damage didn't appear major. The efficiency of the air scrubbers that removed the carbon dioxide from the air had been reduced, but with just the two of them they should be sufficient.

If they had been able to save the rest of the crew, her crew, then that would have been a problem. A guilty thought prowled in the dark of her mind: perhaps it had been better this way.

She didn't recognise that thought as her own and forced her attention to more immediate matters.

The main drive now operated in low-power mode and the system didn't report any problems. That meant that lighting and heating should be fine as well.

Despite the urgency of her current situation, Samantha worried about how the rest of the crew had fared. Even if they had somehow survived the destruction of the ship, none of the other modules had the ability to leave Mars orbit. She felt sure that that nothing could survive being amidst the alien (or whatever it was) for long. The rest of the crew had to be dead.

Still she needed to be certain although she so desperately wanted to be wrong.

It went against everything she knew to leave her crewmates behind, their fates unknown. The practical part of her asserted that she had barely escaped herself and her duty was now to ensure that she and Piotr made it back to Earth.

Even with knowing the correctness of her decision, it weighed heavily upon her. Would the weight be lessened by knowing the crew's fate?

As they departed Mars space, Samantha reviewed their situation. They'd lost access to the crops, but the ship had four months worth of supplies for the return journey. All of those supplies were stored in this module and for the crew at its full complement. Between the two of them, they should have enough for the year-long journey.

She inventoried the stores, satisfying herself they had adequate food, water and medical supplies. It also provided her with the benefit of keeping busy. Although being busy didn't prevent thoughts of her crew infecting her thoughts.

The lack of spin meant they now had no artificial gravity, a fact which at least made the task of moving Piotr to his quarters easier. In theory she could have used the thrusters to rotate the ship, but the module was so small it would have caused motion sickness.

She didn't mind the lack of gravity, it made some things easier. Sometimes she just floated in the air, unable to focus. It seemed that it required all of her strength to simply exist. She felt so tired, the stress of the escape had drained her. Tired as she was, she couldn't sleep. Sometimes she napped for a few minutes, but when she did the crew visited her in her dreams and she had to waken to escape their accusing stares.

Samantha returned to Piotr every couple of hours to check his condition. Each time she hoped that she would see some improvement and that by some miracle she would find him conscious. Every time she tasted bitter disappointment.

Besides Piotr's critical condition, she faced two additional major problems. The first was that she had no communications; the entity had destroyed the main antenna. Her second problem was that she had no access to flight control. When she executed the diagnostics, they didn't provide any clear understanding of what the fault was.

Neither problem was immediately life threatening so she filed them away as problems to be solved later.

For now she needed sleep, but she couldn't retreat to her quarters. Instead she sat next to Piotr's bed and dozed. At least she'd be there if he woke up. She hoped that her dreams would remain silent, if only for the one time.

Chapter 30
Red Sky in Mourning

19th January 2023, 03:16 ship time

Colette awoke awash with pain. It hurt even to open her eyes.

To her surprise, she found herself prostrate upon the hard ground looking up at a pale sky which shimmered with ribbons of green. Every part of her body hurt. With care, she moved her limbs one by one, testing each to ensure they still worked. Each movement provoked a fresh wave of pain. Thankfully nothing felt broken though.

She took her time in moving, but turning over she saw the wreckage of the landing module. It looked like a child's toy hurled against the ground. Wreckage from such a small machine covered a disturbingly wide area.

How she hadn't been killed in the ruin that was once a space ship, she couldn't imagine. For a brief moment she almost wished she had been. It would have been so much easier to surrender to the darkness to escape her pain and the coming struggle to survive a bit longer.

Somehow she had been thrown free, although it was hard to imagine how she had survived the impact. More likely the craft had fallen apart during the descent and she fell separately.

With a hiss forced through gritted teeth, she climbed to her feet and stumbled over to the crashed vehicle. Each step more painful than the last, but she pushed herself onward.

When she reached the wreckage, she leant against a collapsed strut and rested for a minute. As she recovered, Collette looked across the horizon. The rocky, desert scene appeared darker than she'd expected.

Like the rest of the team she knew that despite being called 'the red planet', Mars didn't have the red sky and horizon that most people thought. NASA publicity shots often enhanced the colour to provide the public with what they expected to see. The practice had faded over the previous decade but in most people's imaginations, the planet should be red.

She'd dreamed of this moment, and indeed had worked hard for years to reach this point. A small part of her exulted at being the first person to step on Martian soil. The greater part of her suffered from her injuries and wrestled with the problem of how she might survive this.

They'd come here to see an alien life form, the first that mankind had ever discovered. Colette wondered if one of those worm-like creatures at this very moment burrowed beneath her feet in the Martian soil.

Above her, an even greater being illuminated the sky with ethereal flames. In orbit floated a being unlike anything ever found on Earth. She hadn't believed Stephen's theory and now felt guilty about that. Would things have been different if she had?

Of course not, but it was a fine fantasy to have, if only for the briefest moment.

After a while her breathing returned to normal, and once it had she examined the wreckage. Where to start? The lander had once comprised of two sections, the landing module and the return capsule.

The return capsule had been crushed in the impact, there was no way she would be able to use it to return to orbit. She saw that the lower entrance hatch had burst open and scattered debris around the crater caused by the crash.

Colette crouched low and peeked inside, but everything appeared smashed and broken. Perhaps she could scavenge some supplies, but what good would that do her?

Her suit contained a water pack, but no way to eat anything. She sipped some of the water, it was delicious and cool, and it washed the sour taste from her mouth. The refreshment provided a stark contrast to the mounting concern for her situation. She glanced at the suit readings in the panel attached to her left forearm.

Less than two hours of oxygen remained.

She must have been unconscious for three hours. Three precious hours vanished into unremembered darkness.

Colette pulled herself together and took stock of her situation.

She was the first human being to reach the surface of Mars.

She had no way of leaving.

There was no way to communicate with anyone.

That thought caused her think of the crew, her friends that had travelled all this way. Had any of them survived? She was sure that Stephen was dead, there was no way that he could have survived the destruction of the module.

What of the others?

Where they in orbit?

What of the alien?

Less than two hours remained.

Maybe she could extend those hours somehow.

Inside the mess of twisted metal and smashed polymer plates were the tools she needed to extend her life. The first item she needed was the emergency shelter. This was a bright yellow inflatable tent, similar to emergency rafts used at sea.

Once inflated, the shelter would provide an airtight capsule where she could survive for another 48 hours. Two days wasn't much, but it was a start. It would also provide protection if a dust storm arrived.

Like the Moon landings, dust posed a significant threat to astronauts. It was a fine powder that worked its way into joints and fittings were it would abrade and, if allowed to, cause damage. Unlike the Moon, Mars possessed an atmosphere capable of whipping the dust into dust devils and even vast storms.

With the protection of the emergency shelter she would at least gain some time to develop other options. She could extend that time further if she recovered the other space suit. If she was lucky she could also extract additional oxygen from the lander's life support system.

A spark of hope restored from her conclusions lifted Colette's spirit and she set to work with renewed purpose. The hatch frame had deformed in the crash and she wouldn't be able to fit through. She stepped around the lander, searching for the key to the puzzle, there had to be a way inside. She pulled at the twisted struts. The mangled ruin of the lander thwarted her every attempt. Even more annoying was the knowledge that inside were the tools that would make the task easier.

One frustrating hour later, she gave up in disgust.

There was no way in.

Less than one hour of oxygen remained.

Colette turned away from the crash and looked across the landscape. The Sun appeared so small in the sky, signifying how far from home she really was. She knew that she wouldn't live long enough to see the Sun set.

She wished she could somehow send a final message home. Her mother would be alone now, just as Colette was on the surface of this alien world. She couldn't even contact her crewmates in orbit.

Her suit contained a recorder, to be used for recording observations if she was out of contact with the landing party or Mars Voyager in orbit for a short time. The solid state memory would store her message indefinitely. If another manned mission came to Mars then perhaps they would recover her body and the message with it.

She recorded a short and final message to her mother. A message that her mother would never hear.

That left only acceptance.

Or was it surrender?

A rock nearby provided her with a seat. Not the most comfortable place to wait to die, but still better than standing. Colette thought about the mission. It was a bitter irony that they'd come all this way to investigate alien life and a different alien would be her undoing.

Was the worm they'd come all this way to see beneath her now? It seemed unlikely, after all it had been discovered in the clay at the base of an ancient water course.

Her vision seemed darker than it had before.

Colette sat and watched the Sun sink lower, while her vision continued to darken until she could see no more.

Chapter 31
Flying Blind

22nd January 2023, 08:45 ship time

Three days passed and Piotr still hadn't regained consciousness. Samantha connected an IV drip to at least put some fluids and nutrients into his system. She bathed and cleaned his wounds, as well as applying burns and antiseptic cream several times a day. There were never any signs of improvement. Every so often, he moaned or cried out, but his eyes didn't open.

Inbetween caring for Piotr, Samantha worked to restore the ship to working order. As she was maintaining the ship alone, this was more than she could handle even if it had been in full working order. So she had to prioritise.

The readouts for life support still looked within tolerable limits, so she focused on the flight controls. The return trip hadn't factored in the additional burn she'd needed to escape the alien. She wasn't even certain that the ship was heading on the correct course.

She knew they were heading in the roughly the right direction, but at the distance they needed to travel, even being a little off course meant big trouble. If they had to course correct, it was imperative that she restore flight control and the navigation systems as soon as possible.

Naturally that was easier said than done.

During their training, they had all learned how to fill the other crew member's roles should the need arise. Well, now the need had arisen, but what they hadn't trained for was the fact that Samantha was the only functional crew member on the ship.

She'd received the training, but that didn't make her as expert as Ronald at engineering or Stephen with electronics.

Both were skills she desperately needed.

Still, she was familiar with the systems. She had received considerable training and her tablet stored all the documentation for the Mars Voyager components. Somewhere amongst all the training and data were the answers she needed.

She first had to determine the cause of the problem, so she started with the obvious. She turned it off and then on again. It failed to reboot.

Of course it wouldn't be that simple.

Next she checked the power systems. She knew that main power was operational, otherwise she would be alone in the dark and cold, rather than just being alone. Power to the command console also appeared fine as she could access the other systems, except communications.

For three hours, Samantha traced the power conduits, looking for a fault or any physical damage. She found nothing.

Next on the obvious list were the system's connections. She'd checked the network from the terminal already, but the diagnostic routines reported no errors. To be certain that the software wasn't misreporting, Samantha examined each of the main ports and connections. Every single one of them checked out okay.

Tired and discouraged with the constant failure to solve the problem, she returned to Piotr's quarters. Whenever she could, she mopped his face and replaced the IV bag. She sat beside him and tried to eat, but she had no appetite. Samantha dozed fitfully and dreams of death and despair tormented her for the short time she slept.

Barely rested, she returned to her task. The only option remaining to her was the components of the navigation system and flight control themselves. The temptation was to just replace all of the major components, but she understood that would be a false economy in the long run. No point using her limited inventory if she didn't need to. They still had a long journey to complete.

And so she began the drawn-out task of switching out the different circuit boards one by one. Two laborious hours into the task, she yelled a foul-mouthed version of eureka at her stupidity. She continued to curse as she propelled her way through to the main storage compartment and retrieved the board checker.

This was a laptop device with various connections. With it she could plug in any control board, except for the large mounting panels, and run a hardware test. She stopped cursing her mistake and focused on testing the boards.

Her progress improved and she soon located the damaged circuit boards; there were only two of them which she quickly replaced. She rebooted the system again and after several anxious minutes, both the flight control and navigation displays appeared on the console.

Relief formed a happy wave that passed through her and she shouted a little whoop of triumph. The joy settled into professional calm and she executed the diagnostics suite on the restored systems. It seemed funny that she had been working patiently for days, but now found it difficult to wait for a few short minutes.

When the results were displayed, they revealed fresh cause for celebration. Their current course was within the tolerances of their remaining fuel. There was, however, a slight wrinkle for their arrival. Instead of the aero-braking manoeuvre to slow them into Earth orbit, they would need to perform a retro burn earlier in their flight.

This would extend their travel time by three weeks, which was far from ideal, but their supplies should last that long.

Feeling better than she had since the disaster at Mars, Samantha decided to celebrate. She showered and for the first time on the trip, the two-minute timer caught her out. It didn't matter, she reset the timer, who would complain?

Without the spin, she had to shower within a bag designed for that purpose. It wasn't as convenient but she luxuriated in the warm spray anyway, allowing it to soothe and wash away the tensions of the past few days.

When she felt clean again, she dressed in fresh clothes and prepared something to eat. She chose a light meal of some of the remaining fresh food. She now had no way of cultivating any fresh produce, so she intended to enjoy what she had while she could.

After eating she returned to Piotr's room and gently bathed him with a damp cloth, then changed his bedding and clothes before settling down and telling him the good news.

Samantha prayed that he could hear her.

Chapter 32
Is There Anybody Out There?

24th January 2023, 08:45 ship time

"Today I'll try and get the comms working," Samantha told Piotr as she examined his drip and administered more antibiotics. He remained unconscious and that worried her. She didn't know what to do. His condition was beyond anything they had trained for, and without communications she had no-one to provide advice.

For the past few days she had focused on ship's maintenance. The constant work tired her, but she forced herself to keep going. Her training and Piotr's survival insisted on it.

Samantha had decided that fixing the communications system could wait. If she let the routine tasks go for too long, she would quickly become overwhelmed. The ship represented some of the finest technology that humanity had ever developed, however it was vulnerable and required constant care.

She had hoped that Piotr would show some signs of recovery and when he didn't, the need for communications became a more pressing concern.

That morning while she showered inside the plastic bag, she thought about the events in Mars orbit. They had never truly been far from her thoughts. She now recognised it as a living entity, although if asked she wouldn't be able to prove it. That didn't matter, sometimes you needed a little faith.

Samantha considered the fact that it had also been Piotr's theory which swayed her change in opinion. She couldn't deny it to herself and it brought the guilt of what might have been different had she accepted Piotr and Stephen's ideas before approaching Mars.

Coming to the understanding that the events were caused by an interaction with an alien entity revealed a new truth. A more deadly scenario.

If it was concentrated at Mars, but had never been encountered before by any earlier probe. That meant that the alien had travelled to Mars. Or maybe it had been dormant somehow and had recently awakened. She leaned towards the travelling theory, although she wasn't sure how it could have done so. It possessed no appreciable mass or means of propulsion, which should have made travel against the solar wind impossible for such an insubstantial creature.

Yet they had encountered it on their route to Mars.

There was a leap involved in that conclusion. However she considered the possibility of two separate phenomena with similar characteristics unlikely.

She pondered what that might mean, but her mind couldn't put the pieces together. In any case, Mission Control had to be told what had occurred and she needed their help in saving Piotr.

"I'll get it working and I'll let Earth know what happened."

She worried that Piotr didn't seem to be getting any better. His wounds were infected, so she cleaned them as best she could, but the pus returned by the time she cleaned them again. The antibiotics weren't working, but she hoped they were at least preventing the infection from getting any worse.

What concerned her even more was that he no longer moaned. Indeed he made no sound at all. To Samantha, it appeared as if he had given up whatever internal struggle he had engaged in. He had to fight, to want to rejoin the living or he would never recover at all.

She wanted him to rejoin the living, and more than that she wanted him to return to her. Without him, she didn't know if she would be able to do this alone.

The thought of a trip so long alone filled her with despair.

He needed a focus to encourage him to return and as she tended his wounds, inspiration hit her. She activated his wall screen, which wasn't password protected. With the touch screen controls, she selected all of the videos he'd received from his granddaughter. If anything could get through to him, it would be his little angel. She played the selected videos and put them into a continuous loop.

At least he'd have some company while she worked.

After a few hours, the diagnostics on the communications system identified the problem and the news wasn't good. The failure registered in the high-gain antenna. One of the cameras positioned near the antenna showed her the cause. It was no fault, the mounting look crushed. She thought she recognised some scorch damage as well.

Unfortunately for her, an EVA was out of the question. The module had suits, but no way to get out. There was an airlock in the nose of the module, but the ship reported a malfunction with the door.

She spent the morning working on the airlock, trying to find a way to open it. The door housing had been damaged in the attack. The only way through to the outside would be to cut through. She had the tools to do that, however she lacked the temporary airlock system used in the other modules. Forcing an opening would create a catastrophic loss of atmosphere. A loss that she wouldn't be able to replace.

She doubted that she could repair the mounting even if she could access it. Samantha didn't have the required tools for engineering work. Cutting through the door was one thing, rebuilding the antenna mounting and the complicated orientation mechanism presented a completely different matter.

The wireless data network lacked the range to reach Earth, so the only other available option was the experimental laser communications system provided by the European Space Agency. Although the system had worked well in Earth orbit, it had proved less reliable as the distance between the ship and Earth increased.

Transmission alignment had proved the major issue. Reception had been fine, the ship was covered with detectors, but keeping the laser aligned with Earth had been difficult. Stephen had improved the alignment software, allowing it to align with greater reliability. Not for the first time, she wished she had him there with her.

Or any of the other crew for that matter. Everything seemed so much more difficult when you had to do it alone.

It required feedback from the Earth stations, which with the current signal lag meant an hour's wait, assuming the laser was on target. This would be a long process, but all she could do was wait while the software did its work.

When she established contact she wouldn't be certain that the link would be maintained, so while waiting for the connection to be established, she gathered all the data that Stephen and Piotr had amassed on the alien. She compressed it for quicker transmissions and then read through their notes while she waited.

Although they had worked from the same data and agreed that it was an alien, they had both differed in their theories about it. The most significant disagreement had been about the alien's origin.

Stephen believed the alien had been created in the magnetic fields of Jupiter. The strong magnetic belts contained energised plasma streams within the flimsy rings around the giant planet. Dust from the rings created patterns in the plasma, the flows created symmetrical structures, helical in form like DNA.

Piotr disagreed, not so much in how the creature came to be, but where that formation took place. Due to the highly active thermal and electromagnetic signature of the entity, he considered it impossible for such a creature to have existed within the Solar System for so long and remain undetected. There had been many probes to the giant planet over the years.

Stephen responded that the entity was a being of magnetic fields and plasma, with a microscopic crystalline structure. All things that were well-known to be around Jupiter in abundance. Well, except for the crystalline structures, but no probe had tried to sample matter from the rings of Jupiter or carried the equipment able to detect them.

When she read Piotr's notes, she learned that he thought that the alien was not from our Solar System, but had originated from the interstellar medium, the vast expanse between the stars.

Stephen had scoffed at the suggestion, claiming that there was no way the alien could have crossed the heliopause. The pressure from the solar wind would have prevented entrance to the Solar System for such an insubstantial being.

The same solar wind that hadn't prevented its travel from Jupiter to Mars.

She wondered if there had been any data from observations of Jupiter that would aid their theories. Samantha discovered that Stephen and Piotr had already downloaded gigabytes of data from space probes from the past few decades. They'd also conducted a preliminary analysis of that data, which hadn't confirmed their theory, but didn't seem to contradict it either.

Neither of their notes provided any clarity on how the entity moved against the solar wind. She wished that she'd taken the time to learn more about their specialisations. If Piotr regained consciousness then she hoped that he could help her understand the alien more.

The urge to understand what she had encountered at Mars now caught her attention, for if she comprehended what had happened then perhaps it would mean something. Where she sat at that moment, it seemed like it had been for nothing.

As she read their theories on how the entity reproduced, the computer received feedback. She shouted to Piotr that they now had contact with Earth again. She then transmitted Piotr's medical status and the data to Earth and waited for a response.

Chapter 33
Nursemaid

1st February 2023, 08:45 ship time

Mission Control hadn't finished analysing the data she had sent back a few days ago, so she waited. She decided that it did no good to wait idle. Her life and Piotr's depended on her keeping the ship operational.

Contact with Earth had sparked a new routine for Samantha. The routine she hoped would carry her and Piotr back to their home planet. In many ways it resembled the routine they'd established during the journey to Mars. The key difference was that she had to do it alone.

The day began at 07:00. Her first task of the day was to look in on Piotr, and every morning she hoped to see a change in his condition. She changed his bedding and clothes if he needed it. She then cleaned him with a quick sponge bath. While she ministered to him, she told him about her plans for the day.

With the renewed connection with home, the first information she had sent included the medical details she had gathered on Piotr's condition. They were preparing a plan for her to tackle his condition. They had changed his drug regimen and had warned her that surgery may be required.

She hadn't liked the thought of that.

There was still no improvement in his condition. When she changed the dressings on his wounds, she thought that they looked less infected, although they still looked swollen and oozed with pus. She checked his breathing and replaced his IV so that at least he was kept hydrated.

During the night she turned off the playlist, but in the morning she created a new one, a fresh playlist every day. She included songs from his collection as well as video messages from his daughter and granddaughter. That morning she also included lectures from his collection as well as films and TV programmes. She hoped that something would stimulate his mind and bring him back.

Yesterday she'd even included songs that she knew he hated, usually rock songs from Ronald's collection. He had liked his music loud and heavy and she hoped they might shock Piotr out of his coma. A faint hope indeed.

On this particular morning, she faced an arduous task. She intended to write condolence letters to the families of the crew members. They didn't know for sure that the other crew were dead, although she considered it a grim certainty.

David Richards back at Mission Control had already messaged her to say he would take care of it, but as mission commander she felt that she had to try and provide some comfort.

Could she really provide any comfort?

All night she had tossed and turned as she wrestled with what she would write. David had warned her that she couldn't say anything about the alien, not that they were saying much about it either. Samantha thought that wasn't so much about keeping its existence a secret, but that the team back on Earth didn't believe it was an alien entity.

She'd received a video message from Jake the night before. She did wonder why it had taken so long for him to contact her, but she had burst into tears the moment his face appeared on her wall screen. Despite having the whole module to herself, she still retreated to her quarters for privacy, or was it for comfort? In the video, Jake had talked about the events as if it was some freak occurrence.

So what could she really say about the loss of the crew?

Mission Control had also been sparing in the news from Earth. She could only imagine what the reaction to the mission's end would be. They assured her that everyone was concerned with making sure that she and Piotr arrived home safely.

After taking care of Piotr, she showered and dressed. Breakfast was often reconstituted eggs, sometimes scrambled, sometimes cooked into an omelette for a little variety. The fresh vegetables hadn't lasted long, but she had enough dried and preserved foods to last her for the journey home.

Most important of all, she had ample supplies of coffee, that most essential boost in the morning.

After taking care of Piotr, she spent her mornings checking messages from Mission Control and working through her chores. For the most part, the messages were requests for more information. It annoyed her that those requests remained a one-way street. She wondered what they were keeping from her, then tried to dismiss the concerns as paranoia.

Communication was a frustrating affair; the laser system often lost alignment. The software routine that Stephen had written usually fixed the alignment, but it often took an hour or more, making communications sporadic at best.

One of this morning's tasks was for Samantha to expand the routine so that the system would realign itself automatically if it lost the connection. There'd still be additional delays as the system wouldn't know for an hour that it had lost the connection. It at least meant that she wouldn't have to constantly monitor the connection. The delay would also reduce the nearer the ship travelled to Earth which would make the realignment a quicker process.

She focused on that task rather than the letters of condolence. Mission Control had provided the code update. Software upgrades had to follow an established procedure for testing and implementation and that consumed most of her morning.

As always, she had a continual list of maintenance work that she had to work through. For the most part, it was small tasks that if left undone would accumulate into serious issues for the ship. By lunch time she was exhausted and looked forward to the short rest.

For lunch she made soup and ate it while sitting next to Piotr's bed. She missed the artificial gravity, even the minimal gravity they'd had before made everything so much easier. Now she had to eat her food from tubes or closed containers, since loose crumbs and bits of food would clog the filters and make cleaning even more difficult.

The afternoons were set aside for domestic chores, although she worked on them whenever she had time throughout the day. She didn't have any food to grow, but she still had to keep the place clean and in order. She also inventoried everything she used. As with their journey to Mars, she recorded her food intake and also measured her physical activity. It was a long trip ahead, and everything had to be organised. As she was alone, even the small jobs mounted up.

Mission Control helped her prioritise what needed to be done.

Before making her lonely evening meal, she read through any new messages from Earth. The program she installed earlier had done its job. The laser had lost alignment, but the connection was now restored.

Today she received two messages. One was a message for Piotr, a new video from his family. She copied it to his personal folder and she would play it to him later. The other was a request for more medical data on his condition.

Back on Earth, the medical team were attempting to diagnose Piotr's problem. They requested that she send them more detailed scans of his head. Their current theory was some sort of brain injury, which didn't amuse Samantha as she'd figured that much out for herself. Most likely a hidden infection working in tandem with the damage from his wounds. She'd already come to the same conclusion and she'd hoped that they would have provided some more clarity, but maybe the scans would help provide that. The module did have a small medical bay and it was equipped with a multifunction scanner.

To get him to the medical bay would be difficult on her own, although the microgravity would help rather than hinder in this instance. She decided to do the scan now, before eating and settling for the night.

The sooner they had the information then the sooner they would formulate a plan.

"Hi Piotr. We've got to take a trip to the medical bay. When we're done, you've received a new message from your granddaughter. I'm sure that she misses you and wants to hear her grandpa's voice again. In fact you could save me a lot of trouble by waking up and saying hello. No? Ah well, let's go, it shouldn't take too long."

She released the ties holding him to the bed and gently pulled him free of the sleeping bag. She backed out into the central passageway, towing carefully him behind her.

"Okay, this is the tricky bit. I need to get you up the stairs."

She mounted the ladder and with deliberate movements pulled Piotr up after her.

"We're almost there. It's all right; I won't bump you on the way."

Once on the second floor, getting him to the medical bay was a simple matter. She strapped him onto the bed again and then retrieved the scanner. The latest in medical imaging technology, it allowed a variety of scans to be conducted at different wavelengths. While it fell far short of most modern hospitals' equipment, it was compact and superior to anything available on previous space missions.

With the scans completed according to Mission Control's detailed instructions, Samantha fed the results into the computer. She watched as the images flashed before her. They all showed the same thing.

Samantha was no expert, but even she understood a black patch on the back of his skull was not good news.

Chapter 34
Prep for Surgery

2nd February 2023, 03:34 ship time

Samantha sat with Piotr in the medical bay throughout the night, waiting for Mission Control to respond. In the early hours of the morning the message arrived, along with a video file. The message was concise; it confirmed what she had feared when first seeing the images.

Fluid had built up in Piotr's brain.

The message urged immediate action, as the build-up appeared quite advanced and needed to be relieved as soon as possible to prevent permanent damage. They feared that it might already be too late.

The video would show her how to do that.

A distinguished looking old man spoke with exaggerated diction towards the camera.

"The procedure itself is quite simple. We'll talk you through each step, although we recommend that you complete a few dry runs to familiarise yourself.

"The first step is to prepare the patient. As you'll be operating in microgravity, you should make sure to secure the patient."

Samantha frowned at the screen, why couldn't they refer to Piotr by his name?

"You should also make sure that you are secured to the floor. While the procedure isn't difficult, it is easier to make precise movements when you are stationary. Drifting means you could easily slip.

"You should first shave the patient's head. Then clean the area thoroughly with an antiseptic solution, there should be adequate supplies in the medical bay.

"You will need to scrub up for the operation and also make sure that you are wearing sterile clothes and disposable gloves. Again, you'll have what you need in the medical supplies."

Samantha paused the video. They'd trained in various branches of emergency medicine. They'd even observed shifts in emergency care wards, but they hadn't practised this. They hadn't practised brain surgery. And they hadn't practised anything close to this without additional help.

She worried that she couldn't do what Piotr needed.

With a frown, she resumed the video playback.

"Normally we would use a general anaesthetic for this procedure, however with only one person active we believe this would be too risky. Because of this, you must make sure that the patient is tied down so that even if he does move accidently he won't complicate the procedure.

"While we advise against the general anaesthetic, administering a local would help reduce the pain and thus any involuntary movements from the patient. The medical supplies on board contain the required injections. The message includes a scanned image of the labels to look for.

"When you are ready, inject five doses in a circle ten centimetres around the planned incision point. The injections will take less than five minutes to take effect.

"You will find it easier when making the incisions if you mark the cuts first, then you just need to follow the lines. Draw a dot on the centre point, then draw five radial lines from the point just short of where you injected the local anaesthetic.

"We understand that you haven't performed any surgery, so it is natural that you will feel hesitant. After drawing the planned cuts, take a new scalpel and mime the moves. You must make single clean cuts to create the folds. You will have to overcome your hesitancy as the cuts must be firm and continuous.

"Head cuts tend to bleed a lot, so be prepared for the blood flow. Mop the blood away between each cut. Don't worry, where you are cutting there are no major veins or arteries.

"Now bleeding in zero gravity will be a problem for you, especially without any assistance."

She hadn't considered that, although it made perfect sense. Any uncontained liquid would float in the air, separate and get everywhere. Back on the ISS there had been a small leak from one of the water tanks, and she learned how difficult mopping up could be.

"To prevent blood floating in the air, keep plenty of towels to hand and mop up any bleeding as often as possible.

"Once the incisions are complete, peel back the folds of skin and use the clamps to secure them in place. Clean away any excess blood and then prepare to drill through the skull. You don't have the tool we'd normally use for this procedure, but the mini-drill you use for maintenance should do the job. Make sure that the drill bit is well sterilised before you start the operation."

Oh Christ, could she really do this?

"The standard procedure is to drill guide holes and then cut a larger hole in the skull. You don't have the required equipment for that as you're alone for this. Instead you should drill a single hole.

"This is the trickiest bit – "

No shit.

" – you need to drill all the way through the skull to form a drainage hole. From the scans we have determined that this is the best place to drain the fluid. You need to be very careful as you drill. Don't use any force to push the drill through. Drill slowly with the lowest speed setting and the moment you feel any reduction in resistance remove the drill.

"After the hole stops weeping, you should scan the patient's head again and send us the scans.

"Shortly the video will show a recording of the same operation performed in a hospital. Now I have to urge you to perform the procedure as soon as possible."

Samantha watched the remainder of the video with mounting trepidation. In the video, the surgeon had a team of nurses in support. She would have to do it alone, and she wasn't sure that she could.

That doubt shook her and she wasn't used to that feeling. She re-watched the video three times before preparing herself for surgery.

Chapter 35
Guilty Relief

2nd February 2023, 06:17 ship time

Samantha forced herself to eat before she prepared Piotr for surgery. The extra time helped her to prepare mentally. As she had on many occasions during her life, she fell back on her training. This didn't mean that the training made her a robot. Anyone who couldn't think for themselves had no business being in space. Sometimes though, a situation reached a point where the ability to act became more important than the process of making a decision.

In this case, Mission Control had determined the course she had to follow. Collectively, they possessed knowledge beyond her own. So while she didn't have any desire to cut Piotr's skull open, the deed needed to be done. She wasn't squeamish, but the thought of screwing it up and ending any hope for his recovery weighed heavily on her.

The act of eating helped calm her nerves a little, and once done she scrubbed her hands as best as she could and prepared Piotr for the operation. She made sure that he was strapped to the bed in the medical bay. Around the bed were footholds she would use to ensure that she had a firm footing.

The ship's designers had thought of everything.

She cleaned his head, then shaved off his hair. She'd never shaved a man before, so she took exaggerated care not to nick his skin. That seemed a little ironic considering she was about to cut his scalp open.

All the while she tried to bury her nervousness under calm professionalism.

She cleaned his now-bald head with antiseptic solution. She felt a tremble through her hand. For a moment she thought it was her, she felt anxious enough. None of her years in the Air Force and then with NASA had prepared her for cutting a man's skull open.

The tremble happened again.

The monitor attached to Piotr beeped.

A grimace of pain creased his face.

The monitor beeped again and then shrieked an alarm.

Samantha checked the monitor's screen.

Piotr's heart rate had flatlined.

Samantha's training kicked in once again.

First she checked his breathing. He wasn't breathing, so she felt for a pulse. When she didn't feel a pulse she grabbed the portable defibrillator attached the wall. In a swift movement, she connected the pads to Piotr's chest and then checked to ensure that his airway was clear.

Samantha activated the defibrillator. The charge pulsed through Piotr's body and convulsed his muscles. It registered on the monitor as a single blip then returned to the flat line.

While the device recharged, she performed rapid chest compressions. Every twenty seconds she stopped and breathed into his mouth, inflating his empty lungs. Her air blew back at her as his chest deflated. She then checked his pulse again. Nothing. She repeated the cycle for three minutes and then activated the defibrillator.

Another shock convulsed Piotr's body with the same negative result.

She then resumed CPR.

With each cycle the kernel of fear inside her grew a little more.

She tried three times, nothing.

Four times, still nothing.

Five times and intellectually, she knew that Piotr was dead.

Still she tried again.

She didn't want to accept the reality.

And again.

A voice inside her head shouted at her to stop.

Samantha tried again as if in defiance of the voice. She wanted the voice to be wrong.

One more failed attempt and then she stopped.

Unable to process what had happened, she pulled out a seat folded against the wall and sat down. Without realising she bounced off and floated above it.

At least I don't have to cut him open.

A rogue thought, a guilty thought, which arose unbidden from the secret places of her mind.

The fact that her mind could create such a thought hurt more than the devastating loss of Piotr's passing.

She was now alone out here in the depths of space with only voices an hour away to provide any form of company.

Samantha forced her thoughts onto more practical concerns. What should she do next? A stupid question really, as a procedure already existed for her to follow. The body, Piotr's body, needed to be packed away. In one of the many drawers, just out of reach, lay ten body bags.

Why ten?

There had been just six people for millions of miles. There was redundancy in every part of the mission, including the wrapping of corpses. Of course, there was only one person left now, so even though she had nine left, who would put her in a body bag when the time came?

It would be nice to think that the others had somehow survived. For an all too brief moment, she allowed herself to indulge that comforting delusion. It soon collapsed under the weight of what survival would mean. It would mean a lingering death, waiting for a rescue that could never arrive.

The comfort existed only for her own selfishness.

Another guilty thought to dance with the one that resurfaced when she looked at the pen marks on Piotr's skull.

Samantha stood up, drifting off the floor as she did so. The lack of gravity made the act of putting Piotr into the black plastic sheath difficult. She should have acted quicker and then he would now be awake and watching the latest video from his two favourite girls.

She didn't notice the tears that streamed down her face and floated in the air as she packed Piotr's body into the bag.

Chapter 36
Fragrant

3rd February 2023, 08:35 ship time

Samantha discovered an unexpected, yet significant flaw in the mission plan. The ship stores contained more than enough body bags, but nowhere to store a body. She reported that problem in the same message in which she informed Mission Control of the Russian scientist's death.

The return messages contained sympathy from the team and a solution to the body storage problem. She moved Piotr back to his quarters and set the temperature as low as it would go. It wouldn't stop the decomposition, but would at least slow it down for a while.

That was the theory at any rate.

Samantha now found herself in a grey limbo.

She didn't know what to do, so she followed the routine and found herself heading to Piotr's quarters after she woke and before meals. At these times she'd stand by his door until she remembered that he was dead and returned to the routine.

Except it wasn't a routine, not any more. She drifted through the day. Her training kept her motivated enough to keep the ship running. For the most part the ship ran itself, but it did need constant care and attention to keep operational.

Mission Control tried to engage her, to divert her focus on something other than her grief and loneliness. They also needed her to help them with the investigation of what happened to the ship in Mars orbit. She downloaded the messages as they arrived. Jake sent her video messages, which she ignored. She couldn't face him even though they were just videos.

For three days she existed in this fugue state. Since the night Piotr died, she hadn't cried. She couldn't cry even though she knew that she should. Somehow she had to release the blanket that threatened to smother her.

The morning of the third day saw her standing in front of Piotr's quarters after leaving the shower. As she stood there she detected an odd smell in the air. She recognised it with a grimace of disgust, it was Piotr.

The next day dawned and the smell filled the module. It was rank, although it did at least pull her from the fugue state. If only for a short while. The stench was terrible and there was nowhere to hide from it.

The body bag was clearly insufficient to contain the aroma. She thought about wrapping more body bags around him, she hoped that would be enough.

After some reflection she realised that would at best slow the process. The body bags were not airtight, but she realised that a space suit was.

How she wished she had thought of that sooner.

Even wearing an emergency mask, the stench made her retch. It took a huge effort to swallow back the urge to vomit.

The smell hung thick in the air and that paled in comparison to the deluge of corruption that assaulted her senses when she unzipped the bag. She vomited into her mask, the mess spraying into her face and back into her mouth. Bits of her sick floated around her face.

She had to pull off her mask to breathe, then the vile odour hit her with its full force and she had to retreat from the room. It took several minutes for the retching to subside. After washing her face, she collected another mask and entered Piotr's quarters again.

This time she opened the body bag completely. Even though she wore disposable gloves, his skin felt greasy. She pulled him from the bag and it took considerable effort. The task was probably the most disgusting thing she ever had to do. But all the while she wanted to pay Piotr the proper respect as she manhandled his body.

Getting him into the space suit proved even more difficult.

She had to place him in the suit limb by limb. The legs weren't too bad, but levering his torso in required several attempts. Each time her grip skidded on his loose skin, a wave of revulsion pulsed through her. She had to pull the suit over his body before she could put his arms in.

Somehow she held back the fresh need to puke.

The last job was to stuff the rancid-smelling bag into the suit. The relief as she secured the suit's helmet was huge. It didn't reduce the stench, but it still seemed much better.

With the difficult task completed, she built a cocoon of air filters, some of them old filters from the trip to Mars. Others came from her precious stock of replacements for the return journey. With just her breathing, the system shouldn't need as many so could spare a few.

The mound of material should absorb any of the smell that leaked from the space suit. She knew that suit was airtight, but for how long was unknown. She now hoped that the life support system could clear the air.

Before taking a shower to try and clear the stench from her body, she had to remove the globules of vomit that lingered in rotating clumps in the air. If left unattended they could clog the filters of the air purification system, and without the crops she was reliant on that system for clean air.

Once she finished the horrible task, she closed the door to Piotr's quarters and stripped in the shower. She would later pack the clothes away, and would never wear them again. The hot water felt good, but it took many hits of the reset button before she felt clean.

Cleaner, at any rate. She doubted she would feel clean ever again.

Chapter 37
Heading Home

7th March 2023, 10:42 ship time

A month later and Piotr's putrefaction still lingered in the module like an unwelcome guest. It created an unpalatable undertone to the ambience of the desolate ship. More than that, it provided a not so subtle reminder to how alone she was. To her own surprise, this helped restore her balance, as it provided a focus that she could fight. Day by day and piece by piece, Samantha pulled herself free of the malaise that haunted her since the old man's death.

She even resumed her messages to Jake and had come to rely on their renewed contact. They provided a beacon of personal contact in the busy days. For his part he appeared glad to speak with her again.

The long days in the ship stretched her state of mind. Never had she been so alone. At least now she could reach out and talk to someone. She was still too far away from Earth for proper conversation, but the exchange of video messages provided comfort.

For her part, the messages were often morose affairs. She might have found her motivation again, but despair still infected her spirit like Piotr's smell did the air. She talked about the crew and their loved ones. She talked about the terrible events at Mars, although for his part Jake still appeared reluctant to discuss it in the same terms as she did.

Jake kept her informed about the little things that happened back on Earth. She now had access to daily information packages that included the latest news and current affairs.

Hearing news, trivial and otherwise, from Earth helped keep the loneliness at bay.

She didn't pay them too much interest, but she was happy to listen when Jake talked about them. From his lips it sounded more personal, more interesting coming from him.

He told her about the families of the staff at Mission Control. He included choice gossip and the events that were so important to them. She understood what Jake was trying to do: he was providing her with a lifeline. He wanted her to get to know the people back on Earth. He wanted them to become important to her so that she would want to come home.

There was a pertinent question.

Did she want to go home?

What did home mean now anyway?

She lacked answers for those questions and that tugged at her mood. Following the routine helped. It grounded her thoughts and provided focus. Along with the contact with Jake, it helped her to make it through the day.

During the day, she maintained the ship and responded to requests from Mission Control. She repeated the endless toil of cleaning and maintenance day after day. It seemed that no matter how hard she worked, the list never ended.

Despite the additional data she'd been able to provide, Mission Control remained convinced that the phenomenon had to be an unusual interaction with the solar wind. They didn't even seem willing to consider the possibility that it had been an alien entity.

She'd also sent them the private research that Stephen and Piotr had started, but they informed her that their conclusions were wrong. They didn't even explain why. It seemed to Samantha that they weren't even willing to consider the possibility that it was an alien life form.

She brought the subject up with Jake in her video messages, but he never responded to her questions. It frustrated her. What were they not telling her? It seemed impossible after what she had seen that Stephen and Piotr were wrong, no other explanation made sense.

If Mission Control weren't willing to investigate the possibility, then she had to. With that decision, she discovered fresh purpose for her days beyond simple survival. Once the day's chores were done, she continued the research.

She owed it to Piotr's memory and that of the rest of the crew.

Thoughts of the crew surfaced from time to time. Usually at the most unexpected of times but at least they no longer paralysed her as they once did. She talked about them in the messages to Jake, but at other times they caught her unawares.

Over the weeks, she had learned to take the sudden recollections in her stride and continue with her day. Sometimes she felt guilty at being able to function, but pushed through it. It wasn't easy for her. The module was too quiet, only the hum of machinery provided any company and poor company it was too.

Sometimes the memories surfaced as she tried to sleep at night. Alone in the dark, they were more difficult to put aside. If she was lucky they would be pleasant memories of their training and the trip to Mars. On other occasions she imagined their fates, consumed by the entity at Mars.

Piotr and Stephen had accumulated gigabytes of data on the entity. Much of the physics lay beyond her comprehension, but she did discover a puzzle that she believed she could tackle. Perhaps that was a bit ambitious, but at least it gave her something to work on.

Where had the alien originated?

Stephen's theory that the alien evolved in the rings of Jupiter didn't make sense to her. Probes had visited the giant planet many times over the decades of human space exploration. They'd provided no indication of the alien's presence.

That wasn't proof, of course, but in her fragmented state it seemed sufficient reason.

She considered Piotr's theory of it originating from interstellar space. Samantha liked that theory, she couldn't explain why, but she appreciated the elegance of it. Perhaps the grander nature of the thought would in turn raise the memories of the fallen crew.

So she pursued Piotr's idea, and there were two aspects that attracted her. The first was how did it enter the Solar System? The pressure of the solar wind should have made the movement of such an insubstantial creature impossible.

Mission Control's theory was that the effect had spawned either in or near the Sun and had drifted outwards, and would continue to drift until captured by a massive enough body such as Mars.

Throughout every afternoon and into the evening, she examined the data. She'd then break for dinner, a cold and lonely affair. Often while eating, memories of the crew surfaced, in the same way as when she tried to sleep her mind relaxed and the ghosts slipped in. At first they'd ruined her appetite and she'd been unable to eat, but she'd got used to their visitations.

And felt disgust at herself for doing so.

After dinner and another frustrating, but illuminating afternoon of research, she sat in her quarters facing the wall screen.

"Hi Jake. Me again, although I'm sure you'd guessed that."

The words might have sounded light, but her tone belied that impression.

"Today was pretty much the same as every other day. Although I guess that every day brings me another day closer to home. That has to be a good thing, right? I didn't make much progress on my research today. I did have an idea though."

She knew that Jake agreed with Mission Control's conclusions and to be honest it did make some sense. She couldn't shake the feeling that Piotr was right and it had become her duty to prove him so. Even so, Jake was a smart man and she wished that he'd discuss it with her, rather than evading her questions.

"The alien couldn't move as a whole against the solar wind, it doesn't have any means of propulsion. I've been looping through the same problem for weeks and then out of the blue it struck me."

She even smiled at the camera.

"When we first encountered the alien, it wasn't in a coherent mass. No, what we saw was a tendril stretching through space and I've figured out that's how it moves against the solar wind. It grows a tendril against the wind and when the tendril finds somewhere it can anchor, it drags the rest of it and reels it in."

Samantha laughed.

"I know it sounds far-fetched, but I'm certain that's what it's doing. The question is, how do I prove it? I think I can construct a simulation to prove that it is at least plausible. There should be the software here that I can modify, although it's not really my thing.

"I wish Stephen was here, he'd know what to do."

She paused for a while to recover herself.

"Jake, I know you've been avoiding discussing what happened. I think I'm on to something here and I need your help. Mission Control don't want to discuss this either and I guess that they've instructed you to do the same.

"Please Jake, help me out here. It's keeping me from going crazy.

"Anyway, I had beef stew for dinner. No red wine to accompany it, which is always a shame.

"Did David send the messages of condolence that I wrote to the families?"

She'd put the task of writing the messages off for far too long and had now finished them.

First she wrote to Piotr's daughter and granddaughter. She thought that would be hardest one to write so she wanted to get it done first. She told them how happy he had made the people around him with his jokes and stories of all the cold places he had visited around the world.

She didn't tell them about how he had died, or any details of what had happened. What could she have said? Mission Control would no doubt remove any reference to the events at Mars. From the little Mission Control told her, the news had been kept from the public until the full facts of the incident had been established.

The message to Colette's mother was the shortest. Not because she didn't want to write more, but that she couldn't. This had turned out to be the hardest letter to write.

With being so involved in Piotr's death, it had hit her hard and dominated her thoughts. With Colette, her grief had lain submerged until she tried to write to Colette's mother.

They had been paired as pilot and co-pilot for the entirety of the mission training. The crew had trained together, and indeed lived together for many years before departing to Mars. But the bond between pilots ran much deeper.

Samantha wanted to tell Colette's mother of the times that they had spent together, about that unique bond they shared, but she struggled to articulate those feelings. The message as a result was terse, and not what she had intended to say.

The letter to Ronald's brother had proved easier. Not because of lesser sentiment but because he had inspired so much happiness in life that he was easier to write about in death. Ronald had been such a joker that she almost enjoyed recounting his antics and how he had helped keep the crew's spirits high.

To Juliet's younger sister, Samantha described Juliet's excitement for visiting Mars. As a geologist this had been the ultimate journey, to investigate the surface of an alien world. She reminisced of their training together, and wished that she had got to know the gifted geologist better so that she could have written more. Juliet had been a solid member of the crew, quiet compared to the gregarious Ronald. She had been happy to keep out of the limelight, but always there when something needed doing.

When writing the letter to Stephen's twin sister, she wanted to tell her of the amazing discovery that he had made. She couldn't, not until she had the proof to validate his research and prove him and Piotr right in their thoughts. Instead she told Laura of his brilliance and how essential to the mission he had been.

Too many platitudes written, and now she felt like a cheat. She thought of the brief instant of relief she had experienced when Piotr had died. That split-second still repeated in her dreams.

She ended the video recording and waited for Jake's next message. It was fleeting human contact across millions of miles, but better than none and for now it kept her going.

Chapter 38
Chimera Slain

12th September 2023, 13:05 ship time

For the next six months, Samantha followed her routine and fortune favoured her with no major malfunctions or catastrophes to hinder her voyage. Life on the ship remained a solitary one, and she now talked to herself a lot, although she didn't notice that she did so.

The act of keeping the ship in working order now occupied most of her time. That left her with little time for continuing her research. This frustrated her, although the routine tasks kept her busy and tired and that kept her sane, relatively speaking.

Over the past few months, she'd constructed a computer simulation of the entity. Jake had finally broken his silence on the subject and had helped.

He'd also enlisted the help of Laura, Stephen's twin sister, and she had contributed her insight into the alien. She had been devastated by the news of her brother's death, and the urge to complete his work had provided small, but necessary comfort. NASA were initially resistant to allowing her access to Samantha, but when she managed to contact Jake, he agreed to help her. Her enthusiasm for the project had convinced him to review in more detail what Samantha had compiled so far.

Together they'd formulated a model that demonstrated a structure comprised of plasma crystals and a binding electromagnetic force to replicate advancing against the pressures of the solar wind.

The process required energy, but their calculations indicated that if the entity could absorb the radiation from the solar wind, that would provide enough energy for limited replication. It wouldn't have been enough on its own to travel across interplanetary distances though.

Her idea that the tendril acted as an anchor that would drag the rest of the entity to the target didn't pan out. The connection between the helical bonds just wasn't strong enough to pull even the light mass of the creature.

So they searched for another theory.

Now less than four months from Earth, she received a large data packet from Mission Control. The packet contained a complete data dump for an hour of telemetry and sensor readings from the Chimera probe they had launched on their way to Mars.

This presented a new face on Mission Control's attitude towards the alien. Up until then, she'd suspected that they had humoured her by allowing Jake and Laura to help her. Their project had provided an intellectual escape for Samantha, an anchor to sustain her for the long trip home.

The data from the probe changed all that.

The probe had been active for almost a year. It had scouted several near-Earth asteroids as it orbited in a wide loop around the Sun. The probe had identified two of the asteroids as promising targets for future commercial exploitation. Chimera Industries had considered the mission a success and hoped to glean further data from more asteroid fly-bys.

Once it had completed its first orbit, it prepared for another pass of the targets. As it approached the first of those targets, its sensors registered a sudden change in the space around it.

Samantha scanned the readings. They looked so familiar. There was the sudden increase in ambient temperature combined with the magnetic fluctuations. Exactly the same as what they'd recorded during the two previous encounters with the entity.

Sixty minutes of data had been provided by Mission Control, however the data was much more coherent than the fragments Samantha had been able to recover from the Mars encounter. Even though the probe was radiation shielded, its systems had been overwhelmed. The probe did have sensors that the Mars Voyager didn't, or at least wouldn't have deployed until it parked in Mars orbit.

Those additional sensors provided enough data to map a high-definition 3D image of the entity. Even at a quick glance, Samantha saw that the data revealed an amazing amount of detail, far more than they were able to construct from her own information.

Better than that, the probe had generated these images in real time. As frame after frame rendered on her screen, she noticed the edges of the entity. She paused the playback and zoomed in on the part that had attracted her attention.

She saw it.

When she skipped from one frame to the next, she witnessed the replication of the helical structures. Here on the screen was the proof she needed.

The 3D image was generated relative to the probe and it showed that growth occurring in the direction of the Sun.

The influx of new information didn't end there.

The data also proved that the entity was self-replicating, and it showed the direction the entity was moving in.

The video message from David Richards which accompanied the data summed it up for her.

"Hi Samantha. I don't know if you reviewed the data before watching this video, if not here's a summary.

"The Chimera prospecting probe is believed to have encountered and been destroyed by the entity..."

The entity! Samantha smiled when she heard that. The team back on Earth now believed the same as she did. The same as what Piotr and Stephen had theorised. Her months of effort had been vindicated. She felt almost giddy at the thought.

"... that you encountered on the way to and at Mars. At first we assumed that the part the probe encountered was a remnant from a solar flare discharge. It's clearer to us now that it is travelling towards the Sun.

"We've taken the work that you have been doing and passed it along to our simulation group. They're already building upon the foundation you've created. There are some messages in this data bundle for you to review and respond to.

"As well as confirming that the entity is travelling towards the Sun, we also believe that the entity is in fact an alien life form. The evidence of self-replication has all of the biologists here very excited. You went out to find a worm and are coming back having found something quite remarkable.

"We all wish that it hadn't come at such a price. I know it doesn't mean much to you right now, but down here you are all heroes.

"Our international partners have been made aware of the findings and the matter is being discussed in a closed session of the United Nations Security Council. For now it is being kept from the public while everyone agrees the correct plan to reveal this astounding news.

"We'll no doubt be needing you to participate in the announcements. Linda will put together the briefing plan which will kick in soon, although we're not sure when. We'll keep you in the loop as things progress."

Samantha already knew that news of the mission's failure was now public knowledge. She also understood that the whole truth hadn't been revealed yet and she worried about the tone of the message from David.

The entity had destroyed her ship and her crew, and she felt sure that it posed a danger to human operations in space. True, it seemed to be heading towards the Sun, but what did it want there?

It worried her that while Mission Control had accepted the alien's existence, they saw it as a grand discovery, not the threat she knew it to be.

Perhaps she was allowing her thoughts to be influenced by the anger she had discovered in the world's news. As she travelled closer to Earth, the connection became more reliable. She could now browse the internet again. It felt like she was part of the world, but the headlines on the news channels and websites had offended her.

That was unreasonable and she understood that, but even so she couldn't let it go. So she buried it and let it fester deep inside. Still, it was good to be connected again.

Chapter 39
One Last Burn

15th October 2023, 23:11 ship time

Three months from arriving back at Earth, Samantha prepared to perform a single retro manoeuvre to ensure she arrived in Earth orbit. It still didn't feel right as she sat at the control desk with an empty seat beside her. The braking burn had to be initiated much earlier than planned in the original mission profile.

In the original plan, the module would use an aero-braking manoeuvre by skimming Earth's upper atmosphere. This would slow the ship into a low orbit where they would then rendezvous with the International Space Station. The ship's current trajectory was far too steep and too fast for that plan to work.

Instead she would flip the ship, as she had when approaching Mars, and burn most the remaining fuel putting the craft into a shallower and slower approach.

She was still too far away to conduct a real time conversation so she talked through the procedure. At least it wasn't being recorded and transmitted across the world. Mission Control had determined that it wouldn't be a good idea to monitor and broadcast her like they had on the outward journey.

As she followed each step of the procedure, the ghosts of the crew sat in the seats around her. Samantha completed every part of the sequence according to the checklist. She waited, ignoring the imagined pale faces around her. When the burn completed, she checked the navigation system and it confirmed her new course and speed.

Now she turned her attention to more immediate concerns.

The Mars Voyager's constant need for maintenance had kept her busy for the past few weeks. What had started as niggles which filled her time had developed into more serious problems. Her new big problem was water. For some reason it appeared that she was running out.

The ship recycled all the water it could from the shower, the toilet and the kitchen sink. There was also a reserve tank sandwiched between the two floors of the module. The recycling system provided enough for what she needed, but not if there was a fault. That possibility looked ever more likely with the increased wear and tear on the system.

As with all the major systems, she reviewed the monitors on a regular basis, even if the ship's computer didn't detect any problem. She also had a schedule provided by Mission Control, to investigate each of the systems by hand.

So far it had been a fruitless task, but yesterday that changed when she discovered that the water level in the reserve tank was half of what the system reported it should be. She reported the fault to Mission Control and overnight they deliberated then responded with instructions.

She had to dismantle the floor to gain access, as the water was stored in reinforced bladders under the floor. Three of the bladders had deflated. She saw a chunk of ice against the inner surface of the hull. When she examined the area, she also found what look like tears in the alloy.

Damage from the alien's attack must have punctured the hull and the bladders. The leaking water would have frozen, thus sealing the leak. She believed that would explain why the system detected no hull breach. Vibrations in the hull must have shaken the ice loose and the water escaped fragment by fragment.

Samantha reasoned that the ship must have been leaking ice all the way from Mars. The good news was that the other bladders looked okay. She searched all round them and didn't find any other signs of a leak.

There was plenty of water left for her.

Another guilty thought seared her mind. If the crew had survived then this would have lessened their chances, her chances, of making it back to Earth.

The ghosts judged her with their grey, gaunt faces.

She buried that traitorous thought in the effort of replacing the floor. By the time she finished, she'd restored her equilibrium. She did that a lot these days. It wasn't so much swinging between depression and mania, she now surfed a maelstrom of emotions that clawed at her sanity.

Samantha had learned that it was best not to fight, but instead to just ride the wave in a delicate balancing act.

Over dinner she read her messages, one from David and another from Jake. She decided to watch the message from David first.

"Hi Samantha. I have some good news from the simulation team. They think they've cracked how the alien is moving the bulk of its body. As you discovered yourself, the tendrils lack the strength to pull the rest of it against the solar wind, more so as it gets closer to the Sun.

"We've pulled in an international team to help analyse the situation, and one them, a radio astronomer called Susan Macintyre, had an inspired thought. She's an old friend of Stephen's, by the way. Anyway she suggested that the alien doesn't move itself, instead it collapses itself.

"The team ran a few simulations based on her idea. It looks like it works, in fact it's a quite elegant solution. If the alien kills its tail, it could transfer the energy it releases along the chain and use that energy to re-grow itself at the other end.

"It would take it a long time to travel, but it would consume far less energy that way. What we don't know is how much of itself it can lose and still remain coherent. We just don't know enough about its internal structure."

Of course! That would be the tendril they'd encountered on the way to Mars. Samantha returned her attention to David.

"Another puzzle we've been working on is how much energy it needs. From the models we've constructed, the solar wind is enough to feed the tendrils that you and the Chimera probe encountered. We think that it's gaining energy to rebuild around major celestial bodies like Jupiter. In particular it would need enough to rebuild itself as a store for its next hop.

"We believe that it is using planets as stepping stones to reach the Sun. Why it's heading for the Sun we don't know yet, but we think it gains the energy from the magnetic fields around planets. Unfortunately Mars is lacking in any significant magnetic fields.

"Jupiter would have been a huge boost for the creature, which must be why it managed to travel from Mars without having fed.

"The bad news for us is that Earth has a very powerful magnetic field, which would be ideal for this creature's last push to the Sun. We have confirmed that there is at least one tendril heading towards us and it will arrive at Earth within the month."

Chapter 40
Pre-emptive Strike

4th November 2023, 09:14 ship time

Mission Control had formulated a plan of defence. Samantha didn't think much of the plan and she spent three futile weeks trying to convince them not to proceed with it. The Deep Space Network continued to track the alien tendril as it approached Earth.

Every space agency and launch-capable corporation on Earth worked around the clock to assemble a series of probes. They'd managed to construct seven, each of them built around the same engine core as used in the Mars Voyager. A monumental effort in so short a time.

Those probes formed the first and only real line of defence. They had launched a week ago and then headed out beyond the Moon's orbit towards the approaching alien.

The plan relied on brute force rather than finesse. The tendril presented a small target. The alien had already demonstrated its adverse reaction to the exhaust from the engines. Additional modelling indicated that the intense radiation from the exhaust should break down the alien's internal structure and prevent its advance.

Mission Control worked on the assumption that the exhaust had damaged the alien when the Mars Voyager encountered it and that a concerted burn would stop the alien in its tracks. If it couldn't reach Earth then it couldn't re-energise and continue its journey.

Samantha hadn't been convinced. The alien had reacted violently on both occasions and she felt sure that it would respond in the same fashion. She'd raised her objections, but

Mission Control wanted the alien to react. They wanted it to burn energy trying to break through the wall of nuclear fire.

She also worried that the plan relied on too many unknowns. On that score, the team on Earth agreed with her. Unfortunately they decided that they had little other choice but to make the attempt.

Mission Control provided her access to the feed so that she could watch the engagement. Not in real time though, as she was still too far away for that. They'd positioned the line of defence a light minute from Earth and she was still eight times as far away.

The seven probes had deployed a cloud of mini-sats in a skirmish line ahead of them. These were fist-sized bundles of sensors and transmitters. They monitored the alien's approach and provided extra data so that a more permanent defence could be formed before the alien, or another like it, encroached on human territory again.

They were already planning for the next encounter.

It was the arrogance of it that appalled Samantha; they'd already assumed their victory.

She watched with mounting trepidation as the line of probes detected the approaching alien. Second by second, they tracked the entity's movement. They analysed and built a detailed map of the alien, compiling a mountain of new data for the researchers back on Earth.

Despite her concern, Samantha marvelled at the incoming readings. She couldn't help but think that the Mars Voyager would have been able to build the same resolution of information if the Mars observatory module hadn't been destroyed.

The thought sparked the flame of memories to rise and threatened to snatch her attention. With an effort she remained focused on the incoming data stream. Samantha feared what she expected to see, even so, a tiny thread of hope dared to raise its voice.

With the time lag on the transmissions in mind, the probes had been programmed to organise and initiate the defence without need of Earth control. With the detailed map they'd constructed, the probes analysed the structure of the tendril and manoeuvred themselves to form a funnel.

The plan was to burn as much of the tendril as possible, in as short a time as possible, and then provide an area defence against any reaction by the alien.

There had been some discussion about implementing a failsafe in the probes. The suggestion had been to include nuclear warheads that would detonate as the line of probes was crossed. The experts were divided on this idea.

Some insisted that this would destroy any of the alien within the blast radius. Others disagreed. They raised the possibility that the EMP of the blast would feed the entity, and so fuelling its drive towards Earth.

Hurried research and modelling indicated that both results were possible, so Mission Control erred on the side of caution. The risk of the failsafe backfiring and undoing the damage of the attack was too great for those in charge of the defence. Samantha wished they had showed the same foresight for the plan overall.

Once the probes completed their deployment, they waited. The computers that controlled the probes were happy to wait. Samantha, on the other hand, felt less sanguine with the delay. On the data feed, she watched as the alien moved slowly into the trap.

Two hours passed until the computers decided that the alien had advanced far enough into the trap. Seven nuclear engines fired within milliseconds of each other. On the visual feeds there was little to be seen, but on the 3D map of the magnetic fields, chaos erupted.

The alien tendril disintegrated under the storm of radiation. Unlike the solar wind, the sheer density of exotic particles disrupted its ability to absorb the energy. Its organised structure collapsed, the remains of the tendril coiling out of the combined exhausts. It lashed out in response, striking towards the nearest probe. The probe jetted one of its thrusters, aiming its engine and consuming the attack.

Again the tendril recoiled and struck, this time it hit the probe. Its blow might have been weakened, but the alien still caused the probe to spin. The other probes reacted, sacrificing their own to scorch the tendril.

The watching mini-sats tracked the alien as it attempted to regenerate and resume its battle with the probes. Each attempt took longer to build up. With a final desperate lunge, it took out another probe and then it vanished.

Samantha smiled as she heard the cheers from Mission Control, her relief at being wrong flooded through her.

The cheers died as almost as soon as they had started. Another tendril approached Earth.

Chapter 41
Arrival

16th November 2023, 18:06 ship time

"It's crazy down here."

Samantha watched Jake's latest video message on the big screen in the living space. She'd grown accustomed to the open area and the way her voice echoed back at her. It some way it seemed like a penance and she embraced the feeling by making the space her own. She now only used her personal quarters only for sleeping. She had tried sleeping in the more open space but that felt too weird.

The time lag on communications had now shortened to two minutes, still too slow for proper conversation. Not that Jake had much time for conversations anymore. In the past two weeks, the new alien tendril had almost reached Earth and the entire world had mobilised in response.

"We're working on the defence satellites. We're ignoring every health and safety rule in the book trying to get this done."

The success of the probes against the first tendril had at least provided some hope for the defenders, but the national space agencies had already exhausted their resources in putting that mission together. Now for the first time in the history of the world, every government acted in unison to try and jury-rig enough satellites together to form a final defence against the alien.

"Chimera have managed to put together a launch vehicle so at least we can evacuate the ISS before the alien arrives. The military are pushing for a nuclear strike against the alien. Some of their own researchers have suggested that the old neutron warheads would be effective, although our simulations disagree with this conclusion.

"They might be right, but we have no way to launch them and hit the tendril before it enters Earth orbit. At that range the EMP will be almost as damaging, if not more, as the alien is likely to be.

"As you know from yesterday's briefing, we think that the alien will remain in high orbit. The alien moved so close to Mars because there was little to feed itself. When it reaches Earth, the energy in the outer magnetic belts should give it enough energy to move on.

"We know we're going to lose a lot of our orbital infrastructure, there's a concerted effort to get it rebuilt and as quick as we can. We are hopeful that the assets in low orbit won't be affected."

Samantha had argued against this assessment. In her opinion, the alien would be desperate for energy after failing to feed at Mars. It would consume all it could for the push onto the Sun. She didn't think that it would stick to the outer magnetic belts.

After the victory against the other tendril, even a hollow one, her opinion no longer counted for much. The fact that she talked to herself without realising it didn't help either. She recognised her strange behaviour and realised that Mission Control watched her closely through the cameras in the habitation module.

"We'd hoped to get some of the satellites into orbit in time, they'd would have been able to repel any minor incursions."

Hope. It was a nice, if distant, thought.

"Anyway. Sorry to cut this short. I hope everything is going okay up there."

'Okay' was a relative term. She wasn't under imminent attack, but the ship's systems continued to degrade. Samantha was now close enough to Earth that the Mars Voyager's sensors detected the alien. They registered that the alien was already gaining energy from the increased activity from the interaction between the solar wind and Earth's extensive magnetic field.

In response, the alien surged.

The tip of the tendril reached into the bountiful harvest of the radiation belts and blossomed. Like iron filings around a magnet, it flowed around the planet. It absorbed the energy and replicated. It developed at a phenomenal pace, and within hours it encircled the globe.

At first it followed the predictions and remained beyond high orbit. Samantha continued her routine, monitoring the key systems and making minor repairs. Whenever she could, she stopped at the command console to review events back on Earth. The alien continued to grow, each time she checked the screens the highlighted areas covered more of the globe.

The alien's effect on Earth remained limited to interrupted communications at this point. It only affected the radio and microwave wavelengths, so the laser link between Mission Control and the Mars Voyager remained open.

As Mission Control had expected, the alien drank deep from the energised particles of the solar wind trapped in the magnetic fields caused by the spinning of the Earth's core.

At that point the growth accelerated once again, an almost geometric increase in volume. Samantha prepared a meagre lunch while this occurred. She had survived for so long on the emergency supplies that even the thought of eating sapped her morale. In truth it felt more like forcing down sustenance rather than eating. When she stopped by the console to eat the meal, she saw with alarm the alien's latest expansion.

A new, much thicker tendril now snaked away from Earth. The research team believed that the alien followed the direction of the solar wind, although that failed to explain how it homed in on planets and other massive bodies as well. She wondered if it felt the shape of gravity, somehow following the wells in space-time created by mass.

If that were the case then it would be a revolutionary type of sense. The wonder at that thought faded as the tendril reaching out to the Sun grew at a pace she'd never seen. The scientists must have been right, the alien had been weakened by not being able to feed at Mars. This was far beyond what they had anticipated.

Then what she had feared most happened.

With the alien occupying the magnetic belts around Earth, it soon drained the energy trapped there. It lapped up the steady stream from the solar wind, but the creature still hungered. It needed all the energy it could find to complete its journey.

Not for the first time, Samantha wondered why it needed to reach the Sun. The stray thought distracted her for a moment from the scene unfolding on the screens before she returned her attention to the horror unfolding on her console displays.

As she had feared would happen, a tendril of the alien probed downward towards the Earth's surface. When it encountered satellites it destroyed them with its touch, their circuits melted by its implacable force. Some satellites, such as the military ones, resisted, but those it crushed with coils of electromagnetic force. It fed upon the electrical energy discharged by their destruction.

The destruction of the satellites in orbit sparked chaos across the world's surface. Radio communications and microwave links collapsed. Most of the world's TV services went off air. The GPS system vanished.

Much of the internet survived the initial maelstrom and via that, Samantha watched the world collapse.

When the alien reached into the atmosphere, it flared into an aurora that stretched across the whole planet. Electrical storms raged through the sky, smashing down aircraft. Thousands died in seconds and that was only the beginning.

And then the connection with Earth went dark.

Chapter 42
Silence Isn't Golden

16th November 2023, 18:42 ship time

At first Samantha assumed that the laser had simply lost its alignment. It still did so on occasion, although it happened far less often the nearer she approached to Earth. The system reported a stable connection and it hadn't triggered the automatic realignment routine. She executed the auto-alignment program and waited for it to complete.

After fifteen long minutes, it completed its instructions without establishing a connection. She cursed out loud, ran the program again and initiated the diagnostics for the communications system.

It took all of her willpower, but she continued with the day's work schedule. She wanted, no, needed to know what was happening on Earth. The abyss of not knowing shadowed her throughout the ship as she worked through the daily list.

She would arrive there in less than a month, but spending so long alone in the ship had frayed her nerves. She'd come to rely on the remote contact. She'd spent too long on her own and the daily messages provided an anchor for her to hold on to. As the ship approached Earth, that need grew.

She was still too far away to use the wireless network. She wouldn't be able to use that system until she arrived in Earth orbit.

Her tasks for the morning were mundane, the same as every day. Dull menial tasks that meant that she would live for another day and she did want to live, despite what the whispers might say.

That morning, while worrying about events on Earth, she checked the water and then made sure the air filtration was working. Chores that had to be repeated day in and day out to keep the ship operational and her alive. The task would have been easy enough with the six of them to share the burden.

Even with the two of them, if Piotr had survived, it would have been manageable. Difficult, but they would have coped. Alone she had to prioritise, that meant some of the tasks went uncompleted. The endless tide of work threatened to overwhelm her on a daily basis.

The principal task which went uncompleted was the stock take. She figured, what did it matter? With just her on the ship there would be more than enough supplies and she would be home soon.

What would she find when she arrived?

That had become Samantha's real concern.

For months she struggled to maintain the ship for one simple goal – to return home. Now that dream appeared to be transforming into nightmare. The more reasonable part of her admonished her to stay focused. Things on Earth would no doubt be serious but it still remained the only place she wanted to be.

She finished the current task, flushing the waste system and returned to the command console. It was lunchtime, but she didn't feel hungry.

The trained part of her mind spoke again and reminded her that she had missed too many meals. The part more inclined to stress at not knowing declared that it didn't matter. Samantha pushed that thought to the back of her mind where she allowed it to fester.

The diagnostics found no cause for the failure to connect with Mission Control. Her modified alignment routine also failed to locate the signal. The logical conclusion was that the ground station was out of action. She knew that the alien's structure might affect radio transmissions, but it shouldn't affect the laser system.

What if the electromagnetic effect had reached the planet's surface?

Of all the dark thoughts that had troubled her that morning, this one chilled her the most.

She summoned the ship's sensor feeds. The habitation module lacked the sensor clusters of the Mars science and observatory modules, and much of what it had was destroyed by the alien attack as they approached Mars, but she still had some. She saw that the alien's form obscured most of the sensor readings on her screen.

The optical sensors provided the only thing resembling a clear view of her home planet. Apart from the aurora in the upper atmosphere, the alien wasn't visible to the naked eye. A faint fuzziness in the image indicated that something unexpected lurked around the planet.

On other wavelengths, the alien showed itself clearly. On the radio and microwave bands it formed a complex cloud around the Earth. The ship's sensors lacked the resolution to discern any structure, but it moved. It was vast, encompassing the orbit of the Moon. And from the planet, no longer a tendril, a vast column of the entity streamed towards the Sun.

When viewing in infrared, it didn't seem so large. She still couldn't see too much of the structure, but the heated plasma created energised coils that wrapped around the planet and formed the core of the pillar reaching for the Sun.

She switched back to visible light and she noticed something strange. Dawn's light highlighted a quarter of the globe from her viewing angle. From the shape of the continents she recognised her homeland. Europe and Africa were fading into night, but Russia and Asia were already shrouded in black.

She didn't realise what the absence was at first. It took a few seconds before understanding slammed into her thoughts. There were no lights. Even with the telescope on maximum gain, she saw no cities. Normally they would stand out against the night with their glow.

She saw none at all.

Chapter 43
One's Company

8th December 2023, 09:23 ship time

The days ticked by in a desolate metronome and as they passed, the Mars Voyager consumed the remaining distance to Earth. Samantha's training kept her functional, although by the thinnest of threads. Every day that passed without contact dragged by a little longer than the last.

In desperation, she pulled apart the communication system in the futile hope that the fault was at her end. She knew it would be a wasted effort as she checked each of the circuits, but she had to do something. The slim possibility that she could change the situation provided a dim beacon and that seemed better than none at all.

She also understood that the effort impacted her maintenance schedule, but being so near to Earth pushed that concern away.

A month didn't seem so long at first, but as the days crawled past it stretched further and further. Even more disheartening was the thought of her arrival. What would she find when she got there? Her mood became trapped between the anticipation of finally reaching home and the despair of not knowing the situation on Earth.

Several times a day she reviewed the sensor readings to try and build a picture of what was happening. The alien still occupied the space around the globe, but more of it travelled towards the Sun. She calculated that it should have departed by the time she arrived.

That and the thought of home provided the edge she needed to maintain the tenuous grasp on her sanity.

She had not been able to establish contact and even though she was closer to Earth, she saw no signs of life through the ship's telescope. What she could see were the vast electrical storms that raged across the planet, triggered, she assumed, by the alien's presence.

Each morning she rose, still tired. She had stopped taking the sedatives, they dulled her thoughts and she thought that was cheating. Her nights no longer brought the comfort of sleep, only the restless tossing and turning and memories of the crew. The dead haunted her more than ever, without Jake and the ground team's contact to hold them at bay.

Too many months alone in the Mars Voyager had taken their toll. The intermittent contact with Earth had provided more comfort than she'd realised. More than that, the messages from Jake had grounded her, provided her with some connection with a life beyond the confines of the ship.

It was funny that what had seemed such a small space to live in on their outward journey now appeared so large. The solemn emptiness that she couldn't fill weighed upon her.

Without the messages, the loneliness exhausted her as much as the lack of sleep.

For the first week, she'd recorded messages to Jake and her other friends. She had intended to transmit them as soon as she established a connection. That routine faded as the blackout continued. She'd slept in that first week, but not since, not in any proper fashion at any rate.

In the second week, she spent more time at the command console. She watched Earth grow larger on the view screens and the alien depart. That moment dared to inspire hope but they quickly faded when she saw no signs of life. The loss of that dimmest of hopes pushed her deeper into a depression.

The medical bay contained a full pharmacy, and there lay a way out, but it didn't seem worth it. This was all her fault. She couldn't define why in any logical fashion, but as the mission commander she was responsible for the lives of her crew. More than that, she felt personally responsible. She should have acted sooner to prevent the disaster. The feeling was a selfish one, but she embraced it and all the dark thoughts that came with it. A tiny voice attempted to argue against this conviction although it lacked any real weight and so she ignored it.

Thoughts of the crew hooked into her mind, dragging it deeper into the abyss. Every so often she pulled herself together enough to deal with urgent maintenance. She became lax with her cleaning and personal hygiene. Sometimes she noticed the smell. The hint of Piotr's putrefaction had lingered since death, the life support system had never cleared the smell from the air.

Now it no longer mattered, since her own ripe scent masked it.

The problem grew worse in the third week. She managed a single shower throughout the entire week. She stank, she knew it, but it didn't matter.

For a few days, she stopped checking the consoles. She barely completed any of the required tasks. The smell in the air wasn't just her and Piotr letting her know he was still around in scent and body, if not in spirit. Without constantly checking the air purifiers, the quality of the air she breathed fell.

She stayed in her quarters, swaddled in her stink. She left to use the toilet and to scrape together the odd quick meal when the hunger pangs speared through her fugue. On the wall screen, videos from Jake and of the crew looped over and over again.

The endless videos fed her misery and held her to the bed better than gravity would have done. For almost the whole playlist she remained unmoving.

In the fourth week, she pulled herself together. Not completely and not even by very much, but enough. In a few days she expected to arrive in Earth orbit. She would be home soon and she needed to prepare.

The good news didn't end there.

Samantha made a rare visit to the command console. The navigation panel indicated she was still on target. The sensors showed something far more important. On the radio and microwave bands, the traces of the alien had almost gone. The bulk of the entity now sped towards the inner Solar System and on to the Sun.

The mystery of why it burned so much energy to reach the star flitted across her mind. It failed to find any real purpose. Even with her improved mood, she still struggled to apply herself to more than just the essentials.

On the optical scanners, she discovered something that restored her tattered hope. She saw lights on the continent shrouded in the night. This time it was America she saw sheathed in darkness, but here and there she saw the glow of electricity. Never in history had the sight of electricity been so appreciated. The light pushed back the darkness that had threatened to smother her.

Samantha now knew that there was something to come home to. That discovery sparked life back into her. She showered and dressed in clean clothing, and those simple acts alone transformed her into a new woman. Samantha also tidied up the ship and that helped improve the smell further, although it remained far from the pristine vessel that had departed from Earth two years ago.

She'd banished the smell, or most of it, but the ghosts of the crew were less easy to dismiss. Not watching the videos on an endless loop helped. She also realised that keeping busy helped her further, pushing the voices to the back of her mind. They no longer blamed her, although she still felt guilty.

Still, being so close to home brought light into her personal darkness. It felt good to be home.

Chapter 44
Homecoming

14th December 2023, 07:22 ship time

The decision to slow earlier in the flight path and arrive at a higher orbit proved to be fortuitous. In the past few days, Samantha's condition continued to improve and she paid greater attention to the information from the sensors on the command console. On the approach she watched with mounting joy as the Earth grew larger on the screen. She still hadn't been able to establish any form of communication, but the few lights visible on the night side offered some hope.

A day away, she observed dark spots against the blue Earth. As the hours passed, the spots resolved into a cloud of dots surrounding the planet. It didn't take Samantha long to figure out what this meant – a cloud of debris filled orbital space.

The alien had destroyed all of the satellites in orbit around the Earth. It had broken them up into millions of fragments. The fragments orbited around the Earth in a belt several hundred miles thick. If she had flown into the debris, it would have been like running into the world's biggest shotgun blast.

The fact that she'd spotted the problem so early had also saved her precious fuel. With so much distance left to cover, she had only needed a few short burns to adjust her approach angle and velocity.

The need to calculate the new vector proved a different matter. She needed to enter high enough that she avoided the debris, but not so high that Mission Control couldn't reach her. The habitation module wasn't designed to land on a planet and it certainly wouldn't survive a re-entry attempt.

On a normal approach, Mission Control would have provided the data she needed to plot the new course, but without it she had to guess. She settled on a medium orbit, a thousand miles up. From that height it wouldn't take much to drop into a lower orbit, but it should be high enough to avoid the belt of debris.

She'd still have to be careful though. While the belt predominantly occupied low Earth orbit, debris from higher orbits could be seen.

As she neared her target orbit, the radar confirmed her decision. The visual feed had only shown part of the problem, the larger pieces of wreckage. With radar it revealed the full extent of the danger. She could ignore the smaller fragments, for a while at least, but they'd abrade the limited protection the Mars Voyager provided if she stayed in the debris field for too long.

The radar imaging showed no clear gap through the debris and that would make a rendezvous difficult but, she hoped, not impossible. Samantha wasn't so far gone that she didn't understand that the lack of communications and the debris field meant that rescue would be difficult, but now that she'd discovered a ray of hope, she was reluctant to let it go.

The lack of lights on the night side still concerned her. No lights meant no civilisation. A few glimmered here and there, but the once majestic sight of human civilisation glowing in the night no longer existed.

The world must have been hammered by the alien attack, although she wasn't sure how. It had to connect with the lack of lights, but across the whole world seemed too much.

She focused the ship's telescope onto the cities below, but it lacked the resolution to determine anything other than the lack of illumination.

On her second orbit, the communications system beeped. She switched her screen to see the cause. The laser system still failed to lock an alignment, which didn't surprise her at all. With all the fragments in orbit, establishing a line of sight channel would be difficult, if not impossible.

Her secondary monitor indicated that the local high-bandwidth wireless network had established a connection. The network completed a handshake with the ship and identified it as the NASA's Earth orbit network system. When the system beeped at her, Samantha was startled and then cried with joy as a voice rang out from the static.

"Hello. Hello. Is that Samantha?"

David Richards's voice had never sounded so welcome.

"Hello, can you hear me Samantha?"

She couldn't speak.

"Samantha, I'm showing the Mars Voyager registered on our network, can you hear me?"

Samantha broke her paralysis and replied.

"David. I can't believe it. I'm here."

"Hello. Samantha, please respond."

"I'm right here, David. Can you hear me?"

"Mars Voyager, this is Mission Control, please respond."

Her mic! Samantha realised she wasn't wearing her mic. She hadn't worn the headset for weeks and now she couldn't remember where she'd put it. In a panic she searched the console, she couldn't have put it far away.

"Mars Voyager, this is Mission Control, please respond. Is anyone there?"

There it was! She snatched up the headset and fixed it to the side of her face.

"Hello, this is Samantha. David, can you hear me?"

"My God, Samantha, it is so good to hear your voice."

"David. Oh my God."

"Samantha, what's your status? We don't have any eyes in the sky, so we can't see you."

"I'm in a stable orbit about forty kilometres above the upper reaches of the debris cloud."

"That's good to hear. We've suffered a complete orbital cascade failure."

"I thought the alien caused the destruction."

"It did. It destroyed many of the satellites in orbit. The wreckage from those took out more, then those took out everything. It didn't take long before everything was destroyed."

"How's everything down there?"

"Bad, very bad I'm afraid. I'll hand over to Jake."

"Jake's there?"

"Yes, Jake is right next to me. I'm passing you over now."

Chapter 45
Catching Up

14th December 2023, 09:14 ship time

"It was awful."

Jake looked haggard on the console screen, his face drawn, his eyes shadowed and he clearly hadn't shaved in a while. Despite all that, she felt overwhelmed by the sight of his face. For a moment she wished she'd tidied herself up a bit more.

"We lost everything in orbit within a matter of minutes. The alien moved so much more quickly than it had against you at Mars."

"We should have listened to you."

Samantha had never felt less like saying 'I told you so'. She would have given everything to be wrong. It was so good to see Jake again, to hear his voice and to speak with him in a real conversation. She was so overjoyed that she couldn't speak to him for the first few minutes.

The sound of his voice broke her heart. His face told the story of extreme stress and sleepless nights. His voice, on the other hand, spoke of loss. He nodded as he recognised the conflict of emotions on her face, she would speak when she was ready and he was happy to wait until she was.

"Without the satellites, the communications networks collapsed. We still had land links at that point but they were so overloaded as to be almost useless. The load on the system caused chaos, everything NASA and the other space agencies had put together disappeared in minutes. We had nothing in the sky, nothing to tell us what the alien was doing. All we could do was wait and we didn't have to wait long."

Samantha recalled the reports she'd read on the internet until her communications failed.

"First the planes fell out of the sky. Its body, if you can call it that, was concentrated at the poles so it was the cross-Atlantic flights that were struck first. Their electronic systems were overloaded by the alien and they just fell out of the sky.

"Most crashed into the Arctic ice or into the sea. We've received reports that the few people that survived the crashes didn't live for long in the freezing water.

"We still had the cable and fibre optic connections at that point. So we received reports from all over the world about the aurora in the sky. If we hadn't known about the planes, it could have been a beautiful sight.

"The world went crazy in so short a time, we couldn't believe it. People around the world claimed on every channel still operating that the world was ending, for all of us. They were right. What amazed me was how they hit the airwaves and the net channels before the scale of the devastation became public.

"As well as striking the planes, the electromagnetic energy from the alien stirred up weather systems all over the planet. Vast electrical storms started everywhere. Combined with the lack of radio communications, it hampered the authorities' ability to respond to the shit that went down."

Jake rarely swore, he considered that a lack of control. If his appearance wasn't enough to show what he'd been through, then that single word made it all too apparent to Samantha. She tried to speak, to provide some comfort to him, but the power of speech still evaded her.

He continued to speak, his voice almost in a monotone. She could tell that was his effort to maintain control, even so, small flinches crossed his face as he recalled the terrible events.

"The surges hit power grids and electrical systems next. It wiped out everything electrical all over the world. All but EMP-hardened systems were overwhelmed. We were lucky, if you can call it that. Working with the Air Force meant that most of our systems had protection against the EMP. Even so, we lost a lot of minor systems and that caused chaos, especially as we'd lost all of our birds in the sky. The systems that remained active meant we received the dubious honour of watching as the world disintegrated.

"Everything went down. I mean everything.Ced, trucks, planes, trains, most methods of travel were instantly frozen. Only those with older vehicles could move around and even they didn't for long. With roads gridlocked, airports shut down and no power for essential services, people panicked."

Jake paused at that point as he remembered the horrors that he and the rest of Mission Control had witnessed. The fact that they had seen the devastation on screen didn't lessen the impact of what they saw.

"Nobody was ready for what happened, the greatest country in the world and we didn't have a chance. I guess it's kind of ironic but the countries that survived best were the ones with the least freedom and less reliance on technological infrastructure.

"With no mission anymore, we watched as order around the world vanished. It started in Asia where it was night. With no lights, no power, no communications from their government, people took to the streets in their thousands. It was like watching something from the Bible, or a film. The apocalypse had arrived, it felt like the end of the world.

"The internet still operated through the fibre optic networks and people posted the chaos that they witnessed and experienced. There was panic everywhere, the world everyone knew collapsed in a flash and to top it all, everyone saw the weird firestorm in the sky. No-one knew what to do, they were scared and so were the people who might have made the difference.

"Perhaps if the governments had reacted quicker it wouldn't have been so bad, it's hard to know for sure. With communications crippled, it would have taken time for the response to reach the streets. In any case, it all went to shit and so damn fast."

He paused again and wiped a hand down his weary face. She wanted to reach out, take his hand in her own. She opened her mouth to speak and failed to articulate the words she wanted to say so badly. She'd spent so long alone, to speak with someone now, especially Jake in his upset state, overwhelmed her.

"The electrical activity in the atmosphere made radio communication almost impossible. In the US we at least had a few hours of daylight to prepare. It helped that we have a hardened communications network. That meant that police, national security and military forces could coordinate in some fashion. Not to a normal level, but enough to hold the line in some key places.

"As night fell, our cities followed the pattern of those in Asia as people took to the streets in panic. The mobilised troops and emergency services did what they could. Pockets of order were maintained here and there, but not everywhere. Fires burned out of control where fire departments were unable to respond. Hospitals soon overflowed with the wounded and police stations and military bases were besieged by people seeking shelter.

"As a hardened communications centre, we became one of the hubs for communications around the country and for local logistical support.

"That was the hardest part for us. It's terrible to say, but when we saw the trouble in China and the other far Eastern countries it was horrible, but still remote, you know?"

Tears now steamed down his face, her own mirrored his.

"All through the night we received reports of the chaos that raged everywhere. The constant stream of death and distress proved too much for some of the operators. We had to operate in shifts, sharing the horror.

"Without emergency services in operation, the death toll jumped into the thousands in a few short hours and continued to climb. People panicked and others took advantage of the chaos. Battles between gangs and riots erupted without warning.

"It was like watching something from the news in some foreign country. US troops and the National Guard patrolled city streets and engaged local gangs. For a while there was open warfare on the streets.

"We were safe, isolated as we are, but for those living in the affected areas, they ran, it was their only choice. The streets filled with residents looking to escape the cities. In some areas, the troops and police managed to restore calm. In many areas they failed.

"Later we heard that on the first night the Department of Homeland Security estimated that over a million people died. Many died because ambulances couldn't reach them or weren't even aware that they were needed. Others died in the street battles, most of them civilians caught in the crossfire."

Jake paused again.

"For us that was the worst of it. We escaped lightly compared to Asia and Africa. Even parts of Europe fell apart.

"We're rebuilding the power networks as quickly as we can. It's a slow process, but it's coming together."

Samantha then found her voice.

"I know, I saw the lights. I was so worried when I couldn't see any of the cities at night."

"I know. The power is down in most areas despite the effort from everyone. But it is getting better. For some, anyway.

"We still don't have any eyes in the sky. We've re-established communications with most of the world's major governments. For the most part, the smaller nations survived the best; it was the big urban centres that exploded. In the rural areas, most people just bunkered down and weathered the storm.

"More importantly for you, we don't know what the situation is up in Earth orbit. We have a few radar systems online, but all that is picking up is clutter. We need you to map the debris patterns. You can contact me any time, like everyone else I'm living in the office at the moment."

For a few more minutes, they chatted about more mundane things and then she got on with her task.

Chapter 46
Hell of a Mess

16th December 2023, 15:09 ship time

She might still be stuck alone in the ship, but being in Earth orbit lifted Samantha's spirits. She was almost home, and talking with Jack on a regular basis banished the loneliness into memory. Even the ghosts of the crew seemed to fade in the presence of the planet's warm blue glow. The routine still dragged at her, but it felt a little bit easier knowing that it would soon be over.

It took longer to build a map of the debris than either Samantha or Mission Control had expected. Mission Control requested that she establish as complete a picture as possible. Much of the debris was tiny fragments and that made the task more difficult. The ship's radar wasn't designed to map this fine detail over such a large volume, so she had to manoeuvre the ship nearer to the bands of debris than she would have liked.

She maintained a height of 500 miles above the Earth. The debris stretched up to 470 miles in places. The thickest band ran at 270 miles, the height that the International Space Station and its Chinese counterpart once orbited. That most expensive of human endeavours, its framework now reduced to so many tiny pieces.

Even worse, those fragments would be lethal. The staging point that enabled them to travel to Mars now provided a barrier to her return. She also had to monitor her own orbit for rogue remnants of satellites.

The module orbited the Earth once every two hours. Samantha adjusted the trajectory so that she could scan a larger volume. It took her two exhausting days to build up enough of a detailed picture that satisfied Mission Control.

As the computer scanned, she continued to maintain the ship as best she could. It didn't seem worth it considering that she wouldn't be in the ship for much longer. Even so, she didn't want to risk a failure in one of the major systems.

Although... they hadn't told her when the rescue mission would be. She asked Jake whenever they spoke, but he always evaded providing any specifics. And truth be told, it just felt so good to be having real conversations again after so many months.

The ghosts of the crew had faded into the deeper parts of her memory. They surfaced every now and again, but they didn't demand constant attention as they once did. She'd asked Jake if she could speak with any of the families. Again he'd changed the subject. She allowed that one to slip by as well, since there'd be plenty of time for more bad news when she felt the weight of gravity once again.

For the return journey, she had been lax in keeping up the essential exercise routine. She had now been in space for so long that walking would be impossible when she landed on Earth. Her body would suffer in other ways as well. Just the strain on her heart under gravity again would be difficult.

With Jake and the medical team's encouragement, she resumed her exercises. It was hard – she hadn't realised how out of shape she'd allowed herself to become. She hadn't recognised how thin and emaciated her body now looked and it came as a big shock to her.

Even more worrying was the thought that she might not be able to return to Earth until she was back into reasonable shape.

She spoke to Jake as often as she could. It felt incredible to just talk. They both tried to keep the conversation light, though all too often the topic strayed to the devastation the alien's visit had caused on the planet below.

The sheer scale of events had taken its toll on Jake. Samantha thought about her own tribulations and how they paled in comparison to the suffering on the surface. She accepted the shame of her selfishness and tried to steer the conversations away from her own worries and to provide some comfort to Jake.

She was still eager to get home and once the map of the debris layers was complete, Samantha waited for the call. While she waited, she examined the 3D model the ship's computer had built from the successive orbits.

Since she'd arrived in Earth orbit she'd known, deep inside, that the debris posed a serious obstacle. She'd suppressed that realisation, smothering it with hope that Mission Control would have a plan. She still clung to that hope and it was Jake that shattered it.

"Hi Samantha. We've prepared a new entertainment package for you. We'll upload it in the next data sync collection."

A new entertainment package? Why would she be needing a new entertainment package?

"There's several hundred hours of the TV shows that you've missed. How you can watch that reality TV crap, I don't know."

He offered a tentative smile, but it looked like a lie.

"That's great Jake, but when are you guys coming for me?"

His smile wasn't strong enough to withstand such a question. Up until now he'd avoided the query. Now she'd find out the truth and she didn't like what the look on his face portended.

"There's no rescue mission, Samantha, not yet. There's no way we can get through the debris."

In reality the news shouldn't have been a surprise, but even so the words shocked her. To be so close yet unable to cross those last few hundred miles came as a bitter blow. One she didn't want to accept.

"So clear a way. You can fire a missile to blast a hole clear."

"That won't work."

It's true, it wouldn't. She knew it wouldn't. Unless they could vaporise all the debris in orbit, the blast would only make the situation worse.

There had to be a way though! She thought about the various experiments which had been conducted in case of such an occurrence.

"So build a sail, launch it into low orbit, unfurl it and clear a path."

He nodded. "That might work, although it would take several missions to clear enough of a space to be safe to launch a module through."

Here comes the 'but'.

"But there isn't enough launch capacity. We've already spoken to the Europeans, the Russians and the Chinese. Between us we have three launch vehicles that might work."

"Might work?"

"They haven't been tested since the attack. We've run some preliminary tests on our remaining Delta V Heavy that was due to launch the next Jupiter probe. Luckily it was still in the assembly facility so it was protected from the alien."

"So there's one vehicle."

"Yes, maybe, but the others we're not sure about. Russia and China suffered more in the aftermath than we did. They're still trying to put down uprisings and won't divert resources to..."

He broke off, uncomfortable. Samantha finished the sentence for him.

"To rescue a lone American woman?"

Jake nodded.

"We even tried the Indians and the Japanese, but they have nothing available either. I'm sorry Sam, but we can't come for you. Not yet."

The fact that he even tried to offer her hope at the end hurt the most. She didn't know what to say, so she turned off the communications.

Chapter 47
Two out of Three

19th December 2023, 12:37 ship time

Anger held the despair at bay for a while.

Samantha ignored the repeated communications requests as she stared at the command screens. Mission Control overrode her lockout so she turned the speakers and her headset off. Rendered mute, Jake's voice mouthed unheard words at her from the screen.

There had to be a way. If they couldn't come to her then she would have to land herself.

That was a desperate thought and she knew it, but she followed it anyway. What other option did she have?

Perhaps she could match the orbit of the debris bands one layer after another. She could use the main drive to clear a path ahead of her and use the thrusters to drop into a lower orbit until she touched atmosphere.

That wouldn't work.

To clear the debris, she'd have to fire the engines at such a rate that it would push her into higher orbit. She then considered what would happen if she used a lower thrust. That might clear enough of the debris to allow her to pass through.

Or so she hoped.

The Mars Voyager was a tough ship. It was better armoured than anything ever put in space before, but it was no tank. It could absorb a lot of punishment, but nowhere near enough to make it through the maelstrom that awaited if she moved towards the surface.

The other issue was the speed of the debris. Some of it had settled into a stable orbit, but not all of it. Some travelled at different speeds so matching orbit would leave the ship vulnerable to the rogue fragments.

If that wasn't enough, there was an even bigger problem. The mission profile didn't allow for the habitation module to land. It was intended to rendezvous with the ISS and use one of the regular transport flights to return to the surface.

Re-entry caused immense friction between the craft and the atmosphere. The ship's hull had been designed to protect against radiation and the occasional meteoroid impact. Even in perfect condition, it would burn up within seconds. There was no way she could use the module as a lander.

Defiance born of anger tempered step by step into acceptance. She still ignored the repeated comms requests and felt herself slip back into her previous fugue.

Acceptance helped stave off the despair for a bit longer, but it waited without urgency in the shadows. It knew that its time would come soon enough.

Her newfound state of acceptance provoked her training to wrestle free from its bonds and provide its help. She needed a plan. She'd already listened to her heart, she wanted to return home now. Her head knew that home wasn't the sanctuary she'd sought through her long, lonely voyage.

They would rescue her, they just needed time. The world was in a bad place, and she wasn't at the centre of it. She had to give them time to restore and then put together a mission. They hadn't abandoned her, despite what the now deflated anger continued to insist.

Her training taught her that a crisis needed a plan more than action. The plan was simple: she had to survive for as long as she could. The ship had the basic supplies and equipment she required, but for how long? That's what she needed to determine.

To survive, her body required three basic things: air, water and food.

The process of checking what resources she had available gave her something to do. It kept her mind and hands busy. She thought that inventorying the food would take the most time so she started there. The mission had to grow a lot of their own food to be viable. The attack and destruction of the ship at Mars meant she hadn't been able to rescue any of the necessary materials before separating from the rest of the ship.

That hadn't been a problem for the return journey. The reserve supplies and prepared stocks of food to supply the whole crew was intended to last for four months. With just herself to feed, that had proved more than sufficient.

For a moment the ghosts of the crew cast a guilty shadow, before she pushed them away, back into the depths of her mind.

With the mistaken belief that she would soon be home, she had cherry-picked her favourite food from the supplies. She still had plenty of food, enough for over six months if rationed. However, she'd have to stop eating only what she liked.

That wouldn't be a great hardship, it would be like being on deployment with the Air Force again.

For water, she was in even better shape. The recycling system operated to a reasonable efficiency. She'd lost half of the stored water in the alien attack, but she still had more than enough. After running the diagnostics, it looked like the recycling system would last for almost a year before she'd have to start using the emergency supply.

Some good news, she could still keep hydrated and clean. The power supply from the main engine would keep the water warm for years. She'd have died of starvation long before then.

The song might have said that two out of three 'ain't bad', but for Samantha it had to be all three. Her breathable air situation didn't look as promising as the food and water. Like the water, the air was recycled. The system was functioning, but she'd had to make various repairs on her return trip and it was far from the efficiency they'd enjoyed on the outward journey.

Those repairs had used key consumables needed for the life support system. She'd repaired the system using fresh parts, so she would have to re-use some of the used filters. That would gain her a few weeks.

At best she had three months of air.

Could Mission Control put together a rescue in three months?

When the despair broke through, it dragged her into its embrace with an eager grip.

Chapter 48
The Darkest Hour

20th December 2023, 02:16 ship time

For hours she floated in the living quarters and in that time, Samantha's mind flipped. She delved deep into her darkest thoughts. The terrible situation made it all too easy for her mind to conjure horrors.

Three months.

She might survive for three months and then what?

Would they come for her?

The prospect of another three months alone filled her with dread. Could she survive for those three months? Would it be worth it? Even worse, would she struggle through day after day of mounting misery only for her life to peter out along with her air?

She needed Jake now more than at any time before, but it wouldn't be fair for her to burden him. The situation on the surface far outweighed her singular predicament. She realised he would already be doing everything in his power to help her.

A stray thought, barbed with poison, wondered if the efforts to help her had caused more lives to be lost in the aftermath below. She wanted to deny that thought, though she accepted guilt too easily and it returned with the ghosts like an old friend.

On the screen in front of her, the comms panel flashed, demanding her attention. It would be good to talk with Jake, but what could she say?

She reached for her headset, but hesitated in putting it on. The channel with Mission Control continued to flash. With a deep breath, she activated the control and put the headset on.

Jake's voice filled her ear.

"Samantha, oh my God! What's been going on up there? We've been trying to get hold of you for days. Why didn't you respond?"

"Jake. I..."

What should she say?

"Jake, I've been taking stock."

"We know, we watched you accessing the various systems."

"So you know how long I have?"

The silence hung between them, betraying his knowledge.

"Can you reach me in that time?"

This time he replied, but even over the camera he didn't meet her eyes.

"We'll figure something out. You can't give up hope."

"Is there?"

"Is there what?"

"Hope. Is there really any hope?"

"There is always hope. Things are getting better here, not in a hurry, but they are. Maybe in a month or so there will be more resources we can devote to the mission."

He offered false hope and that made the situation worse for Samantha. She would have preferred that he had been honest with her, to tell her that she was screwed.

"Have there been any developments?"

He looked grateful at the change of subject.

"Order has been restored in most of the major cities here in the US. As many resources as the government can provide are working on restoring power. They claim they'll have most cities back up and running within six weeks.

"Things are still bad, but in the US at least we seem to be recovering. The President is so confident he's already talking about providing support for other countries."

He believes that as much as I believe him, Samantha thought.

"Can you provide a feed for the internet?"

She wanted to know for herself what was going on. She received the occasional radio transmission, but it was always scratchy, the voices reduced to electronic ghosts in the static.

Again he didn't look at her, but glanced to one side.

"We don't have regular access, all communication channels are reserved for security and law enforcement. We'll compile regular news updates and include them with your entertainment packages."

They were trying to protect her from the reality of what was happening.

"Tell me Jake, what's really going on?"

"I've told you. Look Samantha, it's pretty bad down here, but we're getting things under control."

"I can't do this, Jake."

No, she wasn't going to do this. She'd promised herself, it was better to suffer in silence than add to Jake's burdens.

"I can't live here, like this, for another three months."

"You can, you've already survived longer than that. You need to hold on. We will come and get you."

"Don't lie to me, Jake!"

"I'm not lying to you, Samantha. I'm doing everything possible to get to you. We all are, you must believe me."

"What can you do, Jake?"

Unbidden tears fell down her cheek.

"We're running through every possible scenario. Trust me, we're looking at every possible way."

"So you say, but what are you doing?"

She hadn't expected an answer, but when none was forthcoming it hit her hard. She didn't want to talk to him anymore, so she turned off the channel.

Now she sat alone and contemplated her grim future. There was an option. An insidious proposal that slithered up from the darkness. She didn't need to suffer for months without rescue.

She could end it now; the medical bay contained what she needed for a peaceful end.

Painless sleep and never to awake.

Her training balked at such a thought. Every crisis had a solution and if it didn't then you kept trying until you found one. Years of service, first with the Air Force and then with NASA, struggled to resist the fugue that threatened to drown her.

The same training also fed the despair. She knew what awaited her. She understood the effort needed to mount any kind of rescue. With the world on its knees there was no way Jake, or anybody else, could save her.

Chapter 49
Hope

25th December 2023, 08:50 ship time

For five days Samantha cocooned herself in her quarters. She wrapped herself in her misery and the hi-tech blankets. She mired herself within an illusion of escape and allowed her mind to float free with the ghosts of her crew. They comforted her with their memories, but they also trapped her with her guilt. Guilt for the survival that now chained her to her despair.

She didn't eat and barely drank for that time, allowing herself to weaken. When hunger growled in her stomach, she ignored it. The crew and their families filled her thoughts and weighed heavy upon her mind. On rare trips to the toilet or the kitchen, she'd check the console.

She saw repeated messages from Jake listed on the screen.

On the fifth day she rose and the fugue fell away.

It wasn't a miraculous transformation, although perhaps the fact it was Christmas Day put a bit of a shine on it. While her mind wallowed in her guilt, grief and depression, her training worked on a lower level. It formed an alliance with the most basic requirements of Samantha's brain. When it joined with her instinct for self-preservation, it formulated a new plan.

The plan wasn't complicated and it wasn't even a long-term plan. It started by ramping up her hunger. Starvation can be very insistent, especially when there is available food nearby.

Once she had eaten she felt thirsty, and having already surrendered to hunger it was no great loss to drink some water. It tasted good and refreshing.

Smell spurred her into further normality.

She stank.

Her own body odour repulsed her. She showered and dressed in fresh clothes. Once she'd made that effort, she returned to the command console and examined the list of messages. All had the same content, she had to contact Mission Control as soon as she could.

The last few wished her a 'Merry Christmas'. She hadn't realised the date at that point. Christmas in itself didn't bother her, but it did cast her mind back to the previous Christmas. It seemed so long ago. She remembered the festive spirit shared by the crew with a smile. Most times the ghosts condemned her with their empty eyes, in this memory they were happy and excited to be on the voyage of a lifetime.

David Richards responded so quickly when she called, he must have been waiting for her.

"Samantha, you can't keep going dark like this. We need to keep in contact."

"I'm sorry, David."

"It's all right, you don't need to apologise. You just had us worried. You can't shut yourself off. If you do then you won't get through this."

"I'm not going to survive long enough for you to come and get me."

"Stop that right now. We are coming for you and if you'd kept in contact you would have known that."

"What?"

Once again she'd made the wrong choice.

"We're coming for you."

"Oh my God."

The anger born from worry drained from his voice.

"We're coming for you."

"Really?"

"Yes, of course. The Japanese and the Europeans have come through for us. Both were researching solar sail technology for long-range space probes. They're lightweight prototypes so we don't need heavy lifters. They won't clear all the debris, but they'll remove enough of lower orbit to make it safe enough to pass through."

Samantha couldn't believe it, was she dreaming?

"So how will you reach me?"

"It's not going to be easy and there's a greater risk than I'd like. It'll take a few weeks to get the sails into orbit. We're pulling in favours from everyone we can to make this happen."

"How?"

She couldn't believe. It seemed like too much, as if a dream, but she did want to believe.

David hesitated on the other end, unsure what to tell her.

"Tell me, David!"

"Okay, news has leaked of your return."

"Leaked?"

"The news service isn't what it was. It's generally used for service updates and public health information."

How bad was it down there?

"We decided not to announce you had returned until things had cleared up a bit down here. Some people are already trying to take political advantage of the situation."

Samantha didn't mind being kept secret, as long as they could help her. Although if things were as bad as she suspected, she could see why they would want to keep her arrival secret. With the world falling apart, the space programme would be low on most people's priority lists.

"So how have people found out?"

"We don't know, but you've become the hot topic."

"What?"

"We're not sure how, although Linda is working hard to maintain the positivity."

"I guess that means I'll be making TV appearances again?"

"I'm afraid so."

"If it means landing on Earth again then I'll do whatever Linda wants."

"Good. Now getting the sails up is only half of the job. We have two confirmed heavy lifters that can reach your orbit. We'll use one to clear a path and the other to rendezvous with you."

"How are you going to clear a way?"

"We're still working on that. Don't worry, we have a few ideas, but you have to sit tight. It's going to take ten weeks or so to get to you, but keep it together and we'll get you down."

"I can't believe it."

"Well you should, we're not going to give up on you Samantha, so don't give up on us."

"I won't."

"Good, now Jake's waiting on the line, but before I hand you over let me wish you a Merry Christmas from everyone here on the ground."

"Thanks David, give my wishes to everyone."

She couldn't stop crying, but that didn't matter, they weren't tears of sadness. Hope now filled her and it brought light once more into her existence.

Chapter 50
Eclipse

7th January 2023, 11:22 ship time

The news of impending rescue restored Samantha's routine to something resembling normal. As she had before, she spent most of her day maintaining the ship's systems. She now believed that giving Mission Control the time they needed would be her salvation.

She also pushed herself on the exercise machines as often as possible. The effort hurt after so long without proper exercise, but the pain felt good, like it had when she first joined the Air Force and NASA.

Her routine changed in one key detail. After lunch she appeared on news networks around the world. Her solitary plight provided a focus for the world, something beyond their own misery to focus on.

Samantha found it hard to believe that the world considered her plight greater than their own, but she came to enjoy speaking to the interviewers from around the world.

Okay, not quite enjoy, she'd never be happy being interviewed but it did provide some variation to her day. The contact with people also helped keep her steady and she discovered a joy she'd never felt before in meeting new people. If only for a few minutes each day. The shadows remained, fortunately the light kept them at bay for now.

She filled the rest of her day with continuing her research on the alien and tracking its progress to the Sun. She had let it slide once she arrived in Earth orbit, more worried by the news of the events on Earth and whether she would be rescued.

Mission Control had requested that she resume her study, as their resources were now available to focus on the entity. The problem for them was that few of the solar observatories on the surface were operating through lack of power or damage caused by the alien's attack.

That left Samantha and the sensors on the Mars Voyager as the best equipped platform for studying the alien.

In the weeks that had passed since Samantha's arrival at Earth, the alien had covered an incredible distance. Already it had reached Mercury's orbit and continued its advance towards the Sun. Its feast while around Earth had spurred its growth, and it ignored the inner planets.

The solar wind's energy intensified the closer it moved towards the Sun, fuelling its growth further. It also required the entity to expend more energy in continuing its path. The energy it consumed was immense, many times that produced by the world's energy grids before the alien attack.

No-one knew why the alien was heading for the Sun. It had consumed a vast amount of energy to do so. There were a number of theories, the most common that it needed the energy to breed. The real problem with that theory was that it cost more energy to journey from the outer Solar System than it needed. It could have gathered the energy it needed from Jupiter.

Another theory suggested that the Sun would provide the boost it needed to journey to another star, to look for others of its own kind. An interesting idea, but no-one knew anything for sure.

The alien presented puzzle after puzzle, most of which they had no answers for. Not yet, anyway. She amassed as much data as she could. She wished she still had the sensors from the observatory and science modules. More than that, she wished that Piotr and Stephen were still alive to help research the creature.

She was an intelligent woman, but her talents were for the more practical. Despite that, she wasn't a complete stranger to research. Indeed her research throughout the return journey made her one of the few experts on the subject.

Mission Control had to reduce their research team, their skills now needed elsewhere to help with the rebuilding. Once again she hardly slept, this time not through depression and despair, but instead with determined purpose.

There was another problem, one that people didn't like to discuss, but considering the events it had to be considered.

What if the alien returned?

With the planet reeling from the last attack, surviving another might not be possible. Even if they did survive, millions more would die.

Neither Samantha nor the team at Mission Control had reached any significant insights. They watched the alien approach the Sun like a spear, always pushing towards its goal. Its progress had been slowed by the increased pressure from the solar wind, but far from stopped. Despite everything that had happened, Samantha experienced a sense of awe as she watched the entity arrive at its destination.

If only they knew why it had travelled the tremendous distance to get there.

When it reached the Sun, even her poor resolution cameras recorded what looked like a shockwave as giant plasma eruptions lashed against the tip of the alien.

The alien stopped its forward motion as the inferno raged against it. Eight minutes later as the sight reached her cameras, Samantha leaned forward with interest. The rest of the alien continued its motion until it reached the shockwave. There its mass built into a ball that expanded much faster than she would have thought possible.

The shockwave widened, raging with celestial violence, yet still the alien made no forward progress.

It just kept growing larger.

Samantha didn't want to jump to any conclusions, but seeing the alien frozen as it was battered by the Sun's fire excited her. It might provide a way of combating the alien, if they could determine what was stopping it.

Heat alone seemed doubtful, since when active the alien had high internal temperatures, high enough that the heat of the Sun shouldn't damage its structure.

Samantha thought that pressure could be the key. Pressure from the solar wind provided the alien's biggest obstacle in its journey to the Sun. When it pushed against the stream of energised particles, the effort cost the alien most of its energy. Perhaps there was a point the alien could not pass.

However, that didn't make sense to Samantha.

From all they had seen of the alien so far, its sole purpose had been to reach the Sun. Why, they didn't know, but it had done everything in its power to achieve that goal.

What if it didn't know whether it could attain its goal or not?

Perhaps this wasn't its normal habitat, and it relied upon colder, smaller or less active stars.

Too many unknowns prevented her achieving any clarity.

For seven hours she watched the ball of the alien grow. It was now so large it was visible as a dark spot against the Sun's surface, a mini-eclipse. Reports from Mission Control indicated that the blemish was also visible from the Earth's surface.

Then it flattened.

In a single movement it bloomed, not in the tendrils they had seen so far. Instead vast petals unfurled, stretching deep into space, and pushed out by the solar wind. Five great petals spread, flimsy and dark against the Sun's brilliance.

Long minutes passed as Samantha watched transfixed by the amazing event. What was it doing? Was this to capture more energy? Was the theory that the Sun provided a springboard to a new star correct? Were these new structures a natural form of solar sail?

The petals darkened as they absorbed the intense stream of energy from the Sun and Samantha saw that they thickened. Like sails in a gentle wind they filled, and then without warning they snapped shut, collapsing back into the stem from which they'd sprung.

The stem surged through the shockwave, thrusting as if an over-eager partner into the Sun's surface. At first Samantha lost sight of the alien as it plunged into the firestorm. Minutes later the stem resurfaced and the petals unfurled again. Not outward this time, but across.

Across the surface of the Sun, the petals moved. They stretched thinner and thinner, yet still pushing across the surface. Before long it had spread across the whole surface, but it had now stretched itself so thin it was barely visible.

The petals were so thin that they caused just a slight tint to the Sun, but then they thickened again as they consumed more energy and it continued to grow. As minutes ticked by, the light and heat from the Sun dimmed.

Chapter 51
Change is A-Coming

8th January 2023, 05:24 ship time

The Earth had never been a closed system. It relied on the Sun to sustain life, and humans in particular relied upon its light and warmth. It's true that humans had adapted to extreme temperatures. They had colonised almost every part of the planet. However modern humans, that formed the bulk of the population, relied on their technology.

Human technology had been crushed by the alien's attack. Humanity could have perhaps compensated for what was about to hit them if they had been at full strength, but in their weakened state they stood little chance.

It took time for the change to impact the world. The planet's inhabitants might rely on the Sun's light and warmth, but the planet was very adept at storing it.

For a while, anyway.

Samantha had been up all night watching the alien's transformation as it spread across the Sun. She had detected the energy loss from the Sun eight minutes after it occurred. Unlike those on the surface, she did live in a closed system fed by her ship and its engines. Those on Earth noticed that the sky dimmed a bit, but they didn't start feeling its effects until the following day.

Most people didn't realise how much their world relied on the Sun's input. They appreciated the obvious, direct effects, they felt its warmth upon their skin and they needed it to grow their crops. For those in richer countries, it provided a glorious day at the beach.

Some parts of the world were well aware of how bad a life without the Sun can be. Alcoholism and suicide rates in Arctic regions were much higher than in more temperate climes. And the seasonal loss of light paled in comparison to what was to come.

The Sun didn't go away. Overnight the energy reaching the Earth dropped by a fraction over ten per cent. The alien didn't create a true eclipse, it acted more like a polarised filter in front of the Sun.

Ten per cent didn't seem so bad, but in any complex system even the smallest of changes wreaks havoc. The Earth's weather system provided a classic example of such a system. Warmth from the Sun fuelled its movement, and such a dramatic change soon made itself felt.

Mission Control worked throughout the night with meteorological organisations around the world, trying to establish predictions they could use. Every functional government was desperate for information.

Even their direst of predictions didn't come close.

Most people didn't realise there was any change until the next morning. When the Sun rose, the air didn't warm as quickly as it had on the previous morning. Some realised that the air felt a little colder than usual. Compared to the resulting devastation, it seemed like a small inconvenience.

At this stage, however, the effects were for the most part confined to the upper atmosphere.

People remarked that it seemed like a murky day despite the clear skies and then got on with their lives. After all, they had more immediate concerns, the world was still early in the recovery steps from the alien's attack.

Across the world the pattern repeated, night fell and temperatures dropped.

The next dawn arrived colder than the day before. The skies remained clear, but over the oceans cold pressure cells formed.

They didn't move much in their early phase. Already the trade winds that formed the major air currents started to shift.

In the upper atmosphere, the change was already more pronounced. The vast movements of air drained more warmth from the atmosphere and tugged at the forming storms.

Before the alien attack, the Earth's atmosphere had been monitored constantly by dozens of satellites in orbit. Now the meteorologists relied upon ground stations, weather balloons and the limited observations Samantha provided. They knew some of what was going on, but compared to a few months ago they felt blind.

The next day dawned with an even bigger drop in temperatures across the world. The low pressure cells had twisted into massive storms. These weren't hurricanes, they lacked that eager ferocity. Instead, fat with moisture, they headed towards land.

And the temperature continued to fall.

By the time they reached land, the weather systems were so laden with water that they almost waddled. The weather stations stopped calling them storms, they didn't know what these massive, continent-wide movements were. In America, many received some warning from the operating communications systems. In the rural parts and other countries they weren't so fortunate.

The cloud build-up helped raise the temperature a little, but not in the upper layers of the atmosphere where the temperature continued to plummet. The upper currents pulled the clouds into a looser formation, spreading them farther apart.

Then it began to snow.

The world had not experienced this much snowfall in ten thousand years.

From orbit, Samantha could do nothing but watch in horror as a new and deadlier apocalypse struck the population. Without power, the cold swept through the population like a silent reaper. It hit the old, the young and the sick first.

Horrified, she watched as the world covered in clouds. Her contact with Mission Control kept her updated with events on the ground. Like before, newsfeeds from the internet provided Samantha with every update. She read every report and watched news bulletins from all over the world.

For a week the sky dumped snow, not with any ferocity, but in a constant caress that smothered the world in its frozen embrace. All through those days, Samantha kept vigil.

Occasionally she slept, floated in front of the command console until her eyes opened again. Samantha didn't sleep for long and felt like she shouldn't, she had to watch the events unfold. She felt compelled to do so.

Throughout it all she remained in contact with Mission Control, providing them with what information she could. The first breaks in the cloud came as the temperature differential between the upper and lower airstreams ripped them apart.

With the clouds gone, she now saw that the world had transformed from pole to pole into a land of white. Only the great oceans separated the snow and ice. As the clouds dispersed the temperatures plummeted even faster, freezing and locking the snow in place.

One of the great joys astronauts experienced in their careers had been the view of the world beneath them. The richness and the variety in colour and texture was a sight that many described as what the view from heaven must look like. Never had anyone seen the world so uniform in colour.

Chapter 52
Frozen

29th January 2023, 07:55 ship time

Throughout January, the temperature persisted in its terminal decline. Day after day, Samantha watched the situation on the surface deteriorate. At first the cold snatched only the weak and the infirm, but even in developed countries the death toll rose.

Efforts to restore power around the world faltered. Crops froze in the fields. The huge snow falls faded away, but no rain replaced them and the ground remained locked in snow and ice. Populations already suffering from lack of power and transport now faced starvation and the life-stealing cold. Fresh water in many countries had to be thawed from ice, burning precious fuel needed for warmth.

As hunger weakened the population, more people succumbed to the bitter weather. The extreme freeze had one positive aspect: it slowed the spread of disease from the mounting piles of corpses, stacked like frozen firewood out of sight.

Samantha's routine changed as February loomed. She had to focus most of her time on keeping the Mars Voyager operational. Many of the systems were throwing up problems, minor issues for now, but they kept her busier than ever before. She found herself unable to keep up with the mounting pile of issues and that increased the stress of her situation.

Most worrying of the issues was the life support system. Her stock of filters was depleted, so she had to recycle the used ones. They were better than nothing, but operated at a much lower efficiency. At the current rate of consumption she had less than a month's worth of clean air left.

Her daily interviews had now stopped. Most of the news channels had gone offline. Even in the US, the news was limited to a few radio stations and even fewer websites. Power was now rationed and so only strategically selected news stations were allowed to broadcast.

She was no longer a worthy enough news item.

That in itself didn't bother her. She understood what was happening and to be honest, she preferred having one less thing to worry about each day. She needed all of her time and focus for maintaining the ship. The act of cleaning filters wasn't difficult, but it did consume a lot of her day.

Whenever she could find the time she continued studying the alien, or at least providing observations of the surface. As the days passed, she slept less. Strangely she didn't feel wearied by the lack of sleep. The mounting work kept her busy and her reduced sleep at least proved restful.

Her dreams remained haunted, but not in an accusing way. The ghosts of the crew advised her on what she should do. Piotr and Stephen helped her with her observations with the alien.

The alien had developed a spider web of tendrils across the Sun's surface. Over the past few weeks, the growths had thickened. What looked like a thin film of dark material spread slowly between the threads.

As it spread, the Sun's light dimmed further.

As the Sun darkened, so the world grew colder. People now died even where communities had power. Once again law and order collapsed, but this time it happened in a more localised fashion. Nobody possessed the energy or the will to do more than try and hold what they had or take it from their neighbours.

The cold had reached such depths that even where transport or fuel was available, most vehicles couldn't operate. Only military vehicles or those specially adapted to the frozen conditions were able to struggle on in the treacherous conditions.

She no longer thought of what she did as research. The lack of meaningful data frustrated her, although not as much as her lack of understanding. She wanted to crack the puzzle, and find a way to help those on the frozen world below. More than that, she wanted to feel useful, to feel like she had a purpose other than waiting to die.

The evening calls with Jake provided the highlight for Samantha's day. He kept her up to date with the latest news, but for both of their sakes, they tried to keep the conversations light. The evening meal followed by the call had become more than routine, it was a ritual that made the day worthwhile.

Jake's face appeared on the console screen. He looked drained, his face shadowed from strain. He always appeared exhausted. Mission Control operated on a minimal crew and he worked as many hours as she did. Most of the engineers and medical personnel now helped the nearby population along with the civil support teams.

From the limited news reports, she knew that they faced a losing battle. The country lacked the infrastructure to provide supplies to anywhere farther than a few miles from the military bases where civil aid was provided.

It didn't stop them trying, though.

The NASA centre was fortunate to still have power. In the scheme of things, supporting a lone astronaut was low on the priority list.

Today he looked tired, more than that, he seemed weary and she guessed that something was wrong before he said anything.

"Hi Samantha."

Whatever was wrong infected his voice as well as his facial expression.

"Jake. How's it going down there?"

On screen Jake sat bundled up in layers of winter clothing. Despite that, his face was still pale from the cold. Mission

Control might have power, but not enough to maintain heating as well as keeping the computers and communications running.

"It's colder than a polar bear's nuts down here. At least it's above freezing in the office."

He attempted a smile.

"What's going on, Jake?"

"I'm sorry Samantha, it's too cold."

For a brief moment she allowed herself to believe that he meant the temperature in the office. Deep down she'd been waiting for this. Since the freeze began, she'd known that the mission would be scrubbed. The Russians had the most experience in dealing with launches in cold temperatures, but nothing as severe as what the world now experienced.

Knowledge, however, wasn't the same as acceptance.

"There must be some way, Jake. I can't die up here."

"I'm so sorry, Samantha, there's nothing we can do. If we tried to launch, the vehicle would just fall apart."

"There must be something. You can't leave me up here."

"We've examined every possibility. Every space agency still operational on the planet has investigated every option."

"I can't believe there is nothing that can be done."

"I don't want to believe it either."

"I have three weeks of air left up here. If the mission isn't launched now I will die. I don't want to die, Jake."

She said it in a calm voice that belied the turmoil within.

"If there was a way then we'd be there. I'm so sorry, Samantha."

Silence hung between them, stretching across the thousands of miles.

"I'm afraid that's not all."

He'd saved this news for last. What could be worse than what he'd already told her?

"We're being shut down."

"What?"

Her calm facade disintegrated.

"We're being closed down. Orders from above."

"What? Why?"

"The situation down here is getting worse."

"You tell me I'm going to die up here and now you're saying that you're leaving me to die alone!"

Jake couldn't reply, he couldn't even look at her.

"Answer me, damn you!"

"Space operations are no longer a national priority. The power is needed elsewhere, where it can be used to save lives."

Of course it made sense, she understood the mathematics of survival. She also appreciated the situation on the ground, but that didn't make the news any more palatable.

"I'm sorry Samantha, but this is the last call I will be able to make, there will be no more communications."

"Don't leave me alone, Jake."

His visible misery mirrored her own.

"I'm so sorry..."

"Stop fucking saying that!"

An uncomfortable silence passed.

"What about the other agencies, can they keep in contact?"

"No, Samantha," he said, his voice tired and gentle now. "Their difficulties are greater than ours. We have warships docked and providing what power they have to local power grids. The power we're using here is going to be re-routed."

"There's nothing I can do."

"Then this is it."

"Yes, we'll pray for you."

And then she heard only static.

Chapter 53
Alone, Again

19th February 2023, 10:46 ship time

The hours might have dragged by too slowly to bear, but in a terrible paradox, three weeks passed before Samantha realised it. The thought of her earlier mental collapse shamed her, so she refused to succumb to despair and worked hard, trying to keep the air filtration system working.

The spare filters had long been used, their chemical potency diminished. She recycled them as best she could, cleaning the micromesh and soaking them in a solution that became ever more diluted and useless.

She maintained her observations of the alien as best she could in the limited time remaining in each day. The Sun continued to darken, the alien now a vast blemish on its fiery skin. Her observations told her one thing, that the alien was growing bigger and stronger. As it did so, the world beneath her froze further and claimed more lives.

From the latest news she received from faint radio broadcasts, she learned that the death toll had reached the millions. Who knew how many more bodies lay frozen in the snow away from the supply efforts?

Samantha continued watching the world below get colder. In those weeks a new ice age had gripped the planet. At night she saw precious few lights. She kept trying to establish contact, but without any success.

The ghosts of the crew kept her company. They made sure that she didn't remain alone and they promised that she wouldn't die on her own. That provided more comfort than she expected.

When she wasn't working on the filters and other maintenance tasks, she retreated to her quarters and watched recordings of her conversations with Jake. She had so many things she wanted to say to him.

Those things would forever remain unsaid. Not that she loved him, or anything so simple. They were friends, friends with benefits for sure, but true friends nonetheless. She wished she had thanked him for all the times he sat and listened to her vent during those quiet hours of the mission.

She wished she had paid more attention to what he said. Now as she watched the recordings, she registered some of the nuances of what he'd said to her.

Most of all, she wished that their last words had been more meaningful. She wasn't a believer, but the thoughts of his prayers provided small comfort. She had no way to return that favour, but she hoped that the fact he was in her thoughts would be enough.

Her dwindling time wasn't all hers. The ghosts of the crew intruded. As part of the price for their support, they demanded to share their lives with her and so she watched their messages as well. Instead of sleeping, she replayed the videos she'd seen so many times before. On those occasions she'd watched them saddened with her grief for them, now she watched them with fresh eyes while grieving for herself. She would drift into a few hours of snatched rest and then startle when one of them spoke to her.

Before she'd watched them in a trance, the numb armour providing some limited protection from the pain caused by watching these fragments of her friends' lives. This time she experienced pride as she absorbed the experiences of the crew. The anguish of it helped keep the abyss at bay. If she slipped now, she would die as surely as if the oxygen had run out.

There was the irony of it.

Before, with longer to go, she had considered suicide. Now with less time to go, death didn't seem so attractive.

"I'm running out of time," Samantha told the ghosts that followed her.

"I'm feeling a little light-headed, I guess we're running out of clean air."

She nodded at the ghosts' reply.

"You're right, I need a clean oxygen source, but where from?"

She nodded again as she listened.

"A spacesuit, yes, there are two in the module. As you say, it's standard procedure."

A terrible thought struck her.

"I've already cannibalised the suit in here, although I haven't used the oxygen in the tanks. That gives me two suits worth, that's another ten hours of air if I'm lucky."

She listened to Ronald's ghost.

"I know there's another suit, but Piotr's using it."

Again she nodded as Piotr told her that it was fine, that he didn't need it anymore. Samantha pushed her way to Piotr's cabin. Inside he lay where she had left him all those months ago.

She hesitated as she approached his body. It had drifted from the bed; the straps must have loosened somehow. She hoped he hadn't been space sick.

What was she thinking?

"Guys, I think I'm going a bit crazy here."

They told her that she needed oxygen, hypoxia was making her think funny. She had to get into that suit now.

Samantha unclipped the helmet and vomited as the rank stench smashed into her nose and mouth. Even when she retreated and tried to escape the smell it followed her, forcing her from the room.

With the door closed, it held the stench at bay for a while. She'd caught a brief glimpse of the ruin that was once Piotr's face. The sealed suit had prevented complete decomposition, instead leaving a greasy sludge slopped over his skull.

The thought of it made her vomit again. Globules of bile floated around her, some splashed onto the door.

"I can't do it," she told the ghosts.

Then you'll die.

"I'm going to die anyway."

Inspiration came from Stephen's ghost. She'd already used up the emergency masks, using their filters to help patch the main scrubbers. They'd already bought her another day, but that was three days ago.

If she could fix the mask to the suit tank then she'd be okay, for a few hours anyway. The solution was so simple, why didn't she think of this sooner?

Maybe she should rest for a few minutes.

The ghosts shouted at her and spurred her into action.

Her fingers kept slipping and connecting the mask to the tanks proved much harder than it should have been. Her vision blurred and she was almost lost.

Then the cool, fresh oxygen filled her lungs and life had never tasted so sweet.

Chapter 54
Special Moment

19th February 2023, 12:11 ship time

Clean oxygen filled her lungs and cleared Samantha's mind. Her thinking became crisper, but it didn't dispel the five ghosts. She considered herself grateful that the millions of dead on the surface didn't visit her as well.

She'd braved Piotr's room again to retrieve the other oxygen tanks. Piotr's rotten smell now filled the entire ship. The mask she now wore all the time kept most of it at bay, but enough filtered through to make her feel nauseous.

For the first time in her life, she wished the seconds would slow down. They flew by too quickly, charging into minutes that consumed the hours. At least she didn't have to keep working on the maintenance list and so, for her remaining time, she observed the alien.

Perhaps she would discover something of importance in her last few hours and if she didn't, well what else was there for her to do? The view down below of the Earth growing whiter wasn't what she wanted to be her last sight.

The darkened orb of the Sun filled her main console screen. On the other screens, readouts of the ship's main systems reported impending failures across the board. Samantha ignored them. She had less than three hours of breathable air left. The chores could wait for now.

A crack of light appeared on the screen.

She didn't notice it at first. The black of the alien's bulk wasn't absolute, it twisted and squirmed within itself, a billion serpents coiled around the Sun.

Another splinter of light appeared and this time she saw.

The sliver of the Sun's imprisoned fire bloomed bright against the alien. She zoomed the image. It looked as if the edge of the tear glowed, suffused with some magical power. The glow of blazing plasma, she assumed, but if there was ever a time for magic then now would be it.

Two tears peeled away in opposite directions, unzipping the alien. The motion began slowly then accelerated until the line of fire bisected the black coiling mass.

There was a pause, as if the alien experienced some hesitation, and then the two halves peeled apart. Two great petals blossomed and curled away from the Sun.

Whatever the alien had come to do seemed to have ended.

Samantha found her earlier wish granted. Time slowed and she experienced every second with wonder as she realised what was happening.

Each half separated and drifted apart. They appeared to move at a snail's pace, but considering the distance and sizes involved, she knew that the movement was faster than it seemed. Samantha had seen something like this before. It reminded her of a cell dividing, but this was no simple cell. The alien was a vast, complex creature, its scale far beyond anything known on Earth.

In the same moment of realisation, she comprehended the alien's journey. It was a salmon that had swum its way upstream. The stream of the solar wind was a great obstacle the alien had overcome, but why?

Two reasons sprang to mind. The first was that replicating itself required a massive amount of energy, but still, it could have gained the energy from Jupiter. Not as quickly, but given time.

Now the two aliens had pulled clear of the Sun's surface. Samantha continued to watch, as her brain burned through her remaining oxygen trying to solve the puzzle.

The salmon metaphor provided the clue she needed. Salmon laid their spawn in the upper streams to give them the best possible chance in life. Upon their birth, they had the time to develop as they travelled back towards the sea.

Samantha thought that the same strategy was being applied here. She watched as the solar wind pushed the aliens away into deep space.

And where there was once darkness there now came light.

Chapter 55
Spring's Dawn

19th February 2023, 12:23 ship time

The release of the Sun from the alien's shroud was the best sight she could have imagined for her last vision. The first burst of warmth took eight minutes to reach the Earth. It wouldn't change things for those on Earth for several weeks, but in those glorious rays, hope was reborn.

Not hope for herself. She knew that she had less than twenty minutes to live. She felt light-headed, not overly so, but enough to realise that the oxygen supply was running out. The dial on the tank confirmed her assessment.

Perhaps it was the lack of oxygen, or maybe it was a vision of the future, but she watched the Sun's rays strike the atmosphere.

It was the future she saw. On the screen in front of her, it showed the two aliens. They were now clear of the Sun and moving into deeper space. She knew that they wouldn't visit any planets on their way out of the system. Instead they would be pushed by the solar wind, its energy feeding them as they travelled beyond the planets.

Eventually they would cross the very edge of the Solar System and from there they would seek new systems to repeat the cycle.

Samantha wondered how many of them existed in the galaxy. How often did they revisit the system of their birth? Did they return at all?

That would remain a puzzle she'd never solve, but others of her kind might. Her vision shifted to the world below, the frozen hell the world had all too quickly become. The human race had been dealt a savage blow. Billions of people dead as their technology failed them.

A planet of corpses, but it wasn't the end. The Sun shone again, and over time its warmth would restore the more temperate climate. Humanity would rebuild, aware of lessons, not only of their own hubris, but with the knowledge that they were not alone in the galaxy.

To be ready for another visit would be difficult, it would require every bit of humanity's ingenuity. Samantha hoped there would be time. She believed there would be enough.

Every breath she took now killed her, her brain was already dying. It didn't matter. A sight such as this was worth the price.

Thank you for reading Sun Dragon. I hope you enjoyed reading it. If you did then please leave a review or a rating on Goodreads, Amazon or wherever you share the books you read.

You can find out about my other books and keep up with my latest news on my blog:

http://thecultofme.blogspot.com

Printed in Great Britain
by Amazon